Pediatrician Mabel Aphrodite Brown adores kids. So when a childhood friend asks Ditie to babysit her kids for a few days, she jumps at the chance. She never imagined she'd be solving a murder too...

Despite growing up together, Ditie hasn't seen Ellie Winston in two years, and she didn't even know Ellie was living in Atlanta. But when Ellie asks her to take care of Lucie and Jason for the weekend, she thinks nothing of it. They'll bake cookies together, play with her dog—it'll be fun! Until the police call with terrible news...

Ellie may not have been the best friend, but who would want her dead? Could it have something to do with the vague get-rich-quick scheme she mentioned to Ditie? Or the men in a black truck following her and breaking into her home? Not sure who to trust other than her best friend, Lurleen, Ditie's buried maternal instincts kick in to protect the kids and find their mother's killer—before they're orphaned again...

Includes Family-Friendly Recipes!

Too Many Crooks Spoil the Plot

A Ditie Brown Mystery

Sarah Osborne

LYRICAL UNDERGROUND
Kensington Publishing Corp.
www.kensingtonbooks.com

LYRICAL UNDERGROUND BOOKS are published by

Kensington Publishing Corp.
119 West 40th Street
New York, NY 10018

All Kensington titles, imprints, and distributed lines are available at special quantity discounts for bulk purchases for sales promotion, premiums, fund-raising, educational, or institutional use.

Special book excerpts or customized printings can also be created to fit specific needs. For details, write or phone the office of the Kensington Sales Manager: Kensington Publishing Corp., 119 West 40th Street, New York, NY 10018. Attn. Sales Department. Phone: 1-800-221-2647.

Lyrical Underground and Lyrical Underground logo Reg. US Pat. & TM Off.

First Electronic Edition: May 2018
eISBN-13: 978-1-5161-0807-7
eISBN-10: 1-5161-0807-8

First Print Edition: May 2018
ISBN-13: 978-1-5161-0810-7
ISBN-10: 1-5161-0810-8

Printed in the United States of America

For Judith Simmons, who gave me a reason to write

and

Sarah Shope, who taught me how to do it

Acknowledgments

Sometimes it takes a small city. I am very grateful to the people who have made me a better writer through their unique contributions. They include Ellen Albanese, Judy and Bill Alden, Larry Allen, Deb Ayer, Philip Bechtel, Linda Benanti, Lyn and Wayne Brown, Sally Byrne, Marjorie Bufkin, Sue Eliason, Jayne Farley, Mary Louise Klimm, Jeanne and David Lee, Kathy Mosesian, Linda Newton, Lynne Rosa, Margo Schmidt, Kathy Shands, Ann Specht, Virginia Taylor, Patrick Todoroff, Jean Wentzell.

My deep appreciation to John Scognamiglio, who has been a pleasure to work with and who gave me my ticket into the world of published authors.

My love and thanks to Dan and Alix who encouraged me and gave me the space and time to write.

Chapter One

Nothing warned me that my world was about to tilt on its axis and never tilt back again.

Early spring in Atlanta was a magical time, and this morning was no exception. A few cumulus clouds drifted overhead, the temperature was near seventy, and my garden was already in bloom. I got up with the sun, so I'd already made cinnamon rolls, some of which might actually last until the next day, Saturday, when I could take them to work. I planted myself on the open porch of my Virginia-Highland home to drink in the scent of my gardenia bush and watch my tulips sunning themselves. No work for me today, just pleasure.

Hermione, my half German shepherd, half collie bodhisattva of a dog, put her head in my lap, partly to say she loved me and partly to see if she might get a bit of cinnamon roll. I gave her what I had left and sipped my coffee. I would not let this perfect morning be ruined by the hit-and-run visit of my brother. Tommy came when he wanted something and always left me with collateral damage. This time the visit had been on his way to work to see if I'd finally agree to sell the family farm in Iowa.

"We could make millions in condos," Tommy said. For him, everything was about the dollar sign. No, I told him. I hadn't changed my mind and wasn't likely to. The dairy farm had been in our family for generations. We had a good tenant. While I didn't love the farm, our mother had. It might have been the only thing she really had loved. Tommy left in a huff, driving over my Texas bluestar on his way out.

I did my best to breathe new life into my half-flattened plant and then sat on the porch musing about the future. Was it time to leave Atlanta? I'd stayed in this city longer than most that I'd lived in. First for medical school and residency. Later for a job in a refugee clinic. I loved my work, but as a pediatrician, I could work anywhere. Why had I come back? To try once again to mend fences with Tommy? Clearly that was not going to happen. Was it because I loved being near my best friend, Lurleen? She and I kept up through Skype and visits wherever I landed.

I really didn't need to stay any longer.

The desire to roam was getting stronger. I could feel it like an itch that I couldn't quite scratch. Sure, I loved my garden, my house, my work, Atlanta. But there were other homes and cities I could love just as well.

"Ditie?" someone called. I stood up. No one but my closest friends called me that.

My dad called me Aphrodite, Ditie for short, because he thought I was beautiful. My mother said that was absurd. She christened me Mabel Brown after her hard-working grandmother. "You're no Aphrodite," she told me later, "and it's a sorry day your father put those thoughts in your head."

I looked up and down my tree-lined street. I lived in the perfect neighborhood on a street that had little traffic. I saw no one.

"Ditie. It is you!" someone called again.

This time I saw her emerging from behind my neighbor's dogwood tree, running toward me, arms outstretched. Ellie! Tall, slender, her magnificent blond hair swirling around her face, her deep-set blue eyes the color of the Gulf of Mexico. It was how she always appeared. Out of nowhere. Unexpected.

She threw her arms around my round body, squishing my head against her ample breasts. The last time I'd seen her was two years earlier when she'd called for help with a bad-news boyfriend—getting away from him, that is. Eleanor turned up when she was in trouble and not much in between. I'd learned to accept that, sort of, but it was hard.

Ellie was the person I wanted to be from the time I first saw her. I was five years old and she was seven. She stood in the doorway of our classroom with her long blond hair catching the light. She was a goddess to me, the real Aphrodite. I followed her around like a lost bear cub. I was pudgy and short, with curly brown hair. I think I'd just chopped it all off to spite my mother, who insisted that girls had to wear barrettes and dresses when they went to school. Once I saw Eleanor, all I wanted was long silky hair. I didn't cut my hair short again until I was sixteen and headed off to college.

"How did you find me?" I asked. "I tried to call you when I moved back to Atlanta, but they said your number was disconnected."

"Hi, sweetie. I googled you and there you were. Funny how we all ended up here—you, me, Tommy. I live ten minutes away in Little Five Points. Small world, huh?"

Small world maybe, but I wondered if Ellie had moved to Atlanta in hopes of working something out with Tommy. They dated in high school and then broke up when Ellie got a better offer from the quarterback. Loyalty wasn't Ellie's strong suit. Forgiving wasn't Tommy's. She eyed me, and as usual around Eleanor, I wished I'd combed my hair and put on makeup.

"Tommy was just here," I said to get the focus off me. "You missed him by thirty seconds."

"I thought I saw his car," she said.

"So you two have been in touch?"

"No, no," she said quickly. "Haven't seen him in a year. Tommy doesn't have time for me."

"You and me both. It's funny though—I thought Tommy just bought that Mercedes."

Ellie shrugged. She looked over my yard and my 1920s brick bungalow. "This is a big house. You live here all alone?"

"I don't have a man in my life right now if that's what you mean. But I do have my cat, Majestic, and my dog, Hermione." I looked around. "Where are the kids?"

Eleanor seemed to be out for a stroll with no kids in sight. She looked good. Her hair was shorter and her figure was as great as ever. The only thing that looked off was her smile. It didn't light up her face the way it usually did.

"What's wrong? Are the kids sick? I'm seeing a lot of norovirus in the clinic these days."

"No, no. The kids are fine. Thank God. Nothing with the kids, and I want to keep it that way. They're in school. I just stopped by, so we could . . . chat a bit."

"Chat a bit" was Eleanor-speak for "I have a problem."

"Come on in," I said after giving her another hug. I could hear her gasping for air. "Sorry, sometimes I forget my own strength. I'm just so glad to see you. Where is your car?"

"Repossessed. I took a bus. You're right on the line from Little Five."

"Why didn't you call me? I could have picked you up."

"I wasn't sure I'd actually have the nerve to see you. Not after how I left the last time. I never thanked you for saving my life. Again." She gave me a momentary mea culpa look and then shook it off with a quick twitch of her slender shoulders.

Occasionally, Eleanor spoke the truth. This was one of those times. I had rescued her from a thug who would have been happy to beat the crap out of her for promising something she didn't deliver. That was the story of Ellie's life. She promised and didn't deliver.

"Something smells delicious," Ellie said as I ushered her inside. Hermione wagged her tail and then settled on the couch.

"Home-made cinnamon rolls. Can I get you some along with coffee, tea?"

Eleanor shook her head. "I can't stay long. It's a wonderful house," she said, looking around. "Just the house I'd expect you to have—a house with character."

Eleanor knew all my soft spots and most of my vanities. Houses mattered to me. God knows I'd lived in enough of them. Majestic, my large orange cat, swished his way past Eleanor and sat down beside the open door to preen and see what the birds outside were up to.

Eleanor stood near the front door. "I have a favor to ask. A big one."

"Maybe we ought to sit down first," I said.

Ellie perched on the edge of my grandmother's rocker, and I squeezed onto the couch where Hermione was sprawled. "Okay, shoot."

"I know this is a huge imposition, but I don't know where else to turn. You've always come through for me in the past. It wouldn't be for long. Just till I got a few things sorted out."

This was going to be quite a favor. "Tell me, Ellie."

"Do you think the kids could stay with you for a few days?"

I stared at Ellie. She looked desperate. Frantic—if the way she rocked back and forth on the edge of the chair was any indication.

"Of course," I said. That was always my first response to Eleanor. Tommy said I picked up trouble the way other people picked up a favorite book to read. He swore I had a deep-seated neurotic need to be everyone's rescuer, the bigger the problem the better. That was Tommy's latest interest—shrink talk. Ever since he'd gone to therapy for about two weeks, he understood the world of the psyche.

"But why do you need me to do that?"

Ellie fidgeted. "There's just something I have to do. And I can't do it with the kids in tow. I need to know they're safe."

"Safe?" Now I started to fidget. "Ellie, what are you up to this time?"

"Don't press me, Ditie. You're the only one I can turn to. The only person I know I can trust. The only person I'd leave my children with. Lucie talks about you all the time. When will she get to see her Aunt Di?"

Ellie found another of my soft spots—a kid who likes me. Kids in the practice like me well enough, but they're a lot less enthusiastic after I poke them or give them a shot.

"Lucie must be eight or nine by now. And Jason is what, five?"

"Jason turns five in a couple of days and Lucie will be nine in September."

I was silent, and I'm sure I looked worried.

Ellie glanced at her watch and stood up. "I have to go. I've got something I have to handle, and I don't want the kids in the middle of it. If you can't help me out, I'll find someone who can."

"Take it easy. Of course, I'll help you. But I need to know what's going on with you. You look frightened."

Ellie composed her face. "Not frightened," she said. "Excited. I'm about to make a killing. Maybe I'll buy a house next door and we'll become the sisters we were always meant to be."

I smiled. Ellie *was* like a sister to me. Not always an easy one, but one I loved.

"The kids won't be a burden," she said. "They go to Morningside Elementary. They take the bus from our apartment, but they could walk from your house. Lucie is very responsible. She's as much a mom to Jason as I am."

I nodded. She'd been a mom to Jason the last time I saw them. Lucie got her responsibility gene from somewhere, but it wasn't from her mother. "Do the kids ever see their father?"

"Of course not. He's no good, you know that. Doesn't pay child support, much less alimony. I don't even have a current address for him."

Eleanor, for all her looks, never had good luck with men. Her father was a run-around, and maybe that's just what she expected and got from the men she hooked up with. She left her husband before Jason was born and I never knew why.

"When shall I pick up the kids?" I asked.

"At five or six, if that works for you."

"Sure." Why did that word fall so easily from my lips? I didn't actually know how this would work. It was Friday, my day off, but I had a morning shift at the Refugee Clinic on Saturday, and what about Monday?

Ellie read my mind. "Like I say, Lucie can walk Jason to school and home again. No problem. They're used to being home alone."

"I'm not comfortable with that. I can probably get my friend Lurleen to help out in the afternoons, and I can drop them off at school on my way to work."

"You're such a problem solver. That's why I love you. Here's the address." She handed me a slip of paper on Sandler's Sodas letterhead.

"You work for Sandler's?" I asked.

"Used to. Long story. They are about to make me a very good retirement offer. I have to go."

"Do the kids know about this arrangement?"

"Well, sort of."

"Sort of?"

"I didn't want to tell them until I was sure about you. They'll be fine."

"I'll drop you at home," I said.

"You don't need to drop me off. I have an errand to run first. If I'm not home when you get there, Lucie can help you get everything you need. Not to worry."

Not to worry. Right. I could feel my shoulders tense—a sure sign that something wasn't okay.

Ellie flicked her fabulous hair back from her face and gave me her megawatt smile. "I'll explain everything when I pick the kids up in a few days."

Explaining wasn't part of Eleanor's vocabulary. I nodded. I'm no shrinking violet, but with Eleanor I seemed to lose my adult self and become her five-year-old slave again.

She got ready to leave with a kiss on my cheek and a promise to call in the evening. The sky had darkened and we were in for an afternoon storm. I could hear the first drops on the porch. I offered again to take her wherever she needed to go. She refused.

"At least take my big umbrella," I said as she headed out the door.

Probably to get me out of her hair, she grabbed the umbrella, gave me another peck on the cheek, and darted down the front steps. She headed up the road toward Highland Ave., and I went into action mode.

That meant calling Lurleen. I explained the situation. Besides being my best friend, she lived a block away. She hadn't worked since her aunt left her a small fortune and she was always ready to help.

"Oh, *chérie,* you know I would do anything for you." I could envision her twisting one strand of her luxuriant auburn hair. "Anything at all. But children? What do I know about children? They are so little and squirmy." The usual excitement in her voice took on a new timbre of anxiety. Something I hadn't heard before.

"It's okay, Lurleen," I told her. "They aren't babies. They've been looking out for themselves their entire lives. I just need a responsible adult to stay with them when I'm at work. They'll have a great time with you. You're so much fun."

"You think so?" Her voice settled down into a soft southern drawl with French highlights that was music to my ears. Her full name was Lurleen du Trois. I never knew if that was her given name or something she created. I did know her French accent had never seen France, or Quebec for that matter. It was pure Lurleen. "*C'est vrai.* I can be very *amusante* when I try. But kids—I'm not sure what kids find amusing. Maybe we could play badminton or croquet or charades. I'll make a list. And what shall I feed them? Do they eat regular food or do I need to buy something special—like those little fish crackers and alphabet soup?"

"Regular food will be fine," I said. "I can't tell you how much I appreciate this, Lurleen. Do you have time to stop by tonight and meet them?"

"*Bien sur.* Anything for you, *chérie.* When you make your chocolate chip cookies, will you save some for me?"

"Of course. How did you know that was next on my list?"

"My dear girl, you always bake—when you're happy, you bake. When you're bored or upset, you bake. I think today you're worried about your friend Ellie."

"I am."

Lurleen said she'd stop by around seven.

I picked the kids up at five in a run-down section of Little Five Points. They didn't know I was coming and there was no Ellie or babysitter in sight.

"It's okay," Lucie told me. "We don't need a babysitter. I can look after things."

Ellie and I would be having a long discussion about this when I saw her next. We gathered up the few things they had. Jason brought his action figures and Lucie brought her stuffed monkey but only when I insisted. "I'm really too old for that, Aunt Di," she told me.

"Well, I'm not," I said and tucked it in her book bag.

Lurleen arrived on the dot of seven.

"I hope I'm not late," she said and grinned at me. Lurleen was never late. She wore a jaunty beret that sat atop her massive auburn curls, and she stooped to kiss me on both cheeks. Lurleen was six feet tall, slender—a sharp contrast to my five feet of well-rounded flesh.

"*Bon soir,*" she said to Lucie and Jason. She knelt down beside them and shook each of their hands with great solemnity. They looked at her as if she might be from another planet.

"That's French for good evening," she explained. "Ah, I see you have the latest action figure, Jason. The Transformer, isn't it?"

I could imagine how Lurleen had spent her afternoon—searching the Internet for what little boys liked to play with. That was all it took to hook Jason. He showed her the intricacies of the Transformer, changing it around from human to machine and back to human again.

Lucie was equally enthralled with her. "I took French once in school," she said shyly. "But only for a few weeks until we had to move."

"Ah, no problem. Or should I say, *pas de probleme.* We'll speak French every day, and you'll catch on in no time."

Lurleen's first encounter with the kids was a glowing success. I had no doubt it would be. Lurleen could charm a cow into giving more milk, a coop full of chickens into laying more eggs, a judgmental mother into being kind to her daughter. When my mother came for my med school graduation—after Lurleen called her and insisted she come—I never heard one word of criticism. Lurleen entertained her, sang my praises. She had my mother laughing out loud, something I'd never heard before. That had been a good visit, two weeks before my mother died of a massive stroke.

After Lurleen left us, I ran a bath for Jason, who insisted he needed no help in the tub.

"I'm five years old in two days. I'm big now."

I left the door ajar, so I could keep an eye on him.

I got them tucked in bed by eight and kissed them each good night.

"Can Her My Only sleep with us?" Jason asked.

"Of course. Hermione would love to sleep with you. She may jump up on the bed and want to sleep there."

Jason grinned.

"Is that okay?" Lucie asked.

"Fine with me if it's fine with you."

I closed the door, poured myself a glass of wine, and gave way to my frustration with Ellie. Where was she? She was supposed to call this evening. She'd left her children in a terrible place. Lucie was resourceful but she was an eight-year-old child, not an adult. No child should be left in that flea-bitten apartment alone at night.

I must have dozed off on the couch. It was midnight when I got the call.

I grabbed the phone so it wouldn't wake the kids. "Ellie?"

A detective corrected me and asked if I knew an Eleanor Winston. Then he asked if he could come over. He already had my address.

I met him on the porch, so he wouldn't ring the bell and start Hermione barking.

"I'm Mason Garrett," he said. He showed me his credentials and waited patiently while I examined them.

"I have the kids inside. Can we talk here?" I nodded to the swing, but he remained standing. He suggested I sit down.

"Something's happened to Ellie," I said.

He nodded. He was a kind-looking man, in his late forties, with a bald head and a sturdy build. His gray eyes said he'd seen it all and didn't care for most of it.

"I'm sorry to tell you this. We found a dead woman we believe to be Eleanor Winston, shot in the head on a street in midtown. She had your address in her purse and a message that said you were to take care of her kids if anything happened to her."

Chapter Two

Every word felt like a bullet slamming into my own brain. I sat very still on the swing, staring at my hands, determined not to cry. Not until I was alone. As a doctor, you learn to put your feelings to one side. You don't help a mother struggling with the serious illness of her child by breaking down in front of her.

"So she knew she was in danger," I said.

"What information do you have about that?"

"Ellie had some scheme to make money. She said she'd worked for Sandler's Sodas, and they were going to make her a nice settlement offer. I hadn't seen Ellie for two years until this afternoon when she asked me to watch the kids. I tried to get her to tell me what she was up to but she wouldn't."

"You knew her well?"

"We grew up together in Iowa and then lost touch for a few years after high school. I've seen her off and on since then, mostly when she had a problem. She always wanted to make it big. First as an actress in Hollywood and later in whatever way she could to get rich."

"Did that include drugs or other illegal activities?"

"No drugs. They killed her brother. As for the illegal part—I can't say for sure. She liked the good life and could never seem to afford it. Took up with some questionable guys and did some stupid things."

"I see." The detective was jotting notes in a small notebook. "Is there anything more she said to you this afternoon that might help us find her killer?"

I shook my head. "She asked if the kids could stay with me for a few days. Said she had an errand to run and wouldn't let me take her where she needed to go. It started to rain, and I made her take my umbrella."

"We didn't find an umbrella near her."

I shrugged. "Maybe it stopped raining."

"No, not in midtown. A pretty steady rain all evening."

"It was an unusual umbrella, sky blue with a carved wooden handle. I'd recognize it if I saw it again." I didn't add that it was a gift from my father before I left for college or that it was carved from the branch of a linden tree that shaded our house. "So you won't forget us, no matter how far you travel," my father had said. He meant him.

Even then it was clear the cancer was working its way through his body. His hands shook, but he didn't stop carving that handle until it fit my grip perfectly. And he wouldn't hear of my postponing college to stay home with him. My father. As if I ever could forget him.

The detective must have thought I was still in shock. He waited until I looked up at him. "You never know what might help," he said, referring to my description of the umbrella. He closed his notebook and looked at me intently. "Are you all right?"

I nodded.

"I'm sorry, but I'll need you to identify the body."

"What about the kids?"

"We can send someone to stay with them."

"Some stranger? No. Let me see if a friend can come over. Will the children be allowed to stay with me for now?"

The detective gave me a concerned look. "As far as I know. That's what Ms. Winston requested. We'll check with Family and Protective Services. Do you know about her next of kin and how we can reach them?"

I went inside, got out my old address book, and jotted down the name and number for Ellie's mother. I didn't know if it was still accurate, but it was all I had. I handed the address to the detective and told him the name of the children's father, John Winston. No address. No phone number.

Detective Garrett sat on the swing while I called Lurleen. She was at my house in five minutes. She looked shocked, of course, but she didn't pepper me with questions.

The detective drove me to the morgue in his Jaguar. It was an old Jaguar, but it was still a Jaguar. Nicely maintained. He saw me examining his mahogany dashboard.

"I have a thing for old cars," he said. "It's how I spend my spare time, when I have any. Life can get pretty hectic with my job. Yours too I'm sure. You're a physician?"

I nodded. "A pediatrician."

"Where do you work? You have a private practice?"

I tried to focus on his questions, anything to keep me from thinking about Ellie. "I work in a refugee clinic. For many of the families it's their first exposure to Western medicine and a doctor who has time for them. What I do feels important, and the parents are always so grateful."

"Must be hard when you lose a patient."

"It is. Fortunately that doesn't happen often. We can usually send them to the hospital if that's where they need to go. Most of these kids are survivors. That's how they made it to our clinic in the first place."

Detective Garrett nodded.

"Your work must be hard for you too," I said.

Again he nodded. "Sometimes it's very hard." He looked at me. "I'm sorry about your friend."

That was all it took. I could feel the tears coming, and I couldn't stop them.

Detective Garrett handed me some tissue as he turned into the parking lot. "It's okay," he said. "We can wait as long as you want before I take you into the morgue."

Well, that really set me off. A kind cop and the mention of the morgue. I sat in the car and sobbed silently for five minutes. Then I wiped my eyes, blew my nose, and we went inside. We walked through a metal detector operated by a policeman in uniform.

"Hi, Mason," he said while he searched through my purse. He gave the bag back to me and nodded.

The morgue was in the basement. Detective Garrett and I waited for an elevator that took us into the bowels of the building. It was cold and dark with minimal lighting. A city tightening its belt, he informed me. The morgue itself was brightly lit with overhead fluorescent lights that would have given me a headache in five minutes. At a small desk, a young woman checked us both in and walked ahead of us into one of the rooms. She looked at a number on her roster and pulled out a metal gurney. The whole experience was surreal. Not the morgue part. As part of my training, I'd been in morgues, witnessed autopsies. It was the fact that a friend might be lying there, a friend I'd known all my life. A sheet covered the body, and Detective Garrett asked if I was ready to see her. I nodded.

Maybe it wouldn't be Ellie.

The unveiling happened in slow motion. The attendant turned down the sheet inch by inch until I saw the face with a terrible, horrible hole in her left cheek. An exit wound.

The face was disfigured, but it was Ellie's. Eyes closed. Hair matted around her head. So dead.

"Yes," I said. "That's her."

"I'll take you home," Garrett said. He must have thought I was about to faint because he put his hand under my arm and steadied me as we walked out to his car.

We were at my house in ten minutes. There's not much traffic on the road at two in the morning.

"I'm sorry about all this," he said after walking me to my door. "Here's my card. If you think of anything that might be helpful, call me. And if any . . . problem arises, call me as well."

"Problem?" I could feel my skin start to prickle. "What do you mean? Are the kids in danger?"

"We don't know anything about the person who did this. He dumped the contents of Ms. Winston's purse on the street, but he didn't take her money. We don't know what he was looking for or if he found it. I can't say if the children are in danger. I'll call you when I have more information." He briefly touched my hand. "Feel free to call me anytime."

"Thank you," I said.

I went inside and sank onto the sofa with Majestic by my side and Hermione at my feet. Lurleen sat on my other side, one arm around me, handing me tissues with the other as I cried and told her what had happened. She teared up when I told her about seeing Ellie in the morgue and as I wondered aloud about what would happen to the children.

"Will they let you keep them?" she asked.

I shrugged. "I don't know. They'll be looking for Ellie's mother. She wasn't much of a mother to Ellie, but perhaps she'll want the kids. I have them for now—that's all I know."

"I can help you with them every day. I want to help you and them."

I squeezed her hand. "What would I do without you?"

Lurleen smiled. "Oh, *chérie*, I'm not going anywhere." She handed me a tissue and kept one for herself. We sat together silently for several seconds. Lurleen squeezed my hand every time I sighed. I didn't have to explain to her how I was feeling; she understood.

I decided I would let the children sleep. It would be the last innocent sleep either one of them would ever have. As it turned out, I couldn't keep that decision. Lucie came padding out to us. I'd made her wear socks to bed. Old houses can be drafty.

"I heard the policeman come and go. I waited until you came home. It's about Mom, isn't it? Something's happened to Mom."

I took Lucie in my arms and sat her on my lap. "Something terrible has happened. I'm so sorry, Lucie."

"My mother isn't coming back, is she?"

"No, Lucie. Your mother isn't coming back. She died tonight."

Lucie buried her head in my neck. I could feel my top becoming wet with her tears.

"I knew something terrible was going to happen," Lucie cried. "I knew it. This time it wasn't going to be okay, no matter what Mommy said."

"I'm so sorry," I said and rocked her back and forth. I was crying too. I stroked her head, and we sat together in silence for a few minutes.

Lucie finally sat up and looked at me with dark blue eyes that reminded me of her mother's. "How did she die?" she asked me.

"Do you really want to know?"

Lucie nodded.

"She was shot, Luce. She probably died instantly."

Lucie nodded again. "What will happen to Jason and me?"

"Your mother wrote a note saying she wanted you to stay with me. That's where you'll stay until the police find your grandmother or your father."

"I don't want to live with them." Lucie started crying again. "Or with anyone else. I want to live with you, Aunt Di. Jason and I won't be any trouble. I promise."

I hugged her tighter. "It's not about being trouble, honey. You couldn't be any trouble if you tried. I'd love you to stay with me always, but I may not have that right. Let's just take it one day at a time. For now, you're both safe with me."

I hoped that was true.

Chapter Three

Lurleen stayed with us that night. She insisted I go to bed, and she slept on the couch. She had coffee brewing in the kitchen when I woke up.

"Is there anything else I can do?"

"You've done plenty," I said.

We heard stirring in the bedroom, and a moment later Lucie walked out slowly with her monkey in one hand. She looked embarrassed when she realized she was clutching it and started to go back to her room.

"Wait, wait," said Lurleen. "May I see it?" Lurleen took it tenderly from Lucie. "This looks like a sad little monkey," she said.

With that, Lucie burst into tears and let me gather her onto my lap.

Lurleen knelt beside her. "I'm so sorry," she said. She kissed her on top of her head and gave her back the stuffed animal. "Maybe you can comfort each other."

Lurleen reached over Lucie and hugged me. "Call me later. Right now the children need to be alone with you."

I nodded a thank you, and she let herself out.

Saturday was rough.

Lucie understood what had happened, but it's hard to explain to a four-year-old that his mother is never coming back. I tried to comfort them both and answer Jason's repeated questions about when his mother was coming home. Lucie said their mother was in heaven but was watching over them.

"Will she come home for my birthday?"

"No, Jason," Lucie explained patiently. "She can't come home for your birthday. She's too far away."

"I will bring her back from far away. I'm Superman. I can find her in the sky."

"No, Jason. She's in a place even Superman can't go."

Jason's lower lip trembled.

"We'll make a big cake for you tomorrow with lots of candles," I said. "Shall we invite Lurleen and make it a party?"

"Yes." Jason climbed up beside me on the couch. "I want my mommy to come too." He burst into tears. I cuddled him, and he finally fell asleep beside me sucking his thumb. His left hand clutched his Spider-Man figure.

Jason's birthday gave us something else to focus on. Lurleen was thrilled to be included. "I'll bring all the favors and decorations," she said. "You'll have to do the cake, of course, but I'll handle everything else. What favors do five-year-old boys like? Maybe they'll know at Party City. Do children still play Pin the Tail on the Donkey?"

I realized this party was going to be over the top with Lurleen directing the show. Maybe that was what we needed. "Focus on action heroes," I said, "and Jason will be a friend for life."

We settled on three o'clock Sunday for Jason's party. That way we'd have time to make a cake and celebrate with whatever Lurleen had in store. The kids could still get to bed at a reasonable time to go to school on Monday. If they were up to going.

I tried not to cry in front of the children, and Lucie tried not to cry in front of Jason. I called my boss at the Children's Refugee Clinic to cancel my work for Saturday, Monday, and Tuesday.

"I'm so sorry, Vic, for the short notice. I know Saturdays can be a free-for-all." Saturday was often the only day folks could come in. It was a half day of nonstop action.

"We'll make do," Victoria said. "Just take care of the children." Vic was always understanding. It was one reason I loved working at the clinic. No matter how big the problem or how hectic the day, Vic stayed calm and supportive. I promised to call her as soon as I knew more.

Jason was okay for most of Saturday, but at bedtime he wanted his mama. Lucie did too. She didn't say a word, but I've never seen a child look so miserable. I climbed into their bed, put an arm around each of them, and we all cried and held on to each other.

I left them when I could hear the rhythmic breathing that told me they were both finally asleep. It was after nine, and I knew for me it would be another long night. I hadn't bothered to get the mail, so I got it now. The evening was clear, warm, full of stars, the kind of night Ellie loved and would never see again.

Inside the house, with a glass of wine beside me, I looked through a pile of bills and one distinct linen envelope addressed to Ditie Brown. Not Mabel

Brown or Dr. Brown. The handwriting was vaguely familiar. Then it hit me. I knew who the letter was from, and time came to a screeching halt. Phil Brockton. My heart pounded. The only man besides my father whom I had ever loved. I hadn't heard from him in seven years. I didn't want to hear from him now. Now of all times. But I couldn't stop myself. I tore open the envelope.

Hi Ditie,

I know how you love old-fashioned letter writing and I didn't want you to hang up on me or delete my e-mail. I'm coming into town in a few days. I'd really like to see you. Things have changed for me. I can't wait to tell you.

Phil

Phil had left me high and dry after we finished our residencies, his in oncology, mine in pediatrics. I had assumed we'd both be staying in Atlanta. When Phil took me out to dinner and told me he was doing a fellowship in New York and was going to move in with an oncology nurse he'd recently met, I wasn't prepared for the news. He made sure we were in a restaurant, so I wouldn't make a scene. I didn't. I just never spoke to him again.

I crumpled up the letter, straightened it out again, reread it. I studied the handwriting. He'd used a fountain pen, probably a quill pen, if I knew Phil. He loved the 1800s and the Civil War more than he'd ever loved me. He was seriously into reenactments and everything had to be authentic. I didn't know what I felt about the contents of the letter. Angry? Hopeful? Disgusted with myself that I could possibly still care about him?

Time resumed its pace. My childhood friend was dead, leaving two devastated children for me to care for. Phil was of no consequence, except that I couldn't get him out of my head.

I remembered every moment of our last encounter. He gave me the news shortly after our appetizers arrived. He spoke as if I had a rare form of leukemia that he hoped I would survive. Professionally compassionate. I wanted to throw my glass of wine in his face—a very nice cabernet sauvignon—which I'd assumed was meant for a celebration. Instead, it was supposed to be a consolation prize. I gulped it down and said nothing. I was a good girl after all. Never make a scene. Never tell your boyfriend to go to hell. My mother would have approved. My father would have held me in his arms and let me sob. But Dad had also left me high and dry. Not because he wanted to. Because his cancer gave him no choice.

I was drawn to Phil partly because he chose the residency I intended to do—oncology. I wanted to save people the way I couldn't save my dad, but working with children turned out to be my passion. Phil also seemed to have my father's love of history and curiosity about the world. I didn't realize until we broke up that he had none of my father's gentleness or compassion.

I never saw Phil again after that night, and he never wrote. Until now. I tried to shake off the letter the way you might shake off a bad dream, but I couldn't do it. Any more than I could shake off the image of Ellie, dead on a slab in the morgue.

It was a sleepless night.

* * * *

Sunday morning Lucie and I serenaded Jason with our own version of "Happy Birthday" and then the three of us worked on his birthday cake. He wanted chocolate, and there is nothing better than my Mexican chocolate cake if I do say so myself. I'd probably have to change the name to something French in order to please Lurleen. Jason stayed just long enough to learn to crack an egg. Then he was off with his Superman cape rescuing Hermione from danger. He would have done the same with Majestic, but she was too quick for him and disappeared under a bed.

Children are amazing, thank God. Jason played with Hermione and dashed around the house waiting for Lurleen to arrive with all her surprises. He smiled and laughed. Something might remind him of his mother, and then he would grow quiet or ask about her. He'd want to go get her. But Lucie or I would talk to him, and he'd be off again on a new adventure. Of course, the grieving wasn't over. It hadn't really started, but to have a few minutes of joy was a gift on Jason's birthday. Lucie did her best to hide her own terrible sadness. She clung to me like a Post-it note and I hugged her back even though my hands were covered with flour. I'm sure we made quite a picture. Dressed in the best aprons I could find, we were decorated with the natural splatter that comes from baking and sampling—bits of chocolate, flour, sugar, pecans. I'll bet we smelled good enough to eat.

"Mom never had time to cook," Lucie said shyly. "I did all the cooking. It's more fun to do it with someone else."

"I agree," I said. "Now that you're here, we'll try out some new recipes."

"I'd like that," Lucie said.

Detective Garrett called around noon. I left Lucie to keep an eye on Jason and took the call in my bedroom.

"I'm sorry to bother you on a Sunday, Dr. Brown, but we've been having trouble reaching Mrs. Winston's mother. She's on vacation in Costa Rica, according to neighbors. We have no address. She hasn't responded to messages on her cell phone. Do you have any ideas about friends who might know how to reach her?"

"I'm afraid not. I never saw her after I moved away, and I don't think Ellie saw much of her either."

"We haven't found the children's father yet either. According to the ex-wife, they split up a year ago, and she has no idea where he is." He paused. "How are the kids doing?"

He asked the question as if he really wanted to know. I wondered if he had kids. Then I wondered if he was married.

"They're doing as well as can be expected. Have you found out any more about what Ellie was doing?"

"No. We haven't located her cell phone."

"Oh," I said, "that's because she left it with Lucie. It's here at the house. I never thought about it until now."

"I'll come over and get it. Is now a good time? I'd like to talk with the kids while I'm there. Would that be all right with you?"

"Sure."

"What's wrong?" he asked. This guy was good. He could read me over the phone.

"It's Jason's birthday. I hate to upset him anymore than he already is. You could come over and stay for his party at three if that's not inappropriate."

"Unusual, but not inappropriate."

"Great," I said. "Jason will be thrilled to have a real policeman at his party. I'll give you the cell phone then and you can talk to the kids. Do you think you can do that without upsetting them too much? I mean, maybe we could follow up with the heavier stuff tomorrow?"

"I may not know as much about kids as you do, Dr. Brown, but I'm pretty good with them. I'll do my best not to upset them."

I got off the phone and took a quick shower. I no longer worried about my hair, which would do whatever it wanted to do no matter how much gel I put in it. Today it was a mass of dark curls springing out from my head in every direction. I put on makeup with a touch more care than usual. Why in the world was I doing that?

I'd sworn off men after my last encounter on Match.com. Not a match made in heaven. "So you're a doctor. You wanna be my doctor? Maybe we could play doctor." I excused myself to go to the bathroom, never returned, and canceled my account.

Now I was thinking about Detective Mason Garrett with his kind gray eyes. I probably needed something or someone to think about that didn't make me cry.

"You look nice," Lucie said when I emerged from the bathroom.

"Really? Thanks, Lucie. Detective Garrett is coming over. He's going to stay for Jason's party. You haven't met him yet, but he's a very nice man. He's trying to find out what happened to your mother. He wants to talk with you and Jason."

Lucie got tearful but nodded. "I'll get Jason ready."

"Thanks, honey."

Lurleen arrived around two. It took three trips to her little yellow Citroën to bring in all the packages she had, including the one I'd asked her to buy for Jason. My gift to him. An Avengers Action Kit. Beautifully wrapped in Spider-Man paper with silver spiderweb ribbon. A masterpiece.

"You wrapped this yourself, didn't you, Lurleen?"

"Of course I did. Now where is that fine helper of mine, Lucie?" Lucie appeared as if from nowhere and Lurleen dramatically kissed both her cheeks. She held her out at arm's length and twirled her around. "*Tres jolie,*" she said. "That means very pretty."

"I know," Lucie said and blushed.

"And now you must leave us alone," she said to me. "*Au revoir. Tout a l'heure* and all that."

I left them to it and took Jason outside to play. He dashed around the front yard, chasing Hermione until she finally flopped down in the shade.

Detective Garrett arrived moments later with a ball and bat in one hand, a mitt in the other. He looked better than the last time I'd seen him. More rested, clean-shaven, with what looked like a new corduroy jacket over a black turtleneck and gray khakis. His bald head and sympathetic eyes were unchanged.

"I'm Detective Garrett," he said, kneeling down in front of Jason, "and I brought you a birthday present."

Jason looked stunned.

"You do like baseball, don't you?" Garrett said.

Jason nodded. "For me?" he asked, eyeing the gifts.

"For you." He handed them over. "Wanna play?"

Jason's head bobbed up and down. Then he hesitated. "I don't know how."

Good grief, I thought. Ellie didn't even teach Jason how to throw and catch a ball?

"I'll show you," Garrett said. He gave the mitt to Jason, made sure it fit on his hand, and stood five feet away from him. "Here," he said, lobbing the ball into Jason's mitt.

"I caught it!" Jason said.

If I ever needed something to endear me to Detective Garrett, I'd just found it. Good with kids? That was an understatement. Of course, good with kids might mean he had a few of his own. Which meant he might have a wife somewhere lurking in the wings. Of course he had a wife. How could he not have a wife? What had I been thinking?

He and Jason played ball for a few more minutes. Then they moved on to batting practice. Lurleen stuck her head out the front door. Did we want an aperitif? Did we want to come inside? We could do that as long as we stayed out of the kitchen and dining room.

"We'll be right there," I said. "Lurleen, this is Detective Garrett. You met him briefly Friday night."

"*Enchante*," she said. She looked as if she might rush up and kiss him on both cheeks, but she restrained herself. I was a little disappointed—that would have been a sight to see. Instead, she stood at the door and directed traffic as we came inside.

"No peeking, Jason," she said as he started for the dining room. "All in good time."

Lucie stood just inside the door.

"This is Detective Garrett," I said.

He held out his hand and she shook it.

Detective Garrett patted a place on the sofa. "Sit with me for a bit, Lucie? You too, Jason."

I went to the kitchen and started a pot of coffee. Then I found the cell phone and took it out to him.

He placed the phone in a plastic bag and put it in his pocket.

"Are you a real policeman?" Jason asked.

"I am, Jason. Do you know what detectives do?"

"They 'rest people. They rested my mom once."

"Arrested, you mean," Lucie said. "And they never arrested our mom. They just asked her some questions."

"When was that?" Detective Garrett asked.

"A couple of weeks ago," Lucie said.

"Do you remember the name of the policeman who spoke to your mother?"

Lucie thought for a moment. "His name was Schmidt. Detective Schmidt."

"Schmiddy," Garrett said and paused. He looked at me and nodded toward the kitchen. "I think the coffee may be ready. Could you pour me a cup?" I jumped up and followed him through the dining room and into the kitchen. "Remember, no peeking," I said to Jason, who was about to join us. "We'll be right back."

Huddled together over the stove, Garrett whispered to me as I poured two cups of coffee and some tea for Lurleen. "Schmidt was killed a week ago in a drive-by shooting. He was following up on a lead in midtown. We don't know yet if they meant to hit him or someone else."

"You think his death is connected to Ellie's murder?" I asked.

"I don't know. But it's an unusual coincidence. I'll go over his cases when I get back to the station. We still haven't found out who did it. No one claims to have seen anything."

"You think this is some kind of gang or drug killing?"

"Schmidt worked on white-collar crime—not drug enforcement. He was in the Cyber Crimes Unit."

We walked back into the living room where Lucie was sitting expectantly on the sofa and Jason was zooming action figures up and down over Hermione's back. Fortunately, she was a kid-friendly dog, the only kind I would have. I handed the cup of tea to Lurleen, who sat demurely in the big red chair, her long legs crossed.

"Can I see those?" Garrett asked, pointing to Jason's action figures. "My sons used to play with them."

So there were children. No ring on his finger but children.

Jason proudly showed him his Superman and Spider-Man figures.

"I have a new one," he said excitedly. He ran into the bedroom and brought out the slightly larger figure. "It's the Transformer. See, it turns into a man when you do this." Jason flipped it around, and there was a man.

"Wow, my sons would have loved this."

"May I see?" I asked. Jason handed it to me and stood nearby, probably to make sure I wouldn't wreck it. It looked brand new. "Where did you get this?"

Jason looked at Lucie and hesitated for just a second.

"Secret," he said.

"Secret?" I repeated. I've never known a five-year-old who could keep a secret.

"Promise not to tell? My daddy give it to me."

"Your daddy?" Garrett and I said together.

"He means a friend of our mom's," Lucie jumped in. "He gets that mixed up sometimes."

"Do you know the name of this friend?" Detective Garrett asked.

Lucie shook her head slowly. Lucie was not a good liar, and for some reason she was lying now.

I examined the figure more closely. "Can you show me how it works?" I asked Jason.

"Like this," he said. He could have added "silly" because it was clear he thought anyone should be able to turn it inside out as quickly as he did.

I played with it for a while. I got pretty good at flipping it back and forth. On my fourth flip, I noticed a tiny compartment in the midsection of the Transformer. I pushed up the latch that kept it closed and found a paper stuffed inside.

"What's this?" I asked as I carefully unfolded it. Jason looked as dumbfounded as I did.

"Someone played with my Transformer," Jason said. He was angry. "You, Lucie?"

Lucie shook her head.

The message was short and to the point. Like Ellie's note to me, this was also written on Sandler's stationery. *Give it to us. Don't mess around if you love your kids.* I tried to keep my face expressionless and showed it to Detective Garrett.

He pulled a plastic glove from his pocket, put it on, and took the paper from me.

Chapter Four

The air in the living room grew still and I found it hard to breathe.

Detective Garrett read the note and placed it in a clear plastic bag—he seemed to have an evidence kit in his pocket. His expression never changed, although he did glance at me to see how I was doing. I tried hard to mimic his poker face. Next, he examined the figure. "Lucie, did you know about this compartment?"

Lucie shook her head.

"Jason," he said, "I have to ask you a big favor." Jason stopped using Hermione as a launching pad for his Spider-Man and turned his attention to the detective.

"Favor?" he said.

"He wants you to do something for him, something special," Lucie explained. "That's what a favor is."

"You want me to find Mom? You can't find her?"

Detective Garrett looked unhappy.

"It's all right," I said. "Lucie understands, and we've been telling Jason his mother is not coming back."

"She is too coming back. She's hurt. When she's better she'll come home."

"She died," Lucie said quietly. "Like your turtle Oscar died, remember? Your turtle didn't come back."

Jason ran from the room zooming his Spider-Man and Superman ahead of him. "No, no, no! She is coming back! Mommy is coming back!"

We followed him into the spare bedroom. Jason lay on the bed, his action figures held tightly in one hand while he twisted a corner of the bedspread with the other. "I want my mommy," he sobbed as I knelt down beside him. Lucie stood beside me and patted his head.

Detective Garrett sat on a chair near the bed and looked into Jason's eyes. "I'm sorry about your mom. Really sorry. Do you want to help us find out who hurt her?"

Jason stopped crying and nodded.

"Then I need to borrow your Transformer for a while. I'll take good care of it and I'll bring it back to you."

"Okay," he said, rubbing his eyes. "My Transformer will help. He's strong like me."

"Thank you." Garrett left the room to get the figure before Jason changed his mind. I turned on the TV to *Dora the Explorer*. Jason curled up on the bed with a thumb in his mouth.

"We'll be back," I said and kissed him. I motioned to Lucie to follow me into the living room. She wrapped part of the bedspread around Jason and walked slowly out to the living room behind me.

"I don't think Jason can handle much more about his mother right now," I said to Garrett.

"Can you, Lucie?" he asked.

Her eyes got large and she started pulling on a strand of her white-blond hair. "Yes," she said after a slight pause.

"I need to know where Jason got this action figure. Where he really got it. Was it from your dad, the way he said?"

Lucie shook her head slowly. "From some man I didn't know. Mom knew a lot of men. I didn't like this man. He pretended to be nice to us. He brought me a doll. He didn't know I was too old for dolls. And he gave Jason his Transformer. He told Jason to take it with him when he went to day care at Sandler's. He never cared about my doll, but he always asked to see Jason's Transformer when he stopped by. He'd say there was something wrong with it that he needed to fix. He'd take the Transformer into another room and then bring it back. Jason thought it was a game—fix the Transformer. My mom said it was a game."

"Can you tell me what the man looked like?"

"He was big and he was mean to our mom. He made Mom cry once. He twisted her arm."

Garrett nodded. "Do you know his name?"

Lucie was quiet for a moment. She twisted another strand of hair. "Mom called him William. She said, 'Stop, William, you're hurting me.' But she told me to go back to the bedroom when I tried to help. I heard him shout at my mother and then he left. He said, 'If you don't get it for me, you'll be very sorry.'" Lucie teared up. "Do you think he's the one who killed my mom?"

"I don't know," Garrett said. "When did he threaten her?"

"A few times. The last time was a week ago." Tears rolled down Lucie's cheeks. "I should have done something to make him stay away from her."

I hugged Lucie. "There was nothing you could do, Luce. He would have hurt you too."

"Would you recognize the man if you saw him again?" Garrett asked.

Lucie nodded. "He had a scar on his forehead." She moved her hand along her temple. "He tried to hide it with his hair, but anyone could see it."

Garrett looked at me. "I might need her to look through some pictures at the station tomorrow. Can you bring her after school?"

I nodded. "Of course. Can you do that, Luce?"

"I want to find out who hurt my mom," Lucie said.

"I think that's enough for now," Garrett said.

"Thank you, Detective Garrett," I said and shook his hand.

"I think we'll be seeing a lot of each other." He smiled. "Better call me Mason."

"Like Perry Mason," I said.

"Perry Mason? You watch old TV shows?"

"Old TV shows, old movies. It's one of my favorite pastimes."

"Mine too." He smiled again and his gray eyes took on an intensity that made me catch my breath.

"You can call me Ditie," I said.

"Ditie," he said. "An unusual name. I like it. Makes me think of Aphrodite."

I blushed. "My father gave me that nickname. And it was for Aphrodite—funny you'd make that association."

Now it seemed to me Mason blushed a little. "Not so funny."

"Can you stay for some cake and ice cream?" I asked. "I know it would mean a lot to Jason."

"Of course," Mason said. "I wouldn't miss out on cake and ice cream."

At that moment Lurleen burst into the living room. "I thought you all would never finish. And where is the birthday boy?" She pretended to look under the couch and in Hermione's ear. "He must be here somewhere."

Lucie giggled. "Oh, Miss du Trois, he's in the bedroom."

"*Chérie*," she said to Lucie. "You must call me Lurleen. Everyone does. Now let's go get that brother of yours. I've set up all the games outside."

They skipped off to the bedroom, leaving Mason and me alone in the living room. We could hear squeals of delight coming from Jason as they tickled him. We both smiled. There was something about that smile of Mason's. Something wonderful.

I caught myself. Mason had kids, which meant he probably had a wife, ring or no ring. I wasn't in any position to take an interest in him. A childhood friend had died and I had two small children to protect. Here was a smart, kind man, who just might keep the children safe. Nothing more.

I sighed. Mason looked over at me, but he didn't say anything.

I'd had the occasional boyfriend but nothing serious in my thirty-five years—with one exception. Phil Brockton. Some men couldn't overlook the fact that I had a well-rounded figure or the fact that I didn't need to depend on them for my livelihood or much else. It was a fault of mine, as my mother was quick to point out. "You must always let the man think he's in charge." Right. My mother with the iron fist was giving me advice on how to be demure. It just wasn't in my nature. I spoke my mind—too much, I admit—and once I left home, I didn't submit to anyone.

"Are you all right?" Mason asked. "You looked fierce there for a moment. You reminded me of Lozen."

"Lozen?"

"The female Apache warrior from the 1870s. She was a protector of women and children."

"I was thinking about the children, among other things. How do you know about her?"

"I admire strong women. Had to. I grew up with one—my mother. And I read. Anything I can get my hands on. How about you? Do you find time to read, what with your work and your love of old movies?"

Before I could answer, three wild creatures lurched into the living room. Lurleen was doing some kind of dance she'd learned in a Zumba class, and Lucie and Jason were mimicking her actions. She motioned to us, and it was clear we were supposed to follow along, snaking our way through the kitchen, out the back porch to the backyard.

I followed Jason, and Mason followed me. We all stopped and gasped when we saw the yard.

Lurleen had turned my backyard into a country fair. We started with Pin the Beret on the French Artist and proceeded from there to a bowling contest, which Jason won hands down. The pins were small loaves of French bread, and the ball was a French boule of sourdough. Next came a cabaret in which Lurleen was the star. She sang French tunes, leaving one word blank, which we were to fill in. Lucie caught on quickly and won that game. The piece de résistance was a piñata. As I started to inform Lurleen that a piñata was not French, she shushed me and pointed dramatically at the object dangling from the tree. It was a model of the Eiffel Tower she used as her coat rack, and on this occasion it was filled with candy. One didn't so much whack at the tower as pluck candy off its many cornices. This we all did with enthusiasm. And then it was time for cake and ice cream.

We entered the kitchen, sat down at the table, and I lit six candles for Jason.

"But I'm only five," Jason said.

"One to grow on. Now make a wish," I said.

Jason's little face grew serious. I knew what his wish would be. I could have kicked myself.

"Jason," Lurleen said. "Your wish must be something for the future. Something you want to do with me or your aunt Ditie. Or perhaps with Detective Garrett."

Jason glanced at Mason shyly. "Can I ride in a police car?"

We all looked relieved.

"I think that can be arranged," Mason said.

I could have kissed him. Instead I kissed Jason.

We sang "Happy Birthday." Jason blew out his candles, and we ate ice cream and cake until we groaned. Then it was time for my present. Jason loved the superhero wrapping paper. Inside was the Avengers set, complete with four action figures and a couple of bad guys. He ran off with it to his room and then came running back to get Lucie to play with him. Lurleen ushered us into the living room with cups of coffee, insisting she was going to clean up and wanted no one else in the kitchen.

Mason and I sat on the couch like two awkward teenagers.

"I don't know when I've had so much fun," he said.

"Me too," I said. I'm not usually at a loss for words, but I couldn't think of another thing to say.

Mason looked at me. "I'm really glad you included me. And when this is all over, I wonder if I might take you out to dinner."

I hesitated, and he jumped in.

"I'm sorry. I know the timing is all wrong. You're upset about your friend, worried about the children. You probably have a boyfriend. I didn't even ask. Forget I said anything."

"No, I don't have a boyfriend, and you didn't say anything wrong. I'd like that. I really would. You have boys but no wife?"

"My wife died several years ago."

"I'm sorry." I started to say more, but at that instant Jason burst into the living room.

"See 'tective Garrett, the 'Vengers beat the bad guys." He carried in his hand the limp figure of an enemy. It looked a lot like an octopus with a human head.

"Very impressive," Mason said. "We could use an Avenger or two on our team." He looked at me. "I guess I better go."

I nudged Jason. "Did you thank Detective Garrett for the bat and ball and for coming to your party?"

"Thank you. Can we play ball again?"

"I'd like that." Mason shook Jason's hand, waved to the rest of us, and left.

Jason headed back to the bedroom. Lucie stood in the hallway and gave me a funny look.

"Detective Garrett likes you," she said.

I knelt down beside her. "Why do you say that? I'm sure he likes all of us. He's a nice man."

Lucie shook her head. "No, I mean he likes you specially. And you like him, don't you, Aunt Di?"

I nodded. "I do like him." Lucie and I walked over to the sofa and sat down still holding hands.

"I'm glad. I like him too. The men who came to see my mom pretended to be nice, and then they got mean."

"Were there a lot of men like that lately or just the one you told Detective Garrett about?"

"There were two others. One of them always stayed in the car, so I never saw his face."

"Lucie, I have to ask you—why did Jason say his father gave him the Transformer? Have you seen your father lately?"

Lucie took her hand out of mine and sat very still. "I told you Jason got that part mixed up. I have to go check on him, Aunt Di." She jumped up and ran into the bedroom. I heard the door close and nothing more.

So my wonderful Lucie was keeping a secret from me that involved her father. Why? She looked afraid when I asked her about it and when Jason brought it up. Was their dad threatening them? Was he involved with Ellie's death? Ellie called him a deadbeat and said she hadn't seen him. Was she lying to me? It wouldn't have been the first time.

I walked to the spare bedroom and listened at the door. There was no sound but the murmur of the TV. When I peeked inside I saw Lucie lying on the bed with her arm around Jason. He was asleep. Lucie had her eyes closed and lay very still.

I let her be.

Chapter Five

I closed the door and walked down the hall to the kitchen, searching for Lurleen. The kitchen was spotless. Everything was out of sight—including Lurleen. I found her in the backyard cleaning up. The yard looked like a tornado had touched down.

"I don't know how I'll ever thank you for all this," I said.

"Entirely my pleasure. You would do the same for me, and I loved every minute." She stared at me intently. "What's wrong? I know you're upset about your friend, but Detective Garrett seems like a very competent man. He'll find the person who did this. Why do you look so worried? I used to have a boxer, and when he was upset his little forehead would wrinkle, just like yours is now."

I smiled and attempted to smooth out one or two wrinkle lines. "It's not the image I'm going for, but I am worried."

"About what, *chérie*?" Lurleen stopped searching the grass for candy wrappers and stood up to give me her full attention.

"Lucic isn't telling us the truth about her father or where Jason got his Transformer."

"Hmm," Lurleen said, one hand on her slender hip. "This deserves some thought—and maybe another piece of cake when I'm done here. You think best while you're baking. I think best while I'm eating."

"Sounds good. I'll finish up here. You go inside and relax."

"Nonsense. Two hands are better than one. Make that *quatre mains*." She raised her hands, wiggled her long fingers, and began picking up baguettes from our bowling game.

"It's a shame to waste all this French bread," she said. "Waste not, want not, as my aunt liked to say."

"We'll leave it for the birds. They'll be thrilled." I helped Lurleen break up the pieces of bread and scatter them around the yard. Together we untangled the Eiffel Tower from the Japanese maple and carried it carefully to her car where it just managed to fit into the back seat.

"Do you need help on the other end unloading this?"

"No, no. I'm stronger than I look thanks to my interval training and body-sculpting classes." She flexed her muscles to show me some very fine biceps. "I love not working. It gives me time for all the things I do enjoy. If I missed a single exercise class, which I wouldn't, my instructor Wendy would e-mail me to make sure I was all right."

We packed the rest of the supplies in her trunk and passenger seat while I thanked her again for her magnificent party.

"It was nothing. *Rien du tout.* If I'd known children could be this delightful, I'd have had a couple."

We walked together up the driveway to the porch. She settled herself in the swing and looked up at me expectantly.

"Of course, the cake," I said. I grabbed a cup of coffee and a slice of cake for each of us from the kitchen and put them on a tray Lurleen had given me for Christmas. I'd just moved back to Atlanta, and Lurleen insisted I'd finally moved home. She gave me a tray with the picture of what she called her spiritual home. Paris, of course. A black-and-white photo from the fifties shot at night. The city looked like a sparkling jewel.

I left the house door open, so I'd hear the kids if they stirred, and sat beside Lurleen. The sky was an intense blue, and the temperature was perfect. Early April in Atlanta—one of my favorite times in a place that got too exuberant by June and too hot in August. My giant Southern magnolia was getting ready to display her creamy white blossoms. The small patch of lawn in the front yard needed mowing, but that could wait another week.

Lurleen and I rocked gently back and forth on the swing, sipping our coffee and eating our cake. One of the many things I loved about Lurleen was that she was never in a hurry. She could get anxious and buzz around like a copper-colored dragonfly, but when it came to friendship, she had all the time in the world.

She waited for me to begin.

"I'm worried about the kids," I said. "They may be in danger."

"In danger?" Lurleen leaned toward me. "What's going on?"

"You missed some of the conversation with Mason."

"Mason?"

"Detective Garrett. He told me a detective was killed last week. Someone who worked in the Cyber Crimes Unit and talked to Ellie two weeks ago.

Who knows what Ellie got herself into this time? And I have a gut feeling Lucie is lying about where Jason got his Transformer. She says it wasn't from her father, but I don't believe her."

Lurleen looked thoughtful. "She must be scared," she said. "I know—not from personal experience, mind you, just from what people have told me—that sometimes a kid is threatened into keeping secrets."

"I know that too from my work," I said. I looked at Lurleen, and I wondered for a moment if she might be talking about herself. She never mentioned her childhood and changed the subject whenever I asked about it.

Before I could continue, my cell phone rang. It was Tommy.

"Hi, Mabel. Didn't hear from you, so I'm calling you back. You thought about my plan?"

"I've been busy, Tommy. There's a lot going on here. A lot of bad stuff. You remember Ellie Winston?"

Tommy, never at a loss for words, was silent for a couple of beats. "Sure I remember Ellie. The girl you were glued to growing up? The one who wouldn't give me the time of day? Yeah, I remember her."

"Well, she died. She was murdered two days ago. I'm surprised you didn't hear about it." Tommy wasn't exactly an ambulance chaser, but he did keep up with people who might need his services. He was always on the lookout for a case that would put him on the news as an up-and-coming Alan Dershowitz. "Oh, no," was all he said.

"I've got her two kids with me."

"I'm sorry, Mabel. Do the police know who did it?"

"No."

I filled him in on what the police did know. "Don't spread it around that the kids are with me, okay? I'm just not sure how safe they are."

"Who would I tell? Of course I won't say anything," Tommy said. "If I can help, let me know. I really liked Ellie." He sounded genuinely sad.

"So did I. Thanks. I haven't thought any more about your proposal, but my answer won't change. I'm not selling the farm."

"Let's talk about that later. Let me know if I can help you out. I could babysit, whatever you need."

"Babysit? You, Tommy? I've never seen you around kids."

"You underestimate me, Mabel. You always have. You think I only care about myself, but you've got that wrong."

I did think Tommy cared entirely about himself. "Okay," I said. "I'll try to revise my view. How about dinner tomorrow night, so the kids can meet you and then we'll see about your babysitting later on."

"Let me check my calendar." Silence. "Sorry, Mabe. Can't do it tomorrow. Booked. Booked all week, but next week looks good."

"Next week they may not even be with me. I gotta go." I hung up on him. Lurleen gave me that look that said she understood about siblings even though she didn't have one.

"I just don't get Tommy," I said. "One minute I think maybe he really does have empathy for other people, like when I told him about Ellie. He sounded genuinely upset. Then he offers to help and takes it back as soon as I ask him to follow through."

"He's a man with secrets," Lurleen said to me. "Maybe someday he'll share them with you." She swept crumbs off her lap and gave me her full attention. "Now, tell me about everything I missed in your conversations with Detective Garrett, or should I say Mason?" She smiled innocently at me.

"Some men were threatening Ellie. The note we found in Jason's Transformer—on a Sandler's note pad—warned her that the kids would be harmed if she didn't give them what they wanted. Lucie described one of the men—someone named William with a scar along his forehead."

Lurleen put her half-eaten cake down on a side table near the swing. "How does Sandler's figure into this?"

"I don't know. Ellie said she used to work at Sandler's and they were going to make her a nice severance offer. I mentioned that you used to work there, but she said she didn't know you."

Lurleen ran a hand through her thick hair and pushed a few auburn curls behind her ear. "I have a good friend, Marie Vanderling, who still works there. She knows everyone and everything. Whenever anyone left Sandler's, Marie said another one had gotten 'over the wall.' I felt bad about leaving Marie behind, but I think she has her own reasons for staying. And she can help us now."

"Help us?" I said.

"Solve the murder of course. Marie loves intrigue. She has the scoop on everyone at Sandler's, and she'll be glad to help us. You can be Nancy Drew and I'll be your faithful sidekick. Nancy did have a sidekick, didn't she? Remember, you and I watched that old movie of hers, *Nancy Drew and the Hidden Staircase*."

"I think the sidekick was named Ned."

"A minor problem."

"Lurleen, this is too dangerous to play around with. Two children have lost their mother. They may be at risk."

"Point taken. I sometimes get carried away. It's just that I have access. Access that Detective Garrett might not have. And I didn't tell you the most vital piece of information."

She waited for effect. I waited too. It was a standoff between old friends.

"All right, I give," I said after several seconds. "What is your vital information?"

"Lucie mentioned a man named William with a scar. I know one man with a scar like that, and his name is Billy Joe Sandler. We used to call him the Triple B, for Bad Boy Billy. He's William Sandler's grandson. At one point he was being groomed to become the next CEO, but that was before he got into all kinds of trouble."

"Trouble?"

"Drugs, alcohol. Small stuff. Although I did hear he beat someone to a pulp in a bar. That almost got him put in jail for a while. Sandler Senior got sick of his bad behavior."

"Wow!" I said. "You think he's William?"

"Has to be. Probably trying to seem more grown-up with a new name. But a new name doesn't change old behavior. *Plus ca change, plus c'est la meme chose.* He's the same old Billy Joe."

"We have to tell Mason," I said.

"Right. Mason."

"Detective Garrett."

"By all means."

I dialed his number. He didn't pick up, so I left a message.

When I was done, Lurleen took both my hands. "I think he's lovely," she said. "Your detective," she added when I gave her a blank look. "And I will plan the wedding."

"Don't you think that's jumping the gun a bit?" I asked.

"Why? Is he married? Do we have to go through a troublesome divorce?"

"His wife died a few years ago," I said. "But I've known him two days."

"I see," Lurleen said. "Of course, for the French this would not be a problem. You'd have an affair, see where things went, and decide later if this was a permanent or temporary relationship. But you Americans are so much more cautious."

"We Americans?"

"You know what I mean, *chérie.* I may be American by birth but certainly not by temperament."

I nodded my agreement and smiled. "You really like him?" I said.

"*Ooh la la,* I think he's perfect. For you, that is. He's not my type, so no worry there. I like my men a little more out there. And your Detective Garrett is quite self-contained. Steady I would say. Kind."

Lurleen was a very good judge of character.

"I like him too," I said. "But I can't think about a relationship right now, and I haven't had good luck with men."

"What are you talking about? Sure, you had that ridiculous date from Match.com, but who cares about that? And then there was someone else, I forget his name, who soured you on all men. That was years ago, and I could have told you he wasn't a keeper."

"You mean Phil Brockton?"

"That was his name. Phillip Brockton the fifteenth or something like that."

"Phil Brockton the fourth. What do you mean you knew he wasn't a keeper?"

"Phil was always about Phil. And so serious about the Civil War. Of course, the 'War of Northern Aggression' will never be over—not if you live in the south. But Phil took it to a ridiculous level. Dressing up like a Civil War general—"

"Colonel," I said. "His great-, great-, great-grandfather was a colonel in Cobb's Legion. Phil's uniform has buttons from the colonel's coat."

"I rest my case, *chérie.* He spent more time traveling to Civil War plays than he ever did with you."

"They're called reenactments, not plays," I said. "And plenty of people spend their lives doing that."

"Well, I'm sorry for their wives if they have them."

"I thought you liked Phil."

Lurleen shook her head. "Not really. I didn't say anything because you seemed to love him, but you deserved much more. When he left, I thought, Good riddance, *bon debarras.* Don't repeat that—it's very rude in French, but it's the right expression for him. I didn't know you'd be so crushed and give up on men all together. It's a terrible waste, Ditie. You have so much to offer."

"Speaking of Phil, I got a letter from him two days ago. He's coming to Atlanta sometime soon."

"You're not going to see him!"

"I don't know."

"Oh, Ditie, how can you be so clearheaded about so many things and so totally confused about this man? Here is Detective Garrett, ready and willing. And you think about Phil Brockton?"

"I did throw away his letter. Maybe that will be the end of it." I studied her. "How do you know so much about Detective Garrett and his intentions?"

"I saw the way he looked at you during the party. I'll bet he wants to take you out." She smiled. "I can tell by the look on your face I'm right."

"It's the wrong time. He said so too."

Before I could say more, Lucie appeared at the door with Jason beside her. Lurleen and I made room for them on the swing. I cuddled Jason, and Lurleen put an arm around Lucie.

"I bet you two are hungry for dinner," I said. "I wondered if you were going to sleep all night. Why don't we go out to eat? After all, it's still Jason's birthday. Would you like that?"

Both children nodded enthusiastically.

"How about the Varsity?"

The children stared at me as if I were speaking Swahili.

"The Varsity? Hot dogs? Onion rings? What'll ya have? What'll ya have?"

No signs of recognition.

"Okay. Well, the Varsity is a tradition in Atlanta. They claim to be the biggest drive-in restaurant in the world. We'll make it a birthday tradition. Maybe Lurleen will join us." I looked over the children's heads at Lurleen.

"Ah, I would love to, *mes chéries*, but I am stuffed like a French sausage. No room." She patted her flat belly. "Remember, I will pick you up after school tomorrow and then the fun we'll have!"

We all got up at once. Lurleen kissed each of us on both cheeks and we watched as she folded her long legs into her tiny Citroën and drove off down the street.

I asked if the children were ready to go, and Jason looked at me.

"Can Mommy come with us? I want to wait until she comes home. She'll be hungry."

"Oh, Jason," I said, sitting back down on the swing. He climbed onto my lap.

"Mommy missed my birthday party," he said, and with that he started to cry. Lucie wasn't far behind. She cuddled next to me, rubbing her eyes and her nose from time to time. I grabbed some tissues out of the box on the table next to the swing. One for Jason, one for Lucie, and one for me.

We didn't talk. We just sat in the swing, barely moving, crying our eyes out. Hermione joined us, aware that something was terribly wrong, and settled at our feet. Even Majestic jumped up on the swing next to Lucie and crept onto her lap. We were as sad as we could be, but we were a family. I knew at that moment that I couldn't bear to let these children go, and I prayed to God I wouldn't have to.

Chapter Six

The kids woke up early the next morning. I could hear them talking in the breakfast nook. Lucie was telling Jason to sit down and be quiet. It was six a.m. My alarm was set to go off in fifteen minutes. I jumped up, grabbed my bathrobe, and headed for the kitchen.

"You're up early." I gave them each a kiss. "What have you done, Lucie? I was going to make breakfast—you didn't have to."

"Oh, I always make breakfast," Lucie said. "My mom sleeps in, and I get me and Jason ready for school." She hesitated, and I could see she was trying not to cry. "Jason, take your bowl to the sink and brush your teeth." She spoke in a voice that could have been Ellie's, and Jason did as he was told.

"May I have some cereal along with you?"

"Yes. Do you want toast, Aunt Di? My mom always had toast and black coffee." Lucie teared up.

I hugged her and stroked her hair. She leaned against me and let me treat her like the sad little girl she was.

"I miss my mom," she cried. "She didn't say goodbye to me."

"I miss her too. The last thing she said to me was about you and Jason—how much she loved you and that she wanted me to keep you safe."

Lucie dried her eyes with the back of her hand. "She said I was a very good cook."

"I couldn't make anything except chocolate chip cookies when I was your age. I think cereal will be fine for me this morning. Some Cheerios and maybe a banana and some milk. I'll get it."

"No, Aunt Di, I'll get it for you." Lucie dashed to the refrigerator, brought out the carton of milk, and put it on the table. She handed me a banana and placed a bowl and spoon in front of me.

"You are going to make me very lazy."

She smiled and sat down beside me. "Is there a bus we can take to school, Aunt Di?"

"There probably is, but I'm going to drive you. And remember Lurleen is going to pick you up after school. Wait for her in the office. I'll let the principal and teachers know about that. Can you pick Jason up at his classroom?"

"Of course." Lucie gave me a look. "You know, Aunt Di, we can walk home."

I shook my head. "I know you can, but Lurleen wants to pick you up and you'll stay with her until I get home."

Jason came back into the breakfast room in time to hear our conversation. "I want my mommy to pick me up," he said.

"Hush," Lucie said. "Mommy is far away. She can't pick you up."

Jason came over and climbed onto my lap. "When will she come home?" he asked me.

I rocked him. "Your mommy can't come home. I'm sorry, baby."

Jason sat up. "I'm not a baby. I'm Superman. I will bring her home. You'll see."

He jumped off my lap and headed to the bedroom where his Superman and Spider-Man were undoubtedly waiting for him. Lucie got up and didn't seem to know if she should follow him or clean up in the kitchen.

"I'll clean up. You help Jason. We'll leave in half an hour."

The kids were ready ten minutes before I was. Lucie had a backpack by the door for each of them. She gathered them up, took Jason's hand, and waited while I opened the door and ushered them outside. I locked the door and headed for my Corolla.

Parked down the street I saw a magnificent matte-black Dodge Ram. I nudged Jason whose eyes grew wide at the sight of the truck. It was a real beauty built for off-road capacity, something my father would have loved. I could hear the conversation he'd have had with my mother: "Need a new truck for the farm—might as well be a looker." And I could hear my mother's disdainful response: "Nonsense, George. Won't stay new for half a minute. Not the way we work our trucks. A waste of good money." She was right, of course, but right wasn't always fun, and I don't think my dad got to have much fun on the farm.

"Maybe it's time I get a new car," I said to both of them.

Jason's eyes lit up, but Lucie shook her head.

"I love your car," Lucie said. "I remember it from the time we stayed with you in Florida."

"You have a very good memory. It's ten years old. Older than you. I hang onto things as long as I can." Maybe I had a little more of my mother in me than I cared to admit.

"Me too," Lucie said, as she climbed into the car. "See my locket? My mom gave me that and told me to keep it safe forever."

"It's beautiful, Luce. What's inside it?"

Lucie carefully opened it up and showed me the miniature pictures. "It's a picture of Mom and Dad when they didn't fight all the time."

I held Lucie's hand as I studied the pictures. Ellie, smiling, looked beautiful. John, also smiling, looked the way I remembered him—round face, glasses, and hair as blond as Lucie's. Briefly I wondered where Jason got his dark hair and complexion. "I'm glad you have that, Lucie." I closed the case.

"Everyone buckled?" I asked before I got in the driver's seat. They were. As we pulled out of the driveway, the Dodge truck roared to life. The driver tailgated me to the light at Highland. That was weird. I made a right turn. He gunned his engine and stayed behind me. I looked in my rearview mirror, but all I could see were tinted windows.

Something was terribly wrong. I felt my grip tighten on the steering wheel, my focus sharpen. It was the feeling I had when I entered the room of a very sick child. You knew in an instant that something wasn't right.

I took a quick right turn onto a side street to see if the truck was following us.

I didn't have to wait long. He turned, barely missing my back fender. I pulled over in front of a house, hoping he'd drive past. Instead, he pulled up beside me and lowered the passenger-side window. He shouted something, but I couldn't make out what he said over the revving engine. I craned my neck to get a better look and thought I saw someone in the passenger seat. The driver pulled ahead of me to block me in. He had a gun rack on the back of the truck with two shiny rifles.

Lucie screamed. "It's him. The man with the scar. The man who hurt Mommy."

"Get down, both of you," I yelled. They ducked, and I backed up. I swerved around the truck and took off down the narrow road, careening right at the first street I found. I turned again, floored the engine back to Highland, and took a left in front of a Miata whose driver slowed down long enough to give me the finger. The truck had to wait for three more cars before it could get on the road behind me. I tore down Highland, hoping a police car would spot me. No such luck. Traffic slowed at Virginia-Highland and the truck managed to pull up on my left. This time I heard what the guy shouted at me. "Pull over. We gotta talk."

Not likely, I thought. I fishtailed right on Virginia and plowed through a 25 m.p.h. zone. Three more blocks and I skidded left on Monroe. I didn't exactly have a plan, but if I could get to Ponce de Leon, maybe someone would pick me up for speeding. The truck stayed on my tail.

I was all adrenalin. The kids remained crouched in the back seat, Lucie's doing for sure. I turned right on Ponce and for a moment I thought I'd lost him. But in a heartbeat he was behind me again. If I braked, he braked. If I pulled around a car, he was waiting for me on the other side. A cat-and-mouse game. Where were the damn cops when you needed them? I was close to Peachtree when I finally heard the siren. The policeman pulled me over and the truck sped by. But not before I made out the first three letters of the license plate.

"Sh—oot," I said. "I only got the letters."

"I got the numbers, Aunt Di," Lucie said. "Five, three, two."

I could have hugged her. "You're a wonder, Luce."

The officer didn't believe my story until I mentioned Detective Mason Garrett by name. Then he went to his car, made a call, and came back to us two minutes later.

"Detective Garrett says I'm to escort you to his office."

During the drive Lucie was silent, but Jason couldn't stop talking. "A cop. See his car? See the lights? Wow, Aunt Ditie. A real cop. Is he 'resting us?"

"No, Jason, he's not arresting us. He's helping us. He's taking us to see Detective Garrett."

I saw Jason's worried look in the rearview mirror.

"He took my Transformer."

"He'll give it back when he's done looking at it," I said.

"Detective Garrett will protect us," Lucie said. She sat up a little straighter in the back seat and patted Jason's arm as if he were frightened. But he wasn't the least bit frightened. The people who were scared to death were me and Lucie.

The patrolman led us to Mason's office. Mason (or was it Detective Garrett given the circumstances) brought us inside. "Bring a couple more chairs, will you, Joe?"

Joe did, and the three of us sat down. Mason closed the door and took notes on what happened. "You got his license," he said. "Great. Did you get a good look at him?"

I shook my head. "Lucie said it was the man with the scar. William. Lurleen recognized his description when we talked yesterday. She said it had to be Billy Joe Sandler, grandson to William Sandler, Senior."

Mason let out a soft whistle. I didn't know cops really did that. "I got your message. We know him well," he said. "We'll get an all-points bulletin out on the truck. We'll track down Billy Joe with or without his truck. He's always causing trouble, usually when he's drunk. We pick him up and Sandler's lawyers get him off with no charges. This is more serious. We'll bring him in, don't worry."

I nodded. "I think there was another man in the truck but I couldn't make him out. Could you, Lucie?"

Lucie shook her head and stared at her hands.

Mason and I had a chance to talk privately while the kids got hot chocolate out of a machine and sat with a policewoman who clearly had children of her own. They were peppering her with questions—or Jason was anyway. "Are you a real cop? Girls can't be cops—they aren't strong enough. Not strong like me." I heard Lucie's voice in the background trying to smooth the waters while the policewoman patiently answered all of Jason's questions.

"I'm not sure what to do to keep the kids safe. I can take care of myself, but I don't want to put the kids at risk. Do we need to move in with a friend or into a hotel for a while? This guy clearly knows where we live and is after the kids for some reason."

"Or after you," Mason said. "He may think you have whatever it is he wants. I'm going to give you protection for a while. I'll have a police car make circuits by your house during the day and at night you'll have a PI."

"A private investigator? Is that something I should pay for? I'm happy to do it for the kids' sake."

"No, no," Garrett said. "I know a guy owes me a favor—Danny Devalle. He's as good as they get. Part of my job is to keep you and the children safe."

Before I could say anything, he stood up and started to walk me down the hall to the kids. "I'd like to come by tonight to introduce you to Dan and see how you're doing. I'm getting a new Transformer for Jason, so maybe I can bring that along as well."

"Are detectives allowed to have dinner with people they're protecting?" I asked.

"You mean me or Dan?"

I blushed. "I meant you, but Dan could come as well."

Sarah Osborne

"I'm sure he'll be busy, but detectives like me can do what they like off duty except consort with a suspect. I get off work around seven unless something comes up. Always a possibility unfortunately."

"I understand. Come when you're done. I may feed the kids earlier, but they'll be happy to see you. 'Consort with a suspect'—that's a quaint phrase."

"What, are you an English major? Anyway, you should be pleased. It means you're not a suspect. By the way," he said, "you did say you weren't attached, didn't you?"

"I'm pretty sure you did some kind of background check on me," I said. "You probably know I've never been married. And no, I don't have anyone special in my life right now. What about you?"

Mason shook his head.

It was far too early for any involvement, but I couldn't help the warm glow that filled an empty spot in my heart. Mason seemed to read my mind.

"Tonight is not a date," he said. "More of a check-in."

I nodded. "A check-in. Good. I'm not taking the kids to school. I don't want them out of my sight."

"Agreed. Can you stay with someone else until we bring Billy Joe in for questioning?"

I nodded and called Lurleen. She said she was delighted for the company. I gave Mason her address and cell phone number.

"Good. That's where I'll meet you with Danny tonight."

I told the kids we were all going to spend the day with Lurleen.

"What about school?" Lucie asked. "Mom never let us miss school."

"It's okay, Luce. One day won't hurt. I'll go to school and get your assignments. You can work on them at Lurleen's."

Lucie looked relieved.

Mason rode down the elevator with us and saw us to our car. He told the kids how much they had helped with the investigation. He squeezed my hand and told me not to worry.

We got to Lurleen's around ten. Once the kids were settled into her spare bedroom, I told her what had happened.

"Billy Joe has always been a bad apple," she said, "but why is he going after you and the kids?"

"That's the question. There was someone else in the car. Lucie said she didn't see who it was, but I'm just not sure Lucie is telling me all she knows."

"I'll see if I can find out anything." She shook her head and appeared to be lost in thought. "I know how awful it is to be afraid to tell the truth."

I looked at her. "You do?"

She hesitated and for a moment I thought she might reveal something to me. Something about her past—the real past she never talked about. I had my own suspicions about that. Why would someone need to make up an entire history unless their real childhood was too miserable to talk about?

Instead she said, "Of course I know. I watch TV, all the news regarding children and abuse. You can go on to work; we'll be fine. No one knows the kids are here."

"Thanks. I'll stop by the clinic and see if they need me, but first I'm going to the school. I want to let them know what's happening."

Lurleen gave me a hug. She seemed to have dropped all of her French mannerisms. When things got serious, Lurleen became all business. I imagined it was how she behaved at Sandler's as an accountant for all those years.

I talked with the principal at the children's school. Fortunately she knew me from previous interactions. Several refugee families had settled in the area, and we'd spoken from time to time about difficulties the children were having. That was over the phone—this was the first time we'd met in person. I liked the look of her. A large, tall woman, in charge, but with a warmth that came through as she asked for details about the children's situation.

"I hope they won't be out of school for long," I said. "If any adult asks about the kids, could you let me know?"

"Of course." She took down my contact number.

The classroom teachers were equally concerned. I gathered up work assignments for two days and asked if anyone had been around the classroom asking for the children.

Lucie's teacher said no. Jason's teacher took a moment to answer.

"It's odd now I think of it. Some man, dark haired, did approach Jason in the playground. I told him he had to go through the office. Jason didn't seem frightened of him though. I'm sorry I don't know his name or any more about him."

"Did the man have a scar?"

She shook her head. "No scar that I could see. Is that important?"

"It might be. Thank you. If you see the man again, please let me know."

I called Mason with the latest news. He was there and took my call. "We haven't found Billy Joe yet, but we will. It's only a matter of time. I'll send someone over to the school to talk with the teacher."

We left it at that. I drove home, dropped off the worksheets for the kids, and called the clinic.

"I thought you couldn't come today," Vic said. "If you are free for the afternoon, I could use the help. We're slammed."

"Go, go, go," Lurleen said when I asked her about leaving. "We're fine."

I kissed the kids goodbye and headed for work. Every few seconds I checked my rearview mirror, but no one seemed to be following me.

Chapter Seven

Vic was delighted to see me. "I didn't put you on the roster, but I'm glad you're here."

I looked around the refugee clinic. It was always bustling, but today it was busier than usual. The waiting room was full of children and their families—some in Western clothes, others in native dress. It looked the way it always looked, like a mini United Nations gathering. Interpreters were seated by several family members, helping to get their stories straight. Staff members greeted me warmly. I worked at the clinic full time. Victoria had other responsibilities two days a week. I always felt happier when she was around. Not just because we were friends. She'd done this kind of work for years, had an infectious disease fellowship under her belt, and even worked with the Peace Corps in Sierra Leone. She was the doc I aspired to be.

She listened to all that was happening at home and insisted I leave early to be with the kids.

I worked steadily for five hours, triaging patients who needed to be seen by specialists and two who needed to go to the hospital. One of these was a seven-year-old with possible TB. That meant a series of TB tests for close relatives, something the public health nurse would handle. The other child was a ten-year-old boy with severe malnutrition and possible intestinal parasites.

Vic shooed me out the door at 4:30. "We've got the rest," she said. I looked around. Two or three families remained to be seen.

"Aggie and I can handle it. Go."

Aggie was a nurse practitioner who could handle anything. I nodded and took off for home.

My plan was to let Hermione out before I went to Lurleen's. That idea flew out of my head when I saw two cop cars in my driveway. I parked on the street and rushed up to the opened door of my house.

"What's going on?" I yelled at the cops. My voice sounded unrecognizable to me. Splintery. High-pitched. Hysterical. I could barely catch my breath. One cop came from the kitchen and another from the back bedrooms.

"Everything's okay," said the first officer. "I'm Officer Forrest. This is Officer James. A neighbor called us about a possible break-in. We put your dog out back. She was making a fuss, but she's fine now."

"What happened?" I asked.

"We're not sure yet. Your neighbor saw a truck parked on the street. Two guys inside. Apparently they broke into your house."

"Oh God," I said. "It's the men who followed us this morning."

Officer Forrest asked for details and wrote them down on a form. The questions were tedious. Full name. Phone number. Where did I work? Was this my usual time to arrive home? Did I leave the doors unlocked? He took forever writing my answers in the appropriate spaces. Why wasn't he out searching for the men and the truck?

"Look, I know who did this." I tried hard not to yell at the young officer. "It was Billy Joe Sandler. It was his truck. The police have been looking for him all day—you must have that information somewhere." I caught myself. The guy was just doing his job. The children weren't home, thank God, and that was really all that mattered. "I'm sorry." I got rid of the edge in my voice and told him about the early-morning car chase.

"That sounds like Billy Joe. He does whatever he wants, whenever he wants, and Hunter Davis keeps him from going to jail. Best criminal lawyer in Atlanta spends half his time bailing Billy Joe out of trouble. That's what happens when you have enough money. We pick him up at least once a month—but it's always on drug charges, some brawl. This one's different." The officer peered over his sheet at me. "What's he got to do with your kids, and why would he break into your house?"

I told him about Ellie, and then I mentioned Mason.

"You're in good hands with Detective Garrett," Forrest said. He nodded at his partner, who left to call Mason.

"Can't see that anything big has been stolen. Ready to take a walk-through?" he asked me.

I nodded. My stomach lurched at the sight of the kids' room. Billy Joe had stripped the bed. Turned the dresser drawers upside down and emptied them on the floor. He'd torn apart Jason's action figures, and body parts were scattered over the bed as if they'd been in some horrible galactic war.

He was desperate to find something, and by the look of things he hadn't been successful.

"We tried to call you," Officer Forrest said.

"I turn my phone off when I'm working and must have forgotten to turn it back on. I spoke with Lurleen and the kids an hour ago. Everything was fine."

"Lurleen?" James wrote down the information I gave him.

It was disgusting to imagine Billy Joe in my house. I wanted to burn everything he'd touched.

We walked through the entire house. Majestic was hiding under my bed. My room was barely disturbed. A few drawers were dumped on the bed. Nothing more.

Billy Joe seemed to think the kids had whatever it was he wanted. Or maybe he'd been interrupted in his search. Mason arrived as we finished looking over the house.

"You all right?' he said. "The kids okay?"

I nodded. "The kids are with Lurleen. They don't know anything about this, but I feel so violated. I know that's what everyone says when it happens to them, and now I understand why." I took a deep breath. Some punk like Billy Joe Sandler was not going to make me feel like a victim. "Why didn't you pick him up today?"

"We tried. I don't know how he managed to pull this off. We miscalculated. Didn't think anyone, even Billy Joe, would be stupid enough to break into your house in broad daylight."

"I need to check on the kids and talk to Lurleen."

"I'll talk with the officers. We'll dust the kids' room for fingerprints. Give us half an hour. Then you and I can talk."

I drove to Lurleen's house. When she opened the door, she could see something was terribly wrong. She hugged me and whispered in my ear, "What's happened?" The kids were on her heels.

I hugged them and turned away from Lucie before she could take a look at my face. She'd know in a flash that something wasn't right.

Lurleen came to the rescue. "There now. You have said your hellos, *mes petits choux*. I need you to go back to your Chutes and Ladders and play without me. I haven't seen your aunt Ditie all day, and I want to talk with her."

Lucie and Jason ran off without protest to the den.

Lurleen took my hand, sat me on the sofa, and whispered once more, "What is it? Did they find the men who chased you this morning?"

"No, but the men found us. Billy Joe broke into my house, turned the kids' room upside down looking for whatever it is he wanted to get from Ellie."

Lurleen's face went rigid. Her hazel eyes flashed with anger. Her jaw set. Even her hair seemed to glow with a fiery red hue. "You, the children, Hermione, and Majestic will stay with me for as long as you need to."

"I can't put you in danger," I said.

"Nonsense. If you are anywhere but here I will worry about you every minute. I knew there was a reason I took that women's self-defense class along with my Zumba training. No one messes with Lurleen du Trois. Certainly not two men in a beat-up truck."

I might not know Lurleen's real name, but I knew her character and her courage. She'd always have my back.

"It's not a beat-up truck," I said. "And these aren't just any random men. One of them is Bad Boy Billy as you call him. And the other—who knows? Two people have been killed. A police officer and Ellie. It's too dangerous."

"Billy Joe doesn't scare me," Lurleen said. "I've known him since he was a teenager with pimples. He's a big-mouthed bully, nothing more."

"Well, he scares me, and Ellie was afraid of him. I can't let him harm anyone else I love. I wish I knew what to do. Can you watch the kids for another hour while I clean up the mess at home and talk with Mason?"

"Of course. I'll fix them dinner."

Lurleen was a lot of things, but a cook was not one of them. "You'll fix them dinner?"

"Ah, *chérie*." She shook a long slender finger at me. "You know me so well, and yet I can still surprise you. Yes, I will fix them dinner. I have alphabet soup and fish sticks that look like endangered whales. I admit it is a little odd to be eating endangered species, but it will be a very educational meal. I even bought spinach, so Jason can feel like Popeye."

"I'm not sure kids today know about Popeye," I said.

"That's a relief. I find spinach a disgusting vegetable, especially after it gets all limp and mushy."

I smiled. "You are so dear. I'll tell the kids I have a little work to do before I bring them home, and then I'll get back here as soon as I can."

"Take your time. I could get used to this kid thing."

She followed me to the den where Jason and Lucie were still at their game. That was the joy and frustration of Chutes and Ladders. It was a game that could go on for hours. I peered more closely at the board. Lurleen had doctored it so that the children weren't just going up and down ladders, they were climbing Notre Dame, like the hunchback I suppose.

A ladder extended up to two of the flying buttresses. Lurleen saw me studying the board.

"You like? I couldn't resist."

"I like," I said. I gave each of the kids a long hug and a quick kiss. Told them I had some paperwork to finish up at home and would be back soon. Lucie looked at me quizzically but didn't ask any questions.

Lurleen gave me a peck on the cheek. "Please move in with me," she whispered, and I was out the door.

By the time I got back to my house, the policemen were gone, and Mason was seated in the swing petting Hermione. If dogs could purr, she would have been serenading the neighborhood with her obvious bliss. Eyes closed, head nuzzled against Mason's hand, it was good that one of us was content. Majestic appeared at the screen to the front door and then disappeared when she realized I still had company.

Mason motioned to the swing and I sat down beside him. He looked at his watch. "I told Dan to meet us here. That way we can talk without upsetting the kids. You'll be safe as long as he's on duty."

"Do you think the men will be back?"

"It's impossible to say. You'll stay with your friend tonight?"

"Lurleen said I could stay with her as long as I needed to, but I don't want to put her at risk."

Mason was quiet for a while. "You could stay with me," he said at last, almost under his breath. "I have a big house north of Buckhead. My mother lives there. She'd welcome the company."

"That can't be protocol," I said.

"It's not, but I'd know you were safe. My mother was the first female sergeant in Atlanta. She can hold her own."

"Why are you going out of your way for us?"

"I told you. It's my job. It's nothing personal. It just doesn't look good on my record if the people I'm supposed to protect get hurt."

"I see. Nothing personal."

Before he could say any more, someone bounded up the steps. A big man, six-foot-four or more and easily two hundred fifty pounds. All muscle from what I could see. He had a linebacker's physique. And baby-blue eyes. "Hi, Mason. Hope I'm not interrupting something." He spoke with a south Georgia drawl.

Mason shook his head. "Nothing that can't wait."

"Dr. Brown, this is Danny Devalle. Danny, Dr. Brown."

Danny Devalle reached over and shook my hand with an enthusiastic shake. It was abundantly clear he could have crushed my hand or any other part of my body if he wished to. His hands were enormous.

"Pleased to meet you. Call me Danny. I parked down the street just to make sure no one would spot a strange car next to your house. Wanna fill me in?" This was said to Mason.

Mason looked over at me. I looked at Devalle, smiled, and turned back to Mason. "While I appreciate your offer of a place to stay, I think Danny can protect us at Lurleen's. That way I won't have to disrupt the kids or the animals any more than they already have been."

Mason nodded. "Sure." He gave Devalle a summary of all that had happened, from the death of Ellie to the most recent break-in. "You heard about Schmiddy's death?" he asked when he'd finished.

"Yeah," Danny said. "Terrible."

"It seems he talked with Eleanor Winston a few days before he was killed."

"You know what he was working on?"

"Something to do with Sandler's Sodas, according to his coworkers. That's all I know," Mason said. "I can't find the usual case notes. Schmiddy could get sloppy about paperwork, but no notes? That doesn't make sense."

Danny and Mason exchanged a look.

I stood up from the swing and offered to make coffee. It was clear the two of them had something in mind that I wasn't meant to hear.

"Okay with you, chief?" Danny said, looking at Mason. "I'm on your clock."

Mason nodded.

"Then I'd appreciate that, Dr. Brown," Danny said to me, "if it wouldn't be too much trouble."

"How about chocolate oatmeal coconut cookies to go along with that?"

"That would be mighty nice." He grinned and showed off a set of shiny white teeth, perfectly aligned. He brushed a hand over his sandy-blond hair.

His smile was infectious, and I found myself grinning back at him.

"Can I have some of those cookies as well?" Mason asked. He sounded a little peevish. Surely Mason wasn't jealous of a twentysomething, well-put together man with excellent teeth.

"Of course," I said. This was a new experience for me. I walked into the kitchen, humming an old tune from some musical or other, "So This Is Love." Premature, yes, but a nice feeling.

I gave Lurleen a quick call to say I would take her up on the offer to stay with her, given the fact that Danny Devalle would be there to protect us.

I hung up before I realized he was only there at night. Who would protect Lurleen during the daytime? Our attackers had come during the day.

Mason entered the kitchen a moment later. "I've just spoken with Dan. He's finished his other assignment. He'll stay with the kids and Lurleen round the clock until we get this case sorted out."

"You read my mind," I said, "but I don't know if I can afford that."

"I told you. Danny owes me a favor." He paused. "No one needs to know about this . . . arrangement. Danny's an old friend. We help each other out when we can."

I must have looked uncomfortable. I put the plate of cookies on the kitchen table and sat down across from him.

He smiled at me. "Maybe it is a little personal." I thought he might touch my hand, but he seemed to think better of it. He crunched into a cookie and didn't speak until he'd finished it. "These are great cookies. Maybe I'll have just one more." He stared at me. "I've been alone a long time. My boys are grown. I've never met anyone quite like you."

"You don't know anything about me," I said.

"I don't know everything about you, that's for sure. But I know you're smart, good with kids, kind."

We stood up and I hugged him. Spontaneously. Without any thought about what it might mean. He hugged me back and it felt really, really good, like I was standing at one of those chocolate fountains, mouth open, drinking in my fill of the warm, decadent sauce.

I blushed. "I didn't mean to do that."

He smiled. "Do what?"

We took the coffee and cookies out to Danny, who was waiting patiently on the porch, scanning the neighborhood. "Quiet around here," he said. "Reminds me of nights in Forsyth, Georgia, where I grew up."

While we ate, we sorted through schedules—mine, the kids', and Lurleen's. Of course, I didn't really know what Lurleen did during the day aside from her fitness classes. I just knew I wanted her to be protected.

It was after eight when we got back to Lurleen's with the animals and two suitcases stuffed with clothes. The kids had had their baths. Lurleen had given each of them an oversized T-shirt to sleep in. She'd already explained we were going to stay together at her house for a few days. Jason was delighted as long as he could have his new Avengers set. I told him I'd bring it the next day. I left out the part about having to buy a new one.

Danny fit right in. He'd played football at University of Georgia and promised to show Jason how to tackle. He'd also minored in French and didn't seem to mind Lurleen's unique accent. When she babbled in French, he babbled back. Lurleen asked a number of questions about football, a game she had previously described as an American barbaric pastime.

"Oh, please, *Monsieur* Danny, could you show me that tackle? Remember I'm a little frail, so be gentle."

Lurleen, for all her long legs and slender body, was about as frail as one of my mom's Holstein cows. The person to worry about was Danny, but somehow I was sure they could both take care of themselves.

Lucie didn't say much until she got me alone. We were in the bedroom she and Jason were going to share. "What happened?" she asked. "Why are we staying here? It's about the bad men, isn't it?"

"Yes, Lucie," I said. "Someone broke into our house looking for something. Do you know anything about that?"

"No, Aunt Di, I promise I know nothing about that."

"But you do know more about the men than you're telling me. Your dad is involved in this, isn't he?"

"Not my dad," Lucie said quietly. "Jason's dad."

Chapter Eight

I sat on the bed, holding Lucie's hand, staring at her. "Jason's dad?" was all I could manage. That explained a lot—Jason's dark coloring and the break-up of Ellie's marriage while she was pregnant with him.

"You're mad at me, aren't you, Aunt Di?" She burst into tears. "I told a lie." She pulled away from me and hid her face in her hands.

I took both her hands and made her look at me. "Oh, Lucie, I'm not mad at you. If you lied to me it was to protect someone. And, technically, you didn't lie. I never asked you about Jason's dad. I never knew he had a different dad." The person who had lied to me was Ellie. The only person who could ever do that and keep my friendship. I hugged Lucie and asked if she would be willing to talk to Detective Garrett.

Lucie nodded. I wiped the tears from her face with my hand, gave her another hug, and walked her into the living room. Lurleen and Dan seemed to be in a wrestling formation on the floor. Jason was beside them, learning a move apparently, while Mason sat on the couch watching the action. He stood up when he saw me come in with Lucie. Good manners or maybe good instincts. He could see we had some news.

I sat Lucie down on the couch next to him. "Lucie has something to tell you. All of us, actually."

That got Danny's attention as well. "We'll finish this another time," he said to Jason.

Lurleen looked up at me from the floor. "Shall I tuck Jason into bed?"

I nodded. I gave him a hug and promised to be along in a minute. Jason didn't protest. He took Lurleen's hand as she led him off to the bedroom. I could hear her start to sing "Sur le Pont" and Jason's attempts to sing along.

I sat in an armchair across from Lucie. "Okay, Luce. Tell Detective Garrett what you just told me."

"It wasn't my dad who gave Jason his Transformer. It was Jason's."

Mason looked at me.

I shrugged. "I never knew the kids had different fathers."

Once Lucie started, she just kept talking. "He came by to see Mom one day. He brought presents for me and Jason. He acted all lovey-dovey—that's what my mom said. She said, 'You can't just come in here and act all lovey-dovey. We haven't seen you in four years. It's business first and then we'll see.'"

"Do you remember when he came?" Mason asked.

"A few months before my mom died." Her voice trailed off.

"I know this is hard for you, Lucie," Mason said, "but it's really important. You're doing the right thing by talking to us. Tell me what you know about the Transformer."

"He told Jason it was a very special gift and he had to take it to school with him every day. Jason went to the day care at Sandler's, one floor down from where my mom worked. Jason was worried because the teachers didn't like kids to bring toys from home. My mom said she'd keep it at her desk during the day, so it could protect her, and then she'd give it back to him when she picked him up. Sometimes when Jason's dad came to see my mom, he'd ask for the Transformer. He'd play with it with his back to us, and then he'd get mad. He'd say, 'Where is it?' And my mom would say, 'I'm doing the best I can.'"

"Did he come alone?" Mason asked.

"At first. He said it had to be a secret that he came. We couldn't tell anyone or he wouldn't come anymore. The man with the scar came with him later and said if we told anyone, someone would get hurt. He looked at Jason and me when he said that."

"Was it just the two of them, Lucie?" Mason asked.

At this point, Lurleen reappeared from the bedroom. She sat down quietly in a chair across from Lucie.

Lucie repeated what she'd told me. "There were three people sometimes, but the third person always stayed in the truck. I could never see who it was through the tinted windows."

"What is Jason's dad's name?" Mason asked.

"Charles Flack," Lucie said. "My mom called him Charlie."

"What did he want? Do you know?"

"My mom worked at Sandler's Sodas, and I think he used to work there. He kept saying to my mom, 'You can help me get my old job back. You have'"—Lucie searched for the word—"'connections.' My mom said, 'I tried.' And he said, 'Try harder, and we'll all be millionaires.'"

Lucie stopped talking and let out a big sigh. I motioned for her to come over to me. "I know you're exhausted, honey. You did the right thing." I sat her in my lap, and she didn't protest. She put her head on my chest and closed her eyes. I felt as if I were holding a child half her age. More than that, I felt as if I were holding *my* child. My child, whom I wanted to protect from every bad thing that had ever happened to her in the past and that might be heading her way in the future.

Lurleen moved over to me and managed to wedge her slender body next to my more ample one. She stroked my arm as I rubbed Lucie's back. Mason looked as if he wished he could take Lurleen's place.

Lucie's breath evened out and it was clear she was asleep. I glanced at Lurleen. She slid out of the chair like a contortionist. I started to move Lucie to the side of the chair, so I could help her get to bed.

Mason swooped in like one of Jason's superheroes and picked her up from my arms. "I've got her," he whispered. "You lead the way."

We took off her shoes and socks, tucked her into bed beside Jason, and crept out of the room, closing the door softly. She could sleep in her clothes for one night.

Dan and Lurleen were seated side by side on the couch waiting for us. Mason and I sat across from them in two separate chairs, leaning forward, so we could talk quietly and not wake the kids. I'm sure we looked like a gang of conspirators planning our next heist. What we were planning was a way to catch Charlie Flack and Billy Joe and bring them in for questioning.

"We'll get Billy Joe in a day or two," Mason said. "He may have gone underground for a while, but he can't stay there for long. Every cop in the city is looking for him. As for Charlie Flack, we'll see if he's in the system. Did you ever meet him?"

I shook my head, but Lurleen seemed to think the question was meant for her.

"No, I don't think I did," she said. She shook her long hair from side to side. It brushed against Dan's face, which didn't seem to displease him in the least. "I worked at Sandler's for twelve years, but Sandler's is a big place. I was in the USA Fountain Area as an accountant for a few years and then moved into corporate. Kept track of everyone's reports. Made sure they had what they needed, handled their expense accounts." Lurleen caught her breath and looked up at Mason. "I didn't mean to go on and on. I guess you're not really interested in my history. But you may be interested in the fact I have a friend who is the executive assistant to a senior VP—

Marie Vanderling. She might know about your man. Remember, Ditie, she's the one I told you about. The one who kept tabs on each of us as we left Sandler's and congratulated us on our escape."

"Was it really that bad to work there?" Mason asked.

Again Lurleen shook her head. This time several strands of hair lingered on Dan's face, covering one eye and tickling his nose. His fault for sitting so close to her. He moved them gently away. "It wasn't so bad for everyone," she said. "Like Lucie said, they have a day care program in the building. Very convenient. And they even have a wellness clinic with a good-sized gym. But it was cutthroat competition if you wanted to get ahead. That came from the top. You do the job the way the boss wanted you to do your job, or you were out. You increase the value of the company or else. And loyalty was spelled out in capital letters. They would have branded us with it if they could have. I saw Sandler Senior get vicious when someone bucked him or seemed to doubt his authority. He'd blow a gasket, and they'd be out the door in five minutes never to return. I stayed under the radar."

"By all means I'd like to talk with your friend," Mason said.

Never one to miss an opportunity, Lurleen glanced at her watch and pulled out her cell phone.

"It's after ten," Mason said.

"She'll be up." Lurleen started to dial. "And she'll love to hear the info about Billy Joe. She's the one who gave him the nickname Bad Boy Billy. As to Charlie Flack, she'll find out about him in a heartbeat."

"Where does her loyalty creed come in?" I asked.

"She's super loyal," Lurleen said proudly, "to herself and to a few close friends like me. She has so much dirt on everyone, her job is secure for the next twenty years if she wants it to be. She talks about leaving, and frankly there are a dozen people who would pay her big bucks to get her out of there. But she has her own reasons for staying. I think she's involved with someone. Someone high up. She's never come clean about that. Marie knows when to keep her mouth shut."

Lurleen listened to her phone for several seconds. "Call me whenever you get this, night or day," she said and hung up.

Mason handed Lurleen his card. "When she does call you back, please give her my number and ask her to call me."

"*Bien sur,*" she said.

Mason stood up. "It's been a long night." He looked over at Dan, who seemed to be settling in for a comfortable evening next to Lurleen. "I'm sure you have work to do outside to secure the area."

Dan jumped up as if he'd been shot. "Yes, sir," he said. He wasn't being lazy—I think he'd just forgotten for a moment he was on the clock. Lurleen's presence can do that to a person.

Dan gave Lurleen a tender look that said he'd take care of everything and she was not to worry about any intruder.

Lurleen reached up and squeezed his arm, indicating that such a strong young man could provide all the protection she could ever need.

I walked Mason to the door. He leaned in close to me, leaving me a little breathless. "We'll catch these guys," he said. "We'll find Ellie's murderer and keep the kids safe."

"I know." I backed away from him. There were too many pheromones zipping around the room.

He looked a little hurt but left without another word.

Chapter Nine

We all woke up bleary eyed the next morning. Everyone except Jason, that is. He was running around the house at six in the morning shouting at Hermione to be still and wait for him. Apparently, my infinitely patient dog had grown weary of being a launching pad for Jason's action figure adventures. I stumbled out of the guest room, gave Jason a peck on the head, and put coffee on. I was pretty certain Lurleen wasn't an early riser, so I shushed Jason and made sure Lurleen's bedroom door was shut tight.

There wasn't a lot to eat in Lurleen's kitchen. No wonder she stayed so slim. I told Jason to sit tight while I dressed and then he could help me with a mission to bring food from my house. He thought that was a great idea. I took the world's quickest shower, dressed in two minutes, and was back in the kitchen pouring coffee in five. That was apparently enough time for Jason to disappear. I could feel myself starting to panic. How could I lose a five-year-old boy inside a house? Had someone broken in? Nothing looked disturbed. Hermione stood at the front door, sniffing and whining.

Outside I found Jason and Dan whispering on the porch.

Thank God.

"There you are," Dan said. "It was quiet all night. I drove over to your house. Quiet there as well. Jason says you're headed that way. Need a lift?"

"I wouldn't mind the security," I said, walking toward my car. "Let's take my car. I've got Jason's booster seat in the back."

"I don't need no booster seat," Jason said.

"It lets you see better," I said as I buckled him into the back seat. I scanned Lurleen's street. No black truck. No cars of any description on the road. It was just beginning to get light. "It seems safe enough."

We were there in three minutes. Outside my front door was a florist box. Dan said it wasn't there when he checked on the house and insisted on looking it over before he gave it to me. Inside was a yellow rose. *Thinking of you*, the note said. *I'll call later.* It wasn't signed. Yellow roses are my favorite flowers. Could Lurleen have told Mason that? And why would Mason be sending me flowers? Was this his idea of taking things slow?

I stuffed three grocery bags with everything I thought the kids might want to eat. Dan and Jason carted the bags out for me. I carried the box with the yellow rose.

When we got home, Lurleen was standing at the front door, hands on her hips. "Where have you been?" she said to us. She looked a little like the Madwoman of Chaillot, and I said as much. That seemed to calm her down. She patted her mass of unruly curls, wrapped her bathrobe more tightly around her body, and smiled. The smile was meant primarily for Dan.

"I thought you had deserted us," she said to him.

He blushed. "No way."

Lurleen opened the door just wide enough to allow Dan to squeeze through with his bags of food. He couldn't avoid brushing up against her.

"Silly me," Lurleen said. "I haven't given you any room to breathe." She moved about an inch to one side. Jason scooted in behind Dan a second before Lurleen let the screen door slam in my face. It wasn't intentional— she just had other things on her mind. She floated after Dan to the kitchen while I struggled with the catch on the screen door and my florist box.

Lurleen finally registered my existence as I was searching for a bud vase in her butler's pantry.

"What are you looking for, *chérie*? Are you inspecting my kitchen for some reason? Do you now work for the board of health? The children will get no germs from me, I can assure you."

"I know, Lurleen. The kids could eat off the kitchen floor." And it was true. Lurleen was as tidy as she was prompt.

"Did you tell Mason about my passion for yellow roses?" I asked, showing her the box.

"Not me." She examined the rose and then the card. "Nice note, but why didn't he just sign the card?"

"I don't know." I found a crystal bud vase for the rose and left the card beside it on the sill above the sink.

"Good choice," Lurleen said, pointing to the vase. "A gift from Jacques many years ago."

"Jacques?" Danny asked.

"A boyfriend from long, long ago. I was little more than a child at the time. Nothing to worry about." Lurleen smiled sweetly at him. She stood close to him at the island where he was unloading the bags. "I was just whipping up some crepes when Lucie came into the kitchen, wondering where Jason was. Well, that set my head *dans tous ses etats.*"

"Set her head in a tizzy," Dan translated. "*Desole,*" he whispered to her as he started to unload the bags. I joined him, opening cupboards to decide where everything might go. Lucie stood quietly at my side, putting the cold things in the refrigerator.

"You should apologize to Lucie not me," Lurleen said with a touch of righteous indignation.

Lucie remained silent.

"I'm sorry, Luce," I said. "All my fault. I thought I could run over, get some food, and be back before you woke up. I won't do anything like that again."

"It's okay," Lucie said. "When I saw you were gone with Jason, I didn't worry so much. I knew you'd take care of him."

"Thanks, honey. Now, what is this about your fixing crepes for breakfast?" I said to Lurleen.

"Ah *chérie*, you think I am just a little puff of French pastry, but every respectable French woman must know how to cook." She poured some batter into a crepe pan. "Don't you remember I went to the Cordon Vert for a course last summer?" she whispered.

"The Cordon Vert?" I asked. "You mean the Cordon Bleu."

"No," she said and sighed. "They made a special course for me. Vert for beginner. Bleu will be next year I hope. Anyway, I now make very good crepes."

I smelled something burning.

"Oh, no," Lurleen cried. "My crepes!"

I grabbed the pan off the stove but not in time to save her charred crepe. "Everyone out of here," I ordered, "so Lurleen and I can fix breakfast. Lucie, you may stay and help."

Jason and Dan seemed only too willing to leave. Lurleen gave me a look and her lower lip protruded suspiciously.

"Did I rain on your parade?" I asked.

"*Un peu.* I wanted to show Dan I could cook, and then you swept in and took over."

"I'm sorry. Bad habit of mine." I tasted her batter. "This is delicious. Do you want Lucie and me to stay out of your way?"

"No. They sent me home with the recipe for the batter if I promised not to darken their door again anytime soon," Lurleen said. "I only lasted half a day."

"Well, you got the best part of the deal," I said. "May I help you with the cooking part?"

Lurleen nodded. "I followed the directions exactly," she said. "I mixed the batter last night and left it in the refrigerator. And then the *desastre*."

"Not to worry." I pointed Lucie in the direction of the refrigerator. "Find some strawberries, Luce, and wash them. We'll slice them up, sweeten them, and put them in the middle of our crepes. Let's work on the crepes first. The secret is to be quick and confident." I washed the non-stick pan, heated it, coated it with butter, and added the batter to the center, swirling it around the pan. I flipped the crepe over in thirty seconds. In another ten seconds it was done. Lurleen watched my every move as if I were a brain surgeon. "Now your turn, Lurleen."

After two or three tries, Lurleen produced the perfect crepe. She beamed. "I'm a French chef! Look, Lucie, I'm a real French chef!"

Lucie patted Lurleen's arm the way you might pat a younger sibling who had just learned to tie her shoe. "Great job."

Lucie and I finished with the strawberries and invited the boys in for an excellent breakfast. Dan and Lurleen cleaned up while I talked to the kids.

"No school today. I brought home the work you'll need to do. The teachers know you're going to be out another day."

"Why?" Jason asked.

"You know the truck that chased us yesterday?" I said.

Jason nodded.

"The man in the truck may be a bad man, so until the police catch him, I want you to stay with Lurleen. Are you okay with that?"

"I can find the bad man," Jason said.

"I know, but right now I want you to take care of Lucie and Lurleen. Will you do that?"

Jason nodded solemnly and then took off to get his superheroes. When he was gone, Lucie whispered to me, "I'll help you take care of Jason. Don't worry, Aunt Di."

I said goodbye to Lurleen and Danny and managed to get to work early. Vic took a moment to ask about the children. I said hi to the volunteer docs from the Centers for Disease Control and nodded at the interpreters, who were chatting in the waiting room.

I loved the clinic, and it was good to be back for a full day of work. A microcosm of the world, it took care of some of my wanderlust. I suppose it was most of all the underlying warmth of the place that attracted me. Every day was unexpected, full of surprises, but amid the chaos we were all working together. The families knew it, and we knew it.

By noon, I'd seen one child from Burma with undiagnosed hearing loss, two from Afghanistan who were basically healthy but undernourished, and a worrisome infant from the Congo with severe malnutrition and failure to thrive. This one we sent on to the hospital. In between scheduled appointments we had walk-ins and follow-ups. Every interaction took time. I couldn't rush, and I couldn't be half there. I didn't have a minute to worry about the kids at home. I checked in with Lurleen at lunchtime.

"So glad you called. Marie got back to me and does she have news! Can you talk? Is it private? Can anyone overhear us?"

"I'm in my office, and I've just shut my door. No one can hear us. Tell me."

"Well, Marie doesn't know Charlie Flack—she's checking on that—but she did know Ellie. Are you sure you want to hear all this? You may not like it."

"If you're going to tell me Ellie was up to something, I think I already know that. You don't have to spare me."

"Okay then. Here goes. Ellie started working at Sandler's about six months ago as a receptionist in the new products division. It's a pretty high-security place, so Marie isn't sure how she got the clearance to work there or who recommended her. Sandler Senior normally wouldn't allow a new employee anywhere near that division. Especially when there is a product in the pipeline, and boy is there a product in the pipeline! Marie says it could revolutionize the company, set it on a totally new track. All about health and good taste.

"Anyway, Ellie met a lot of bigwigs. They seemed to take a real interest in her, if you know what I mean."

"Ellie was beautiful. And if she turned that smile on you, look out. So you're saying people got interested in her romantically."

"Exactly."

"That would explain all the clothes in her closet. They looked expensive and dressy. Perfect for a night on the town with some executive."

"She started to make the party scene according to Marie. Showed up everywhere with all sorts of men. Billy Joe was one of them. But he wasn't the only one. She didn't necessarily go home with the man she came in with, and that made a lot of the wives mad."

A knock on my door interrupted our conversation. A nurse said we had several walk-ins and asked if I was available to help. I nodded yes and mouthed, *Five minutes.*

"I've got to go, Lurleen. I'll be home as early as I can to hear the rest. You gave Marie Mason's number? And the kids are okay?"

"Of course. You worry like *une vieille poule.*"

"An old hen? That's a French expression? I don't think I've heard it before."

Lurleen paused. "Perhaps I made it up," she said in a small voice.

I realized I'd hurt her feelings by challenging her French authenticity. "Well, it's a good phrase," I said. "I do tend to worry like an old hen. I'll see you soon."

I hung up worrying about my dear friend. For all her bravado, Lurleen had the sensitivity of a wounded child, and I wondered who it was that had been cruel to her when she was young.

The nurse knocked once more, this time with a patient for me to see.

The afternoon was as busy as the morning. A family of five children from Ethiopia appeared without an appointment. Vic managed to triage them to various available staff. I met with the oldest girl, Beza, fifteen. She'd been in the US for several months. She spoke excellent English, but she couldn't seem to be specific about her complaints. Her stomach ached. Her head hurt. She had no fever, no cough. When I asked her about what was going on at home, she burst into tears. A new uncle had come to live with them. She wouldn't tell me more. Vic and I consulted and got a refugee social worker on the case. She would look into things. This was a hard one. Sometimes, medicine couldn't fix things. I finished up around five-thirty and turned my attention to home.

There was quite a reception waiting for me at Lurleen's. Mason's Jaguar was out front. The kids met me on the stone walkway with Hermione in tow. Mason, Dan, and Lurleen stood more demurely in the doorway. Everyone was smiling, even Hermione. It's not every dog that can smile, but when you find one who does, you know you have a treasure.

Chapter Ten

Jason ran along the walkway to me, arms wide open, wanting to be picked up and swung around. I happily obliged. Lucie waited patiently until Jason was back on terra firma, and then she grabbed my right hand and skipped along the grass next to me. What a joy to see both children acting like kids again.

Lurleen, Dan, and Mason stood near the doorway and ushered me inside. Mason brought me a glass of white wine once I sat down on the couch. I half expected Hermione to trot up with a pair of slippers. Instead, Majestic leaped up and settled in my lap.

"Something smells delicious," I said.

"I helped cook," Lucie piped up. "It's beef burg onion. Did I say that right, Lurleen?"

"Close enough. Boeuf bourguignonne," Lurleen replied with a pronunciation that sounded exactly like Lucie's.

"You made boeuf bourguignonne?" I asked.

Lurleen blushed. "Not exactly. Danny is the chef. But I was the sous-chef. I chopped the onions."

Dan smiled modestly. "How 'bout I take the kids outside for a little while and give the dish a few minutes more to simmer. Y'all can talk." Lucie took Dan's hand, and Jason pleaded for a piggyback ride. Dan hoisted him up one-handed.

Mason sat down beside me. "How was your day?" he asked.

"Busy. The way I like it. Those kids and their families struggle with so much. A new country. A language they sometimes don't understand. Thank goodness we have all the support we do in the clinic. One girl in particular worried me today. Fifteen. Trouble at home with some newly arrived 'uncle.' We've got a social worker looking into it, but who knows what's going on at home."

Lurleen sat very still as I told them both the story. "Social workers can only do so much," she said. "Their caseloads are enormous."

"You're right, but we have a good one. She's paid by the clinic, and I'll follow up with her." I watched Lurleen pull on one strand of hair and then another. "Are you all right, Lurleen?"

"Of course. I just hate to see a child suffer."

"So do I." I turned to Mason. "Are you making headway with the case?"

"That's a hard call. I do have some news. Do you want it now or after dinner?"

"Good or bad?"

"Mixed."

"I think I'd better hear it now."

"We found Billy Joe and his truck late this morning," Mason said.

"So you brought him in for questioning? What does he have to say for himself?"

"It's not quite that simple. It seems he missed a sharp curve and ended up in a ravine near Kennesaw. He's dead."

"Oh." It took me a minute to register the fact that Billy Joe would no longer be a threat to us. "Was anyone with him?"

"No one else was in the car," Mason said. "My captain seems convinced it was an accident, but I'm not so sure. There were skid marks that suggest another car might have been involved. That's all I've got right now. I didn't get there in time to see the body."

"I don't know whether to feel relieved or scared," I said. "If it was an accident, then maybe this is finished. But if it was murder, the children could be in even more danger."

"I've been thinking about that," Mason said. "Billy Joe may have been in charge of whatever was going on, but he wasn't acting alone. And if he was murdered, we have a ruthless killer on the loose. We have to figure out what to do about that."

I didn't say anything and neither did Mason. He was a quiet, thoughtful man. He'd tell me what was on his mind when he was ready.

Dinner came first. Lucie and Jason ran in from outside. We waited while they scurried to the bathroom and washed their hands. Then Lurleen ushered all of us into the dining room, where the smell of sautéed onion and garlic from the kitchen blotted out my worries. The table was set elegantly with fine china, crystal glasses, and small bowls of white roses. Even Jason's place had the same fine china and a small crystal goblet filled with milk.

On his chair was a very fat *Larousse Gastronomique*. I helped him up. "So you can see better, like the booster seat," I said as he started to protest.

I looked over at Lurleen. "The table is beautiful. You sure about this?" I pointed to Jason's goblet.

She smiled back at me. "*Naturellement.* Beautiful things are meant to be used, *n'est-ce pas*? If they break, *ca ne fait rien.* They're just objects. Not like people. That's where you want to be careful, if you know what I mean."

When Lurleen talked like that, I knew why she was my best friend. Why she'd always be my best friend.

"I forgot something," she said. She ran to the kitchen and brought back the yellow rose, placing it in front of me along with the note.

"What's this?" Mason asked, glancing at the card.

"You didn't send this to Ditie?" Lurleen asked. "*Ooh la la*," she said under her breath.

Mason shook his head and color rose to his cheeks. He looked at me.

"I assumed it was from you," I said. "It's not signed." Now *my* color rose. "I can't imagine who sent this to me. I have no secret admirers, I promise you."

Mason remained silent. He held my chair for me and then sat down stiffly beside me.

Dan held Lurleen's. "I'll serve," he said to break the tension. "Y'all get comfortable."

It was an amazing dinner—beginning with an apple and walnut endive salad with blue cheese dressing and ending with authentic chocolate mousse. In between was a boeuf bourguignonne Julia Child would have been happy to call her own. It even thawed Mason's cool demeanor. The kids dined mainly on sourdough bread while I savored every morsel and asked for seconds. Mason had brought the wine. White for me and a pinot noir for everyone else. Mine was a Pouilly Fouisse 2005. I'm not a wine connoisseur, but I know what I like. And this I liked.

After dinner, Dan and Lurleen insisted on cleaning up. I got the kids ready for bed, tucked them in, and then settled down in the living room with Mason. We could hear Dan and Lurleen giggling in the kitchen. It's quite an amazing sound to hear a big guy laugh like a two-year-old.

"I'm sorry for how I behaved at dinner. I just thought you said you weren't involved with anyone," Mason said.

"I'm not. I haven't been serious about anyone in years. I've only been serious about one man in my adult life." Finally, the bells went off. One man. Phil Brockton. He knew I loved yellow roses. His letter said he'd be in town in a few days. I was quiet and Mason noticed.

"You know who sent you the rose?"

"I might know."

Mason hesitated and then said, "I'd like to hear about my competition."

"He's hardly competition. Just a man who broke my heart years ago."

Mason didn't ask for more information, but I found myself getting prickly just the same. I didn't need pressure from two men when I had the children to worry about. It wasn't the right time to get involved with either one of them. Besides, the news Phil might want to impart was likely to be that he'd had some children who needed a good pediatrician. As for Mason, he and I had agreed to do nothing until the case was resolved. Even then it was a plan to have dinner, nothing more. I looked over at him. He seemed lost in thought, his brow furrowed.

"What is it?" I asked. "More bad news?"

"In a way. I'm thinking you should move again. I know it's hard on the kids but if this was murder, there's a dangerous person still out there. Maybe more than one."

I sighed. I wasn't surprised by what he said. Just discouraged. "I can call my brother, Tommy. In a pinch I think he'd put us up. He lives in Buckhead in a high-rise apartment with a person at the front desk twenty-four seven. That's about as safe as we can get. But I hate to do this to the kids again."

"It won't be for long, I promise. We're following up on leads. And we're getting some cooperation at Sandler's."

"So you do think all this *is* connected with Sandler's Sodas."

Lurleen came into the living room in time to hear my last remark. She looked at Mason. "Did you talk to my friend Marie?"

"Yes. She's been very helpful. No one seems to know where Charlie Flack is now, but he did work for Sandler's several years ago in their new products division. He's a biochemist. Your friend Marie tracked down his employment file. He was dismissed for a 'lack of loyalty to the company.' That was about three years ago."

"Told you," Lurleen said. "Lack of loyalty will get you fired in about five minutes. And never reinstated. The old man just hates that."

"What does lack of loyalty mean?" I asked. "Was he selling secrets to his competitors?"

"Funny you should say that," Mason said. "Marie thinks he tried to carry out classified information on his computer. His dismissal was hushed up. No charges were filed, but he was blackballed from the company. He wanted to get reinstated. Marie thinks that's where Eleanor came in. She was pleading his case to anyone who would listen. Wrongly accused, etc. Apparently, it did no good. He never got his job back."

I stood up to offer Mason more wine, but he shook his head. "So is that the cooperation you're talking about?" I asked. "Is Marie your inside person?"

"Marie is one of them. The whole place is pretty shaken up by the death of Billy Joe," Mason said, "or at least they claim to be. After all, he was the grandson of the CEO. I haven't gotten a chance to talk with the senior Mr. Sandler yet."

"Well, good luck with old-man William Sandler the Third," Lurleen said. "'WS3' to us. Stuffy and arrogant. He'll never tell you anything. If it's family, it stays private."

Mason nodded. At this point Dan entered the living room with a dish towel over his arm. "All done in the kitchen. What's next?" He looked at our solemn faces and dropped into a chair beside Lurleen. "What did I miss?"

"You know most of it," Mason said. He turned toward me. "Right now, we have to decide what's best for everyone. We have one or more assailants on the loose. And I think they believe you or the kids have something they want. We have to talk about where you'll be safe."

"You don't think they're safe here?" Lurleen said in a voice that was both hurt and frightened.

"Do you?"

"Dan's been great," Lurleen said.

"He's the best there is," Mason said. "That's why he's here. But he's one man and this house is not Fort Knox."

That settled it for me. "I couldn't stand it if I put you or the children in danger," I said to Lurleen. "I'm calling my brother. He owes me, and in his own way I know he loves me."

While I basically believed that statement, I wasn't at all sure how he'd react to a live-in sister with two kids. I made the phone call in the kitchen. Surprisingly he answered on the first ring.

"Hi, Mabel. I was going to call you. Got worried when I heard about Billy Joe Sandler. You all right?"

"For now. How did you hear about Billy Joe? How do you even know who he is?"

"Everyone in Atlanta knows Billy Joe."

"How did you connect him with us? Did we talk about that?"

"Must have. So anyway, are you and the kids okay?"

"I'm not sure. That's why I'm calling. Mason—Detective Garrett—thinks we need to move. Whoever did this may be desperate to get at the kids, thinking they have something he wants."

"Garrett doesn't think Billy Joe's death was an accident?"

"No."

"He thinks his death might be connected with Ellie's?"

"That's what he thinks."

"Does he know what the murderer is looking for?"

"You're full of questions, Tommy. We don't know what they want. It may be something to do with Sandler's. Why are you so interested in the case?"

"I'm just worried about you and the kids. I'm your brother, remember?"

"That's actually why I'm calling. We need a place to stay. Mason doesn't think we're safe where we are. Can you put us up for a while?"

Tommy went quiet, and I could feel my throat constrict. Once again, he might let me down. Like he had so many times in the past. All I ever wanted from Tommy was a brother who cared about me, came through for me. All I seemed to get was someone too involved in his own life to give me the time of day. Unless he wanted something from me—like the deed to the farm. I got ready to blast him.

"Look, Tommy," I started.

"Hang on, sis. Don't light into me. I'm thinking it over. How to make it work. It's a small place but you know that. Two bedrooms. The kids could have one. Can you sleep on the couch in the den? I'd give you my bedroom but all my stuff is in there. I'd just be in and out all the time disturbing you."

"Oh, Tommy. Thank you. I wouldn't dream of kicking you out of your bedroom. And the kids are wonderful. You'll see."

"Slow down, Mabel. You always move so fast. Let me think this through."

Damn him. Could he ever just say yes when I needed help? "We don't really have time for you to weigh the pros and cons about this. The kids might be in danger. We have to come over soon, like tomorrow."

I waited through five seconds of silence. "Sure. Fine," he said at last.

That was the end of the conversation. For once, Tommy was actually willing to help me. Maybe, just maybe, Tommy and I could find some common ground, and perhaps I could find the brother I'd lost when he went away to boarding school and cut me out of his life.

I rushed into the living room, phone in hand. Apparently, Mason had also been on the phone. He was just putting his away and he looked ashen.

Chapter Eleven

Mason didn't wait for me to sit down. "They've taken me off the case," he said.

"What are you talking about?" Dan asked before I could.

"They say they have a more pressing homicide. The coroner's report concluded Billy Joe was drunk, with a BAC of point two five. He also had traces of Vicodin in his system. My captain's designated it an accident and wants me to handle a shooting in Alpharetta. That's about as far as I could get from Atlanta. The Alpharetta police asked for help apparently, and he agreed to send me."

"Why would he agree to do that?" Dan asked. "There are plenty of people they could have sent. You're in the middle of a high-profile case. It's the kind of case they assign you to. Why would they take you off it now?" Dan was pacing as he spoke.

I was sitting next to Mason. Every muscle in his body looked tense. He was straining to keep his voice steady. I'd never seen Mason angry before.

"I have no idea. Whether or not Billy Joe was murdered, Eleanor Winston was. That's a certainty. Along with Schmiddy, who just happened to be working on a cybercrimes issue connected with Sandler's. I've never been yanked from a homicide before. You get Sandler's involved and you have publicity and strings being pulled. This came from someone higher up than my captain. Had to be the chief of police or the deputy chief of criminal investigations."

"I take it they're your big bosses," I said.

"Right."

"What's going on?" Danny asked. "You get the job done and you never make waves. Why would they want you out of the picture?"

"I wish I knew. Boy, I wish I knew." He turned to me. "This doesn't change your plans. Your brother agreed to take you in?" I nodded. He stood up. "I'm not convinced Billy Joe died accidentally," he said. "In fact, I'm pretty sure he didn't. I have to check out the Alpharetta situation, but I'll call you tomorrow."

He looked at Dan. "You'll hold down the fort?"

"You know I will. I'll get them moved tomorrow. First thing."

"Watch your back."

"You know me, boss. No one will follow us."

"Walk with me, Dan."

Mason took my hand before he left. "You'll be okay. I'll get this straightened out as fast as I can."

I nodded. I got the feeling there was a lot Mason wasn't telling me. Lurleen hadn't said a word or stirred from her perch by the fireplace. Now she got up, walked over to me, and put an arm around me. She led me into the kitchen and made me a cup of tea.

"What do you think happened, Lurleen?" I asked.

Lurleen shrugged and shook her head.

"Do you think Mason got pulled from the case because he was spending time off duty with us? I was afraid that could get him in trouble."

"Take it easy, Ditie. Mason is a grown man. He knows what he's doing, but *mon Dieu,* did he look angry!"

"Yeah. Now he's telling Dan everything he didn't want to tell us."

"Don't give me that look. I'll do my best to get information out of Dan, but you and I both know he's incorruptible. Believe me, I've tried."

That made me smile.

Lurleen and I sat at the kitchen table waiting for Dan to come back. It took me a few moments to realize what I was feeling. I was scared. Chilled in a place Lurleen's tea couldn't reach. If Mason was off the case, how would I know what was going on? How would I ever feel safe? How could I protect the children? And how long was I supposed to keep them out of school and hidden away?

As if she were reading my mind, Lurleen jumped in. "I'll home school them," she said.

"Really?"

"What else do I have to do with my time? I was a teacher once, briefly. I bet you didn't know that."

I shook my head. "French?"

"No, no." Lurleen laughed. "Math. It wasn't a bad job, just too many students running around disinterested in the subject. Actually I substituted for a friend, who was out for minor surgery. It convinced me it wasn't my calling. But your two—that's a different story."

Lurleen's lovely face lit up with a smile that I returned. My two—the adjective that gripped my heart.

"You'll do a great job," I said, "but how will you get there every day? You could so easily be followed."

"Really *chérie*, have I not told you about my days as a race car driver?"

I never knew when Lurleen was telling me the truth or part of her more interesting fictionalized past. I sat back and enjoyed the story. Dan walked in as she was wrapping up.

"So once Pierre and I were finished, that was the end of my twenty-four hours at Le Mans."

"You were at Le Mans?" Dan asked. "I've always wanted to see that. And who's Pierre?"

"Pierre is no one," Lurleen said, "and I only made it through twenty-two hours. Wine anyone?"

"Coffee," Dan said. "I'm on duty, remember."

Lurleen poured him the last of the coffee and offered to make another pot.

"No, no, I'm good." He joined us at the table and looked at our expectant faces. "Mason doesn't know what's going on. Hopefully he'll be back on the case in a couple of days. In the meantime I'll keep up with the investigation. I've still got contacts in the division from the years I worked there."

"Dan, is Mason in trouble for spending time with us, with me?" I asked. "After all, I could be a suspect."

"He told me you'd worry about that. You're not a suspect and you're not the one causing him grief."

"Who is causing him grief?" Lurleen asked.

"That's the million-dollar question. No million-dollar answer yet." Dan drank the last of the coffee and put the mug in the dishwasher. "I think y'all should make this an early night. We've got a lot to do tomorrow morning, and the earlier we leave here, the better."

He insisted on spending the night in the car. Lurleen promised to bring him a thermos of fresh coffee and returned to the kitchen with a look on her face that said she was ready for action. It was something about the firm set of her well-defined chin, the slight upturn in her lips, and the way she arched a single eyebrow.

"Mason may be off the case, but we're not," she said. "You and I are having lunch with Marie tomorrow. Can you arrange that at your work?"

"Tomorrow is a half day. I get done around noon."

"Perfect." She dialed Marie's number and put her on speakerphone when she answered.

"Lurleen, I'm so glad you called. It's been ages and I have so much to tell you."

"That's wonderful. I want to bring my friend Ditie to lunch with you tomorrow. She's the one I've been telling you about."

"I know. Ditie is the one with that cute boyfriend Mason Garrett—the detective who spoke with me."

"That's the one, but don't spread it around he's her boyfriend. I'm not sure he knows that yet, and it could get him in a lot of trouble."

"I'm the secret keeper, Lurleen. Don't ever forget that. Anyway I'd love to see you and your friend. Shall we meet at the Boulangerie on Boulevard?"

"Perfect."

"Tell your friend—oh what the hell—you have me on speakerphone, I'll tell her. Ditie, I've got information on Charlie Flack. Shall I call your . . . friend Mason about it or let y'all know tomorrow."

"You can tell us," I shouted into the phone from across the table. "Mason's been pulled off the case."

"That's strange. I talked to him twice and gave him a couple of other contacts. You remember Barry Hampstead, Lurleen, head of the mailroom? Of course you do. He's the one who was crushed when you left Sandler's. He was sure he could convince you to marry him eventually. Anyway, he knows almost as much as I do about Sandler's. Just works at it from a different angle. Between us, and a cute receptionist Mr. Sandler hired recently, we know nearly everything that's going on. Detective Garrett appeared to be on top of things, asking the right questions. Why in the world would someone take him off the case?"

"We don't know, *chérie*. Did he tick anyone off at the company, like Sandler Senior?"

"I don't think they've even met. Mr. Sandler's been out of the office a lot recently and when he's in, it's all about the new product."

"Right, the new product," Lurleen said.

"Very hush-hush at the moment. But a real gold mine. I'll tell you more tomorrow at one. I won't let anyone know about our meeting. I'll get a sudden migraine around noon."

"You're the best, Marie. *A tout a l'heure*," Lurleen said and hung up the phone.

She hugged me. "If anyone can figure out what's going on, it will be Marie."

"What about Barry?" I asked.

"What about Barry? He's a dear sweet boy, if that's what you mean. And he'd do anything for me. Don't give me that look. I never led him on. I've never led any man on."

In a way that was true. Lurleen was a flirt, but she never let things get out of hand. Unlike Ellie, she never used men to get what she wanted. I wondered if Ellie's murder was more personal than we'd been thinking. Was someone furious with her because he felt rejected by her? Some man like Charlie Flack?

"You look lost in thought, Ditie, but we need our sleep."

"I'll go to bed in a bit. I need to call my boss and let her know I might be late tomorrow. And I think I'll whip up some muffins for the kids, so they can have a little nutrition before we head out."

"I understand. You need to try to put together some pieces of the puzzle, don't you? Just don't stay up too late."

"You are the mother I wish I had." I hugged her once more. She headed for her bedroom and I walked into the kitchen. My boss was as understanding as always. "I can cover for you," she told me. "Come when you can." I'd never had a boss quite like her. I thanked her and began rummaging through the supplies I'd brought from home. The perfect bran muffin, that was what I was working on. Healthy and flavorful.

Half an hour was all I needed. With the muffins in the oven, I had time to think. Three people were dead—Ellie, Detective Schmidt, and now Billy Joe. Their deaths had to be related, and all of them had connections with Sandler's. A mysterious new product was about to come on line. Marie called it a gold mine. Something that would send the company in a new direction. Charlie had worked in the new products division, and he'd been fired for trying to steal information. Ellie was sure she was about to make money off of Sandler's. Schmidt had been called in by someone to investigate some kind of cybercrime.

I pulled the muffins out of the oven and let them cool. I tasted one when I couldn't wait any longer. Delicious. I'd found the perfect mix of ingredients. Couldn't a murder investigation be handled in the same way? I had most of the ingredients. It was really a question of how they all mixed together. Ellie's scheme might be about stealing information on the new product and selling it to a rival company. Corporate espionage. She couldn't be the mastermind—she wasn't clever enough to pull that off or get the information she needed on her own. It had to be someone on the inside. Charlie Flack couldn't get inside, no matter how hard he tried. Billy Joe could, and he undoubtedly knew what was going on. But Billy Joe was dead. If it was an accident—too much alcohol and drugs—then maybe that would be the end of it. But Lurleen didn't think Billy Joe was all that smart. So who else might be at the heart of the espionage? Perhaps Marie could point us in the right direction. Someone who needed money or wanted to destroy the company or both.

I cleaned up the kitchen feeling less frantic. The kids would be safe at my brother's. Dan would keep us up on the investigation, and hopefully, Mason would be back on the case in a day or two. Marie might have more inside information when we met for lunch. Another muffin and a cup of warm milk also helped calm me down. The kids were going to love them.

Chapter Twelve

The next day was a big one, but not quite in the way I expected. I called Tommy early in the morning to let him know we'd be arriving around eight with the full entourage.

"Are you kidding me, Mabel? You call me at 6:30 in the morning when I'm sound asleep? You tell me you're moving in within the hour and bringing—who did you say you're bringing?"

Tommy hated two things, always had—waking up early in the morning and surprises.

"I'm bringing the kids, the animals, and my friends Lurleen and Dan. Lurleen will be home schooling the kids, so I can work. Your condo association allows pets and I assume you're at your office all day, so the kids and Lurleen shouldn't be too much trouble."

"The apartment may allow pets, but I don't. And who is this Dan person? Is he the PI you told me about? If he's so good at protecting you, why do you have to move in the first place? This isn't going to work."

"Tommy, you can't do this to me! We're desperate. If you're worried about dog hair on your precious furniture, I'll pay for a cleaning lady every day. Hermione's not a puppy. She doesn't run around and chew, but she will growl if a stranger tries to enter the apartment. You'll never see Majestic. Besides, you're a cat person."

I could picture Tommy seated on the side of his bed rubbing his head the way he always did when he's upset.

"Look, Tommy, are you worried we'll cramp your style—with women I mean?" Tommy had the looks in the family. He had wavy blond hair and a body built from hours at the gym. Girls swooned over that hair and body, along with the fact that he was a prominent Atlanta lawyer. Maybe that was what this was all about.

"You know so little about me, Mabe. No, I'm not worried about your cramping my style, although I will be if this lasts for more than a few days."

I was silent.

"How long is this going to last?" Tommy said. "You're not moving in with me for a month, are you?"

"No, no." I hadn't really thought about how long this might last. "Look, I'll make a deal with you. We'll find a more permanent solution if this goes on for more than a week. How's that?"

"I guess I can live with that. I don't have much choice, do I? But I don't want that detective, either detective, snooping around my place. Is that clear?"

"Clear." My brother and his paranoid privacy issues.

"Tommy, you don't have a gun in your condo, do you?"

"Why do you ask?"

"The kids."

"Oh, yeah, the kids. You don't have to worry. I keep it locked up."

"Could you get it out of the apartment, just while we're there?"

"What else do you want me to do? Take a room in a hotel?"

"No. You know how much I hate guns. Can you do this for me?"

"And what if a bad guy breaks into the place with a gun? The only way to stop a bad guy with a gun is a good guy with a gun."

"Oh, please. We're not going there. Just remove the gun, can you do that?"

"I'll keep it out of the way."

"Thank you." I hung up. How could two such different people come from the same parents? I suppose it was because I was my father's child and Tommy was my mother's. Dad never touched a gun. My mother had a rack full of rifles, all locked in a gun cabinet. She knew about gun safety, but she also believed in protecting what was hers. Each of us kids had to learn to shoot. I hated every minute of it and quit when I was twelve. Old enough to say no and mean it. Tommy thrived on it. It was strange that Tommy was the one sent off to boarding school and not me. I never knew what he did to warrant that kind of punishment. Maybe it wasn't punishment for him. It was one of a hundred things we never talked about.

Lurleen stood in the doorway of the guest bedroom. She heard me sigh. "Trouble in paradise, *chérie*?"

"It's my brother. He's trying to squirm his way out of our agreement."

She sat down on the bed beside me. "I always wished I had a brother until I saw what trouble they could be." She patted my hand. "Perhaps this will be an opportunity for the two of you to mend some fences, get to know each other as adults."

"I've never really known Tommy. I've wanted to. But even as a kid he was so different from me and so closed off. I was the annoying little sister. He hated the fact that I had an easier time in school than he did. I've wondered if he went away to boarding school just to get away from me."

"You don't actually believe that, do you?"

"No," I said. "I don't think I was ever that important to him. I somehow hoped in this crisis, we might get closer, but that's not going to happen." I stood up to shake off my gloomy thoughts. "Let's get this show on the road."

"The kids are getting dressed. And I've given Hermione and Majestic their breakfasts."

"You're terrific."

Lurleen blushed and bowed. "I am always at your service. Dan is packing up a few things from the kitchen he thought you might want to take. Including the muffins you made last night. He and I tasted a couple of them. *Formidable*."

"Thanks. It's a good idea to bring the essentials. Who knows what Tommy has? I've actually never seen him in a kitchen."

"Well, then he'll be in for a treat with your cooking. I bet Dan would happily whip something up as well."

"That might be a problem," I said. "Tommy doesn't want Dan poking through his stuff. I'm sure he won't want him in his kitchen."

Lurleen pulled at her curls as if this idea disturbed her. "But everyone loves Dan once they meet him," she said.

"You're right. Maybe they'll become good friends." I doubted that, but there was no point in borrowing more trouble than we already had.

We got ourselves ready to go. Lucie and Jason did their part with no complaints once I explained we were about to have a new adventure. I offered them my bran muffins, but they were too excited to eat. Lucie would have asked questions but refrained for the sake of Jason. We were packed up by seven. That left us with time to fill before we showed up at Tommy's. He lived twenty minutes away.

"I know the perfect place," I said. "We'll go to the Silver Skillet for breakfast."

"The Silver Skillet?" Lurleen asked.

"You haven't been there? Best greasy spoon in Atlanta. Sometimes you'll see a movie star there."

"In that case, *chérie*, I'm all for it."

Dan nodded. "Might be a good idea. If anyone tries to follow us, we'll spot them at the restaurant."

We had an uneventful breakfast. No movie stars or bad guys. Just good food and great service. "Honey" this and "honey" that. Refills on coffee before you thought to ask. Melt-in-your-mouth southern biscuits, crisp bacon, and soft scrambled eggs. I was in heaven. The kids were on their best behavior and the mothering from the waitresses didn't hurt a bit.

Even Lurleen with her refined taste enjoyed herself. "I'll just have one more little pancake," she said.

Dan guffawed. "That's your fifth little pancake," he said.

"A gentleman would never count." Lurleen put a finger to his lips. "It's your fault anyway for making me order the big stack."

We brought some ham and biscuits out to the animals. Majestic was not happy to be left in her crate and ignored our peace offering, but Hermione gobbled up everything we had. Both animals were happy when we arrived at Tommy's. It was at 8:15.

"You're late," he said when the concierge buzzed us up to his condo.

"Sorry."

I introduced everyone.

Tommy shook hands and mumbled a greeting before showing us to the guest bedroom. I settled the animals while Lurleen helped the kids unpack. Dan said he'd go get the rest of our stuff.

"You mean this isn't all of it?" Tommy was incredulous.

Danny motioned Tommy away from everyone. I followed them and closed the bedroom door.

"Okay, dude, we get it," Danny said. "This is an imposition for you. But you've got a sister in trouble and she's got kids to look out for. If she were my sister, I'd be all over it."

"Yeah, well, she's not your sister. And who the hell do you think you are lecturing me in my own house about how I should act?"

The last thing I needed was a fight between my brother and Dan. "Dan, please get the stuff. Come on, Tommy, I'll fix you a cup of coffee."

Tommy seemed to realize there were children nearby. "Yeah. Okay."

He followed me first to the den where I dropped off my suitcase and then to the kitchen far from the children's room. He sat down at the glass-topped kitchen table and motioned to the Keurig machine. I looked for the strongest brew I could find and popped it in.

"These are for you," I said, placing a bag of biscuits on the table. "They won't be good tomorrow."

Tommy opened the bag and actually smiled. "Remember how we went to the Silver Skillet on Saturdays when you were in med school? Those were good times."

"They were." We probably went there twice during my four years in school and twice more in residency, but for Tommy that was a lot.

"I know I'm being an asshole, Mabe. I'm sorry."

An apology from Tommy? I had to sit down. "I'm asking a lot of you, Tommy, and I know that. To move in here with two children, two animals—it's a big deal."

Out of the corner of my eye, I saw Lucie standing at the doorway. She ducked away as I was speaking. "Come on in, Lucie. I wasn't saying anything you shouldn't hear."

Lucie walked in and I pulled a chair out for her next to Tommy. "You will find that Lucie is incredibly responsible," I said to Tommy. "And you will find, Lucie, that my brother is a very funny person. And a magician. He used to do magic tricks as a kid."

"Still do," said Tommy. He reached over and pulled a quarter from Lucie's ear. He gave it to her.

She giggled and handed it back to him. Then she looked serious. "Jason and I won't be any trouble, Mr. Brown. I promise. We'll be quiet as mice."

At that moment Jason zoomed into the kitchen—his Spider-Man figure leading the way. Spider-Man and the elusive bad guy in Jason's other hand seemed to be having a noisy argument. "Stop right now or I will 'rest you! I won't and you can't make me. Yes I can."

Lucie turned bright red and looked at Tommy.

"It's okay, Lucie," Tommy said. "I was a kid once myself. I was a lot like your brother. We'll get along fine."

"I hope so," Lucie said quietly.

"This is hard on you too, sweetie," I said. "So much moving around. But it will only be for a little while."

"Until you catch the bad guys," Lucie whispered. She didn't want Jason to hear, but before she'd finished speaking he'd already dashed out of the room.

"Yeah," I said. "In the meantime, Lurleen will be over every day to help with school work. I'll get everything you need from your teachers and you'll have Hermione and Majestic to take care of. Not to mention Jason."

"We'll be okay," Lucie said. This time it was Lucie patting me on the arm. "Don't worry about us, Aunt Di."

At that moment the concierge buzzed the intercom to announce that Dan was coming up. The elevator opened onto a private vestibule. "Is this the only way a person can get in?" Dan asked when the doors opened.

"There's a service elevator at the back of the apartment." Tommy showed me and Dan a small utility room with a door that led to a hallway and the service elevator.

"Who can use this elevator?" Dan asked.

"Just staff connected with the condo."

Dan checked the door to the utility room. "You keep this door locked?"

"Yes. Of course."

I could see Dan was getting on Tommy's nerves. Dan noticed it too. He left without another word and distributed his bundles to the guest room and den.

"This'll be handy," I said, pointing to the washer and dryer. "We'll be happy to do your wash as well."

"Thanks, but I've got that covered. You probably won't see much of me. I usually get in pretty late. Only thing I ask is for quiet in the morning, so I can sleep in if I want. You think that's possible?"

"We'll make it work, I promise. I really appreciate this." If he were anyone else, I would have given him a hug. But Tommy always got stiff as a board when I tried to hug or kiss him. Jason saved us from an awkward moment.

"There you are, Mr. Tommy," Jason said. "You want to see my bad guys? Spider-Man just killed this one."

Tommy actually knelt down beside Jason and took the mangled form of what looked like a half man, half monster. "I know this guy," he said to Jason. "Good job. I used to work with a guy like this."

Jason didn't get the joke, but he did get the smile. "I protect Aunt Di and Lucie and I can protect you too, Mr. Tommy."

"I'm glad to hear it. Just call me Tommy." He glanced at his watch and stood up. "Now I've got to get to work. Can we get the excess baggage out of here before I leave?"

"You mean Dan?" I asked.

He nodded.

Chapter Thirteen

Tommy gave me a set of keys and left without another word. Dan wasn't pleased when I told him he couldn't spend the day in the apartment with the kids.

"I mean no disrespect, Dr. Brown," he said, "but how does your brother expect me to protect the children if I'm not in the apartment to do it?"

"My brother is a little paranoid about his privacy. I'll work on him. In the meantime, could you stay in the lobby, see who's coming and going, check in with Lurleen from time to time?"

"I'll take care of it," Dan said, but I could see his jaw working overtime.

We discussed whether or not it would be safe to take the kids out to lunch. They'd go stir-crazy if they didn't get out, and Dan knew just the place. Johnny Rockets in the food court at Lenox Square. He assured me he could keep them safe and that it was better for the kids to be with him than out of his sight. Lurleen could act as another set of eyes, something she was eager to do.

We came down to the lobby together where we talked with Oscar, the concierge on the day shift. I explained that the kids needed a safe place to stay for a few days due to problems with an ex-husband. Dan was there to help if anyone strange turned up looking for them or me.

Oscar seemed to take all this in stride. "Mr. Brown spoke with me about you. If there is anything you need, please let me know." He called to get my car brought up from the garage.

I got to work on time and delivered some of the bran muffins to the break room. They were gone in ten minutes. The morning was as busy as usual. It was supposed to be a catch-up day to complete paperwork and spend some time consulting on projects. Vic worked with medical students and residents interested in international health, and I went where I was needed. Walk-ins showed up as they did every day.

I did find ten minutes to talk with our social worker. She'd made an unannounced visit to the home of the fifteen-year-old girl I was worried about. The family was living in a one-bedroom apartment with another Nigerian family. The "uncle" was nowhere to be seen, but it was clear that Beza remained frightened of him. The social worker said she'd stay on the case. In the meantime, she'd arranged a follow-up visit to the clinic for the girl. I made sure I was scheduled to work at the time of her visit. The clinic doors closed at noon with a sign saying that anyone needing help that afternoon should go to the hospital ER. It was literally down the street, within walking distance. I left Vic still in her office at twenty to one. She'd be the last to leave and the first person back in the morning.

Lurleen and I arrived at the restaurant within minutes of one another. "So how did it go this morning with the kids?" I asked.

"*Un morceau de gateau,*" she said. "A piece of cake," she added in case my French was rusty. "They had leftover homework, so we worked on that. You'll get their current assignments from the school?"

"I'm headed there next."

Marie appeared before we had time to say more. Her smile was nearly as large as Lurleen's and her hair was a lot bigger. She had the bouffant Buckhead look, tailored suit, very corporate.

"Shit, I hope I didn't keep you waiting. Hell of a day. Boss had something up his ass for sure. Anyway, I won't bore you with that. Let's get a table and talk."

I couldn't keep from smiling.

"What? What is it? Is my slip showing? No, I don't wear a slip."

"I'm sorry," I said. "I should have known—any friend of Lurleen's wouldn't be a typical businesswoman."

"You mean my language. Does it offend you? I can clean it up if you like."

"Don't change a thing."

Marie spoke with the maître d' and we got a table in a corner near the kitchen.

"An undesirable spot," Marie said, "unless you want to have a private conversation. And this needs to be private. Let's order before we get into it. I'm starving. Those old farts decided we needed an all-morning meeting to deal with the 'crisis' and that I needed to be present for every moment of it. No time for a bagel or even a bathroom break. Men!"

"Don't you just love her?" Lurleen said to me.

"I do," I said.

"Look, I'll calm down after my first glass of wine. Maybe you could rush that to our table," she said to the waiter. "How 'bout you two?"

I shook my head. "I have to see school administrators and teachers this afternoon."

Lurleen also declined.

"I'm not always like this. But today I need a break from the big boys. You can bet they're drinking it up at Bacchanalia. And was I invited to come along? Not that I would have gone. Not after a morning of their raunchy jokes and mass hysteria. Not if it meant missing out on lunch with you two. But they could have asked. I am sick and tired of their damn boys club."

The waiter brought Marie her wine. I wondered if she needed something stronger.

Marie gulped down half the glass and turned to me. "Was it like this for you in medical school? Lurleen told me that was when she met you."

"Yep," I said. "Pretty much."

"Let's order and then talk," Marie said, downing the last of her wine. "I'm feeling better already."

While we waited for our food, Marie started in about Charlie Flack. "I don't know how much of this you've already heard from Detective Garrett, but I do best if I start at the beginning. It turns out your boy Charlie is well known at Sandler's. He was up and coming for a couple of years as a promising new biochemist—full of bright ideas. Rumor has it he started the ball rolling on our current new product. Then he screwed up bad. Security caught him walking off with a computer full of classified data. What kind of idiot would think he could get through security with that? He swore someone planted the data on his computer. They didn't prosecute, didn't want the publicity, but he was out the door. He spent the next few years somewhere else and then tried to weasel his way back in a few months ago."

Lurleen finished slathering a baguette with butter and pointed it at Marie. "How did Ellie get her job in the new products division? It's the last place a new person would be assigned."

"Good question. And the answer is . . ."

"Billy Joe," Lurleen said. She took a large bite of the baguette.

"I thought Billy Joe was on the outs at Sandler's," I said.

"He was always getting into trouble, if that's what you mean. And he had no hope of becoming head of the whole operation," Marie said. "He burned that bridge a long time ago, but he was family. And Mr. Sandler is all about family. So if Billy Joe recommended somebody as a good hire, that person would come on board. With the exception of Charlie Flack. Even Billy Joe couldn't get him rehired."

"So what was Ellie supposed to do?" I asked.

"I think she was supposed to put in a good word for Charlie about how he'd reformed or been framed. After all, he was her ex-boyfriend. She charmed the bigwigs—the men, that is. The wives hated her. When she wasn't successful in getting him reinstated, I think she was supposed to snoop around on her own."

At that moment our entrees arrived. A salmon salad for Lurleen. Quiche and fruit for Marie. And a croque monsieur with a double layer of cheese for me. No point in dieting when you go to the best French restaurant in town. We sat for a few minutes in blissful silence enjoying our food.

"You were saying Ellie was supposed to snoop around on her own?" I asked.

Marie nodded at the waiter and ordered a second glass of wine. "She'd turn up in places she didn't belong. She'd be flirting with someone in the new products lab instead of staying at her desk to answer phone calls. That's what eventually got her fired. There was a crisis about a breach in security regarding our newest product and Mr. Sandler was suspicious that Eleanor might be involved." Marie stopped to take another bite of her salmon and another gulp of wine. "This was a couple of months ago. Mr. Sandler Senior wanted to keep the problem in house—didn't want the press to get wind of the product or the breach—but someone contacted the Cyber Crime Unit."

"Do you know who did that?" Lurleen asked. "Who would have the nerve to go over Sandler's head?"

"I can think of only one person—Kathleen Sandler."

"Kathleen is Sandler's granddaughter," Lurleen said to me. "She's as tough as Sandler and she's next in line to the throne. I wonder that didn't sour their relationship."

"Oh, it did, believe me," said Marie. "They've barely spoken in the last month. I guess you heard Detective Schmidt was killed, a week before Ellie. He was the detective from the Cyber Crimes Unit. That was the end of the investigation. No one knows if his death was related to what he was investigating at Sandler's or not."

"It was related," Lurleen said. "All of Schmidt's notes mysteriously disappeared."

I gave Lurleen a look, but it was too late. That cat was out of the bag.

Marie noticed it. "It's all right," she said to me. "You can talk to me about the investigation. I'm a one-way drop box. Things come in but they don't go out. Except to you two of course." She smiled, and for just a moment I felt uneasy. Marie appeared to be the epitome of trustworthy. But she was also the self-confessed secret keeper. She hadn't gotten where she was today by being completely forthright. I wondered where her true loyalties lay.

"Back to the new product. It's going to be a game changer. With all this talk about the evils of sugar and soft drinks, Sandler's has been searching for a healthier product to shift the brand. It looks like they've found it. It's being market tested in a few weeks. I think Flack, Ellie, and Billy Joe were trying to get their hands on information about it—to sell to a competitor."

"Corporate espionage," I said.

"Corporate espionage?" Lurleen asked, her eyes aglow.

"I think so," Marie said. "Billy Joe always wanted more money than his allowance provided. And he liked to stick it to the big guys."

Lurleen turned to me. "Billy Joe's parents died when he was young. In a plane crash. We all cut him some slack because of that—Mr. Sandler especially."

"That's right. But I think the old man was getting weary of his pranks. And the idea of espionage would have driven him right over the edge—"

"Company loyalty," Lurleen and Marie said in unison.

I turned to both of them. "This all makes sense. When Ellie talked about making it big, buying a house in Buckhead, she thought she was on to something about the product—something that could be sold to a competitor. And that may have cost her her life." I put my fork down. I'd just lost my appetite.

"That's what I think," Marie said.

"But who was the ringleader, the person who put the plan together?" I asked. "Was Billy Joe smart enough to do that?"

"I don't know," Marie said. "He was never the brightest bulb, but he did like money. He was shrewd enough to get what he needed from the old man. At least until recently. Maybe he came up with another way to get money."

"Where is Charlie Flack now?" I asked.

"Not a clue. If he's smart, he's long gone. Their operation is dead in the water," Marie said.

"Maybe. But someone sure thought Ellie or the kids had the information they were searching for. Who's to say they will stop now, and who's to say Billy Joe was really the one in charge?" I waited for Marie to respond.

"You think Billy Joe may have been working for someone else? Someone who didn't trust him and got rid of him?"

"I am worried about that. And I hope I'm wrong."

"That's why we moved again," Lurleen added.

"We were told Billy Joe's death was an accident," Marie said.

"So were we, but Garrett doesn't believe it." I studied Marie. She seemed agitated.

"I can see your point, but I don't have any answers for you," she said. "I haven't seen anyone else acting suspiciously. The higher-ups are ecstatic about the new product. It's going to make millions for all of us. Why would anyone sabotage that?"

Why indeed? Marie seemed to have shut down, or was that just my imagination? Maybe my brother's paranoia was catching. I wasn't really sure who I could trust, maybe not even one of Lurleen's best friends.

We finished our lunch with promises to meet again once this whole thing was behind us.

Lurleen headed back to the condo as much to see Dan, I suspect, as the children. I went on to school, spoke with the principal and each teacher. Everyone was sympathetic. I left with an armful of books and worksheets.

Mason called me as I was about to leave the school. He was still in Alpharetta but hoped to wrap things up in a day or two. He listened quietly while I filled him in about Charlie Flack and our lunch with Marie.

"You shouldn't have gone to see her without informing me," he said in his most formal detective voice.

"I'm sorry," I said in a tone that I hoped sounded genuine.

"Do you have a description of Charlie Flack?" he asked. "An old address?"

"I'm sorry, Mason. I didn't think to ask for either one. But I can follow up."

"That's all right. I'll get Dan on it. I don't want you anywhere near Sandler's. I'd do it myself, but I'm still supposed to be hands off."

"Have you figured out why?"

"No. How are the kids?"

"They're fine, or as fine as they can be moving every few days. How about you?"

"As good as I can be after being sent on a bogus case. I'd like to come by this evening."

"Better make it as early as you can. Tommy isn't big on detectives. He wants Dan to stay out of his condo, so Dan's camped downstairs in the lobby."

"I know. He told me about it. Maybe we can all go out to dinner."

That cheered me up. I'm not sure why I still hadn't learned that nothing in our lives would run smoothly. Even plans to go to dinner.

Chapter Fourteen

I left the parking lot of the school and wound my way through local streets until I was heading north on Piedmont. I was eager to see the kids, but Buckhead traffic was impossible as usual. It was one of many reasons I'd never live in Buckhead. Too upscale for me and far too congested.

For Tommy it was perfect. Near the action. He could be anonymous and in the thick of things at the same time. Tommy loved his mystique—never tell everything you know. That's what made him such a good lawyer and such an annoying brother. He loved being elusive.

The valet at the condo greeted me as if I were a long-time resident. The concierge Oscar did the same.

"Nice morning?" Oscar asked me.

"Yes, thanks. An easy work day and a great lunch when I was done," I said. "Everything quiet here?"

"Yes, Dr. Brown."

Dan came loping down the corridor at the back of the lobby. "Glad to catch you," he said. He led me to a private space near a large art deco fireplace. "Got some news for you." He looked somber.

"Are the kids safe?" I could feel my hands getting clammy.

"No problem with the kids. Didn't mean to worry you, Dr. Brown. It's not about the kids. We had a great time. No one bothered us. The kids enjoyed themselves. I hope you don't mind—they had hamburgers, french fries, and shakes."

"I don't mind," I said. "I know Jason is thrilled whenever he can spend time with you. And a little junk food won't hurt them once in a while. Thanks. What's the news?"

"It's about Billy Joe. I just checked with my contacts at the police department. Mason is cut off from all sources of information for some reason. It's driving him crazy. But it seems I'm still flying under the radar. I got this from more than one source. Billy Joe didn't die in an accident. He was pushed off the road and into the ravine. And he was dead before he ever went over the edge. Shot in the back of the head at close range."

"Oh, my God! Why would they tell Mason it looked like an accident and then pull him off the case?"

"That's what Mason is trying to figure out." He paused. "I thought you should know. It changes the situation with the kids. They shouldn't be out of my sight."

"I agree. I don't care what my brother says; I want you upstairs with them all the time. Come with me now." I nodded at Oscar and marched to the elevator with Dan beside me.

The kids, of course, were thrilled that Dan would be spending the afternoon with them. Lurleen looked like someone had offered her a free trip to France. She was a little less enthusiastic when I explained the reason for the change in plans.

I had second thoughts about going out to dinner. The kids didn't need to be running around in public, and Tommy needed to understand how serious the situation was. Maybe if I fixed us all a nice meal, he'd soften about having us there. I did an inventory of his kitchen. He had one six-pack of Goose Island Bourbon Country Stout and two bottles of white wine in his refrigerator—Domaine Leflaive Montrachet Grand Cru. Lurleen had already spotted them and told me how expensive they were. In his pantry were a dozen bottles of red wine, equally expensive I was sure. Two Lean Cuisine dinners were in his freezer, and a package of fancy crackers in his cupboard. That was it. How could I be related to this person? Did he even live here? I'd brought food for the kids but not nearly enough to make a decent dinner.

"I'm going to run to the store," I yelled into the den where Lurleen, Dan, Jason, and Lucie were hovered over a game of Clue.

Lucie jumped up and ran to me. "May I come with you, Aunt Di, and help with the groceries?"

"I'd love that Lucie, but I don't think Jason can manage his suspects without you. Besides, I'll be back in a flash, and you can help me make dinner." Lucie seemed to accept that. Poor kids. They were basically in prison. I hoped they didn't realize it. I'd pick up bathing suits for them at Target, and at least they could swim in Tommy's pool.

I called Oscar, who had my car brought up. When I exited the building my Corolla sat in the circular drive, engine humming. A valet waved at me from the side of the building. I climbed into the front seat and was adjusting my seat belt when the man approached from the passenger side, opened the door, and slid in next to me. What was this all about?

"My name's Mark," the man said. He reached over and shook my hand. His grip was a little too firm. He was about my age, late thirties, dark hair. "I work here. I'm a friend of Tommy's. He wanted me to check on you to make sure you didn't need anything during your stay."

I might have believed him if he hadn't added the part about Tommy's concern for my welfare. My hands gripped the steering wheel like they were welded there. "Please get out of my car. I'll be happy to talk with you in the lobby."

"Just trying to be friendly," he said. He didn't move. So I did. I released my seat belt and pushed the door handle on the driver's side.

"Don't," he said. This time the tone wasn't friendly. He grabbed my arm before I could open the door. "Drive." He pulled a gun out of his pocket and stuck it in my ribs. "Now."

I froze and willed myself to stay calm. I stared at him.

Dark hair. Dark eyes. A very familiar face. He was a grown-up version of Jason. "You're Jason's father. You're Charlie Flack!"

"How the hell do you know anything about me? Drive. Now."

I drove slowly to the gate and watched as it opened to let us leave the complex. I tried to remember every movie I'd seen with the bad guy in the car pointing a gun at someone. It didn't help.

"What do you want from me?" I asked. By now we were at the end of the drive and ready to turn onto Wieuca and from there onto Peachtree.

"You know what I want." He sounded frantic. "I don't want to hurt you. I didn't want Ellie to get hurt either."

"I don't know what you want. I swear to God, whatever it is you think I have, I don't."

"Pull into the parking lot at that church."

I turned on to Wieuca and then left into the parking lot of one of the biggest church complexes in Atlanta. There were enough spaces for five hundred cars, but only a half dozen were filled. I turned to face Charlie Flack with my left hand on the car handle, trying to figure out some way to escape before he shot me in the side.

I took a good look at him. He was sweating. He looked scared to death.

"I don't want to hurt you," he said again. He pulled the gun away from my side. I could see his hand shaking. "I know you're looking after my kid. Don't make me hurt you. Just give me what I want."

"Believe me, I would if I knew what it was. I don't know what you're talking about."

"Ellie must have told you something, given you something." He grabbed my purse. It took both his hands to empty out the contents. That was his big mistake. Two seconds. Gun down by his side and I was out of the car running for my life. I listened for a shot but none came. I ran in the direction of the church. Weren't the doors in a church always open? Before I could find out, a security guard ran up to me.

"Can I help you, miss?"

"Over there," I panted. "In the white Corolla. A man with a gun."

The guard grabbed me and pulled me into the foyer of the church, locking the door behind him. Then he called the police. By the time they arrived, Mark, aka Charlie Flack, was long gone. In the meantime I'd called Mason. He was on his way.

Mason pulled up as I finished giving my statement to the police. He hugged me long and hard.

"Hey, Mase. What are you doing here?" one of the policemen asked. He gave us a funny look. "You know this woman?"

"Yes. She's a friend of Eleanor Winston—the woman who was murdered in midtown. The same guy who shot Winston may have killed Billy Joe Sandler. Charlie Flack's a suspect. There's an APB out for him."

"The perp left on foot. We'll get him. The word at the station is you got pulled from the case."

"Don't believe everything you hear, Jerry."

Mason turned to me. "You all right?" He took my arm. "I'll be taking Dr. Brown home."

He got me settled on a bench near my car. "You feel up to telling me what happened?"

I nodded. "I'm just glad to be alive." I told him what Charlie Flack had done.

"If anything had happened to you—" he began.

"But it didn't. You know, when I looked at Flack, he looked like a scared kid. Like one of my patients when I'm about to give them a shot. When I saw him like that, I thought, This guy isn't the murderer. This guy is afraid he'll be next."

Mason nodded. "You may be right, but a frightened man can be just as dangerous as a cold-blooded murderer." He put his hand over mine. "I'm worried about you and the kids. We don't know who's out there, and we don't know what they want."

At that moment, the police officer Jerry approached the car.

"We have to impound Dr. Brown's car for twenty-four hours. And I'm sorry, Dr. Brown, but we'll have to check your purse for fingerprints."

"It's not a problem," I said.

"I'll take you wherever you need to go tomorrow," Mason said. "I'll feel better about that anyway."

"How can you do that with your work?" I asked.

"I'm on desk duty as of tomorrow. One step short of leave with pay." He saw my worried look. "Just until I can talk to my captain. I'll get this straightened out. In the meantime, I'm going to put you in a safe place. You're coming to live with me."

"What are you talking about?"

"You and the kids are coming to live with me. I have an old farmhouse just north of here, off Peachtree Road. My mother is there, and remember she's an ex-cop. Dan will be there too. We'll finally be able to keep you safe. Lurleen is welcome to come as well. If we get everyone under one roof, just until this is solved, then I'll have one less thing to worry about."

"What made your mother become a policewoman?" I said. It seemed to be the only thing I could wrap my head around.

"She went to the police academy when my father died—he was killed in the line of duty. My mom was the first female sharpshooter on the force. She retired two years ago. You remember the standoff in the Grady ER a few years ago?"

"Yes. I had a friend working in the ER at the time. Someone shot the guy before he harmed a single hostage."

"That was my mom. You'll be safe with her. She got the Sharpshooters Commendation five years running."

"Wow! So this police business is in your blood."

Mason nodded. "My dad was a cop and his dad before him. Of course, my being a cop was hard on my wife. When she got sick, she worried about the kids. She didn't want them to lose two parents. I almost quit the force at that point. But Amy lived a long time with breast cancer and pain. The boys were off to college before she died. I think she hung on for me and for them."

"I'm sorry," I said.

"Me too, but time helps."

Mason opened the door to his Jaguar and got me settled inside. He was done discussing his previous life with me, and I had no desire to press him for more information. He checked my seat belt the way you might check on a small child's car seat. I'd never felt so well taken care of. Maybe it's more accurate to say, I never let anyone take care of me before.

"Let's go to the condo and get you out of there. I need to have a long talk with Tommy."

"Why?"

"Charlie Flack said he knew him. It might be a lie, but how did he manage to turn up as a valet at your brother's condo?"

It was a good question that left me with a bad feeling. The feeling I had when Tommy did something wrong as a kid. Then it was little stuff—shoplifting candy, a toy he wanted. I'd find it in his room and take money to the store he'd stolen it from. It was a small town. I knew every shopkeeper. I also knew my mother would go ballistic if she ever found out. Her favorite child stealing? She'd have a heart attack. So I kept it a secret. Maybe I hadn't handled that right. Maybe that was why Tommy never really learned right from wrong.

Chapter Fifteen

Mason dropped me off at the condo and looked around the perimeter of the building before he joined me inside. He showed Oscar his badge and asked if there was a valet named Mark or Charlie Flack working there. Oscar shook his head, said he knew all the valets. There were no new hires and no one who met the description I provided. Mason gave him his card and asked him to call him immediately if anyone showed up who fit Flack's description. Oscar looked concerned and asked if they might need additional security.

"It wouldn't hurt," Mason said.

Oscar was immediately on the phone, and I found myself breathing better.

The kids were excited to see Mason and even more excited when he offered to bring food back for all of us. Mason took everyone's order and headed out the door. Dan and Lurleen knew something was up but waited until we were alone to question me about it. The kids were engaged in Lurleen's Chutes and Ladders game in the den, which meant we had plenty of time to talk in the kitchen.

I filled them in.

"Charlie Flack showed up here?" Lurleen sounded incredulous. "How could he know we were here?"

"How has he known about every move we've made?" I asked.

"You don't think your brother—"

I stopped her. "Flack said he knew Tommy, but no, I don't think he would have put us in danger. At least not knowingly. My brother is a lot of things, but no, I can't believe he had anything to do with this."

I probably would have gone on some more if Lurleen hadn't put her hand up. "I know, sweetie, innocent until proven guilty. And he is your brother."

Dan said nothing.

I told them about the plan to move in with Mason and his mother. Dan nodded his approval.

Mason arrived an hour later with bags of food from the Varsity for Jason and Lucie, the Bistro for Lurleen and Dan, and the Golden Buddha for me and him. Of course, once the kids saw us using chopsticks, they wanted some. Fortunately, Mason had brought along some kid-friendly chopsticks for them to use. We had plenty of food for Tommy, but he never showed up.

We talked to the kids about our move the next day. They were good sports, especially when they heard about the tree swing and the huge backyard to run around in. It didn't hurt that Mason's mother was a cop. Lurleen said she thought she could make arrangements to stay with us. Dan tried not to grin like the Cheshire cat.

After I got the kids to bed, I called my boss at the clinic, this time expecting she might be ready to fire me. Instead, she suggested I take the rest of the week off and keep her posted. She had second-year pediatric residents who were starting in the clinic the next day. She had things covered. I kept expecting Tommy to show up, but when he didn't, I wrote him a long letter explaining why we were moving. I didn't mention Charlie Flack. I just said I'd had a bad encounter. That was Mason's idea. He wanted to talk with Tommy first, find out what he knew. Mason left around eleven that night and was back at seven in the morning. Still no Tommy. We sat in the kitchen waiting for the rest of the household to wake up.

"Do you think Tommy could be involved with any of this?" I asked.

"Charlie Flack says he knows him, works at his condo. And you said Ellie and Tommy were friends."

"She had a huge crush on him growing up. Tommy went away to boarding school when he was fourteen, and every summer when he came home, she'd be after him. They dated for a while in high school, and then she cheated on him with the football captain. Tommy never forgave her for that."

I offered to make Mason a cup of coffee, but he shook his head. He motioned for me to keep talking. "I think Ellie moved to Atlanta to see if she could get him back. He was an up-and-coming lawyer." I sighed. "I loved Ellie but she was always looking for the next gravy train. And she never found it. Tommy wouldn't have anything more to do with her. He's kind of like old-man Sandler. You're disloyal to him one time and you're out the door."

"What makes you so sure they never reconciled?" Mason asked.

"Something Tommy said about how he didn't need more trouble in his life, and Ellie always brought trouble. I think it was after I moved back and tried to look her up. He said I should leave well enough alone. If her phone was disconnected, maybe that was a good thing. Time to leave the past behind."

Something was niggling at me.

Mason saw me lost in thought. "What is it?" he asked.

It took me a minute to remember.

"Ellie and Tommy just missed each other that day she came by. When I asked if they were in touch, she said she hadn't seen him in a year or more, but she thought she'd seen his car go by. Tommy just bought that car. It was his pride and joy. How would she know his car if she hadn't seen him?"

"Hmm" was all Mason said.

We heard the elevator and then a key in the lock. Tommy walked in, looking like he'd been in a fight. I ran to him.

"What happened to you?" I asked. "Are you hurt?"

He shook his head. "You don't want to know."

"I do," said Mason, standing in the doorway of the kitchen.

"Who the hell are you and what are you doing in my condo?"

"This is Detective Mason Garrett. I told you about him. He's investigating Ellie's death."

"I told you, Mabel, no strangers, no cops."

"Something happened to me yesterday. I asked him to come over."

"What happened?"

Mason stopped me from answering. He stuck out his hand but Tommy refused to shake it.

"What happened?" Tommy asked me again.

"She's not at liberty to say right now," Mason said. "She's all right. The kids are all right. What about you? You get in a fight?"

Tommy looked down at his torn shirt, rubbed a hand over his face and what looked like a doozy of a black eye.

"It was a rough night. Finished up a big case and followed it up with too much partying."

"Doesn't really look like you've been partying. Looks like someone beat you up," Mason said.

"Where do you get off? I come into my own house and find you here questioning me about how I look and where I've been. Get out of my house!"

"We're all getting out," I said. "We're moving. You'll have your condo back by the end of the day."

"Why?" Tommy asked.

"It's a long story. We'll talk about it over breakfast," I said.

"Can't stay. Got a breakfast meeting downtown in an hour." With that he disappeared into his bedroom.

Mason and I stared at each other. Tommy could get angry at the drop of a hat, especially when he'd been drinking. He worked out in the gym, but he wasn't a big guy. He knew his limitations and I hadn't seen him in a brawl since he was a teenager. He was more the smooth-talking type. He could annihilate you with sarcasm or legal threats. Maybe someone didn't take to that and let him have it.

Before we could talk, the kids came running into the room. They were dressed and ready for action. The thought of a big house to run around in with a tree swing in the backyard was almost more than they could imagine. Hermione and Majestic followed on their heels as if they'd gotten wind of their new home. Poor Hermione, cooped up all day with only a ten-minute walk from me or Dan. Maybe she knew she was about to get her freedom.

"We're all packed up, Aunt Di," Lucie said to me.

"Great, honey." I hugged her and Jason. "Tommy's here, so you can thank him before we go."

Lurleen and Dan wandered in from the laundry room where Dan had camped out during the night.

"You stayed here last night?" I said to Lurleen.

"It's not what you think," she said, trying to organize her tangled chestnut curls. "*Bonjour, mes petit choux.*" She ignored me and hugged the kids.

"I insisted she stay," Dan said. "You'd already gone to bed. I didn't want her driving home alone."

Tommy called from the bedroom. "Mabel, could you make me a cup of coffee?"

"Sure," I yelled back. I looked at the menagerie in front of me. "I think we might give Tommy a heart attack." I looked at Lurleen and Dan. "Maybe you two can get yourselves ready for the day. Feel free to use the shower in the kids' room. And Lucie and Jason, would you mind playing with Hermione and Majestic in the den? I'll call you when it's time to leave."

When everyone cleared out, I sat with Mason at the kitchen table waiting for the Keurig to do its thing. Tommy joined us there, grabbed the cup I handed him, and drank it down. He looked a lot better.

"Sorry I was so uptight," he said.

"What *did* happen to you last night?" I asked.

"Somebody thought I was being too loud, boasting about my big win. That's all. What about you?"

Mason stepped in. "She was attacked by someone called Mark, a valet here. He held a gun on her and demanded she give him something. He said he knew you."

"Mark? A valet here? I don't hang out with valets."

"His real name is Charlie Flack. Know him?"

I swear I saw Tommy flinch, but he immediately recovered. "No. I don't know anyone named Mark or Charlie Flack. You okay? Did he hurt you?"

"No," I said. "I'm perfectly fine. But we can't stay here. Mason's found us another place to stay."

"Where?"

"It's a ways from here," Mason said. "Your sister will be safe and protected."

"What? You can't tell me where you're going? What if I want to check on you, make sure you're okay?"

"You know my cell number, Tommy," I said. "Besides, I think I'm always the one calling you. I'll keep you informed if you want that."

"Yeah, sure." Tommy seemed jumpy to me. Maybe it was too much alcohol and too little sleep.

"You all right?" I asked him.

"Yeah, of course."

I called the kids in to say goodbye. I thanked Tommy for letting us stay there. It took three trips to get everything packed in the three cars we had—Mason's, Dan's, and Lurleen's.

"Maybe," I said, when Mason and I were alone in his car, "Charlie Flack traced us to the condo and waited for me without anyone else knowing about him."

"Maybe," he said. "But it doesn't explain how he knew your brother's name, knew enough about him to claim to be his friend."

"Lots of people know about Tommy. The more press he gets for a case, the better he likes it." I said that more to reassure myself than to convince Mason. I don't think I convinced either one of us.

Chapter Sixteen

The kids squeezed into the back seat of Mason's Jaguar along with Hermione. I held on to Majestic. He was indignant about the idea of more traveling and howled when I tried to put him in his traveling cage. Lurleen followed us in her Citroën. Dan brought up the rear, the back seat of his Honda piled high with the rest of the stuff. When we arrived at Mason's house, his mother stood on the front porch, an apron tied around her tiny waist. She was about my height, maybe five one, with short silver hair and a grin that was as warm as Mason's. She waved a hand in a hot mitt at us. This was a woman I was going to like.

She gave us time to get out of the cars and come up the steps before she greeted us. Something else I liked. She wasn't going to smother the kids with goodwill or overwhelm us with questions. She took off her mitt, shook my hand, and then hugged me. "I've heard a lot about you," she whispered in my ear. "All good."

She knelt down to greet Lucie and Jason, shook each of their hands, and then said hello to Hermione and Majestic. Hermione, tail wagging, smiled in that winning way of hers and ventured inside the opened door. Majestic allowed Mrs. Garrett to pet him and then began to purr. Anyone who could win over Majestic on an initial meeting was a person to be reckoned with.

"Let me help," she said to Dan and Lurleen as they climbed the stairs, their arms full of bags.

"No, we've got it, Mrs. Garrett," Dan said. "Nice to see you again. This is Lurleen du Trois. She'll be staying here as well if you have the room." He glanced at Mason. "Shouldn't be more than a few days."

Mason nodded.

"Of course," Mrs. Garrett said. "I'm delighted for the company and I'm pleased to meet you." She gave Lurleen a quick hug. "Call me Eddie. Everyone does. I'm not sure why Dan is being so formal. He practically lives here. Another son really."

"Eddie?" asked Lurleen.

"Short for Edwina, but if you call me that I'll have to ask you to leave."

"*Ooh la la,* a woman with spirit," Lurleen said. "I feel safe already."

"You are safe here," Eddie said. "No one will get in or out of this house without our knowledge. We're a cop family."

Lucie stood near the door. "Does that mean we have to stay inside, Mrs. Garrett? I mean all the time?"

"Call me Eddie, sweetheart. Of course not. We'll be outside as much as you want. It's just that an adult will have to be with you. Are you okay with that? I know you are very independent. Can you live with those rules?"

"I can," Lucie said. "But I don't know about Jason." She nodded in his direction. He was already exploring the front yard, eyeing a large magnolia.

"I know about boys," Eddie said. "Jason and I will get along fine." She walked over to Jason and the tree. "You can climb it as long as one of us is watching. Deal?" She held her hand up.

"Deal," Jason said, giving her a high five.

Lucie and I looked at each other. It was going to take more than one adult, even an ex-cop, to keep an eye on Jason. I glanced around the front yard. It was fenced. Hermione could hang with Jason, and while she might not be the bravest dog in the world, she'd have the good sense to bark if a stranger entered the yard. At least I hoped she would.

I thought the inside of the house might remind me of my childhood home, but it didn't. In Iowa, our farmhouse was adequate but spare. Nothing unnecessary. This home was magnificent. A wide porch circled the front half of the house. Old rockers were strategically placed as if this were an inviting bed-and-breakfast. I guess for us it was. Inside were large square rooms off to each side, circa 1900, with a mahogany staircase rising from the middle of the foyer. High ceilings. Not exactly what I would call a farmhouse. I couldn't wait to see the kitchen.

Eddie read my mind. "Come on, my dear. Mason told me what a master cook you are. Let me show you what we have to offer."

Lucie took my hand. Shyly she reached out for Mason's. He squeezed it and walked with us. Hermione could smell bacon and trotted ahead of us toward the kitchen. Majestic had disappeared, no doubt investigating his new home.

No worries about Jason for the moment. He was helping Dan carry in the bags from the car. While Dan led the way to the second-floor bedrooms, Lurleen swished up behind as if she were Scarlett O'Hara, or whatever the French equivalent of that might be.

The kitchen had a fireplace at one end, a large country table, and industrial-sized appliances. Two loaves of freshly baked bread stood cooling on a marble counter and strips of bacon were draining on paper towels beside a six-burner stove. I was in heaven.

Eddie watched me and beamed. "I thought you'd like this. The kitchen is yours any time you want to use it, which I hope will be often."

"She may not look like it," Mason said, "but my mom has the appetite of a truck driver. She's been drooling in anticipation of your visit. And now that you'll be living here, she's beside herself."

"I am," Eddie said. "With two boys, I never got the opportunity to share recipes with anyone. Now I can do that with you."

"And with Lucie." I looked over at her. She was rubbing her hand over the marble counter top and eyeing the bread. "She is already a good cook but with both of us to help her she's going to become the best chef in Fulton County."

Eddie grabbed a spare apron from a drawer and wrapped the tie twice around Lucie's waist. "Want to help me with breakfast? I have a new pancake recipe to test out on this crew."

Lucie glanced at me. "Can I?"

"Be my guest. I'm happy to help as well."

"No, no. You have enough to do to get settled in," Eddie said. "Mason will show you the bedrooms. Lucie, wash your hands and then grab some milk and blueberries from the fridge. We'll get started before everyone faints from hunger."

Mason took me by the arm and led me upstairs. Four large rooms surrounded the upstairs landing. He showed me the first one, where my suitcase was waiting to be unpacked. "The kids have the room next to yours. Lurleen is across the hall and Mom's room is next to hers. Dan and I will sleep downstairs in the den and a guest room off the kitchen. We'll be able to keep an eye on things."

"Am I kicking you out of your room?" I asked.

Mason gave me a funny look. "I haven't lived here for years. I have a condo in midtown. When all of this gets cleared up, I'll show it to you."

"Your mom mentioned a brother. I didn't know you had a sibling."

"I had a brother. He died a long time ago."

"I'm so sorry."

Mason left the room and knocked on the door next to mine before I could ask anything more. I joined him and together we entered what was to be the kids' room. Jason was climbing over Dan on the huge bed, giggling when Dan tried to tickle him. Lurleen was sitting in a chair, her short skirt revealing one of her best features—her long, shapely legs.

"You know," she said sweetly, "this house reminds me of a chateau owned by my great-aunt Therese." Lurleen had never mentioned a great-aunt Therese before or a chateau, but I let it pass. "I'm going to be very comfortable here, dreaming of my summer vacations in the south of France."

"I'm glad," Mason said. He led me to the large windows in the bedroom that looked out on the backyard. "Let's walk out back." He took my arm and we headed downstairs.

The backyard was half an acre with apple trees near a six-foot fence at the back. Mason showed me the outdoor potting shed, padlocked, the lights on the back of the house that would illuminate the yard. "We have an alarm system, but with all of us roaming around at night I might be reluctant to use it."

"You think someone will come after us?" I said.

"I think it's possible. Whoever is behind this believes you have something they want."

"Like information of some kind. Secret information. To sell to the highest bidder," I said.

"And they seem to have an uncanny ability to figure out where you are."

I shivered. "That's what I think as well. Do you know why they've taken you off the case?"

Mason shook his head. "I don't know. I hope I'll get some answers when I talk to my captain tomorrow. I've gone over everything in my head."

"Is it about me? You offered your friendship to me. And I'm connected to Ellie. I could be a suspect."

"It's not about you, but everyone's under suspicion, including your brother."

That made me catch my breath.

"You do know he worked for Sandler's." Mason looked at me in a way I'd never seen before. As if he were sizing me up, wondering how truthful I was going to be.

"I never knew that," I said. "As far as I knew, Tommy moved from one high-profile criminal case to the next. I saw more of him on TV than I ever saw of him in real life. Born for the stage, only his stage was the courtroom."

"Apparently, Tommy got called in by Sandler Senior from time to time, whenever there was an employee who needed to be sacked or sent to jail. Your brother would handle the situation discreetly. No scandal, no bad press."

"That changes everything, doesn't it?" I said. "It means Tommy hasn't been honest with me. If he did work for Sandler's, he must have known Ellie was there, and he never told me. She denied seeing him as well. I suppose that's possible but unlikely. When I told him about Ellie's death, he acted upset and surprised. Like he had no idea what she was up to or where she worked."

Mason shook his head. "How well do you know your brother?"

Chapter Seventeen

I stood still in the middle of the backyard. Birds chattering. Azalea bushes in full bloom. I probably looked like a plump topiary soaking up the sun. But the warmth of the sun didn't reach me. A chill settled in my bones.

"Apparently I don't know my brother well at all. I had no idea he did work for Sandler's."

Tommy at Sandler's. While Ellie was there. She would have sought him out. No question about it. But Tommy didn't say a word about running into her. The chill spread. I saw Ellie as she was the day she came to see me. I saw her dead, on the slab in the morgue, barely recognizable. And Tommy never said a word about her or his work at Sandler's. Why?

I looked over at Mason. He didn't urge me to speak or move on. He just stood there calmly staring out at the trees.

Tommy and Ellie were all about money—that was something they had in common—and they didn't really care how they got it. Did Tommy use Ellie the way he often tried to use me—to do his dirty work? And then what? Ellie didn't deliver the goods? The way she so often didn't?

I didn't want to go to the darkest place, but I couldn't stop myself from going there. Did Tommy have something to do with her death? We were raised in the same household. Whatever might be said about my mother— her criticism, her coldness—no one ever accused her of dishonesty. She was ramrod straight. Not Tommy. He loved the con.

I started to cry. Mason whipped out a handkerchief, the old-fashioned kind. That broke the tension and made me smile. "I can't use this." I never knew what you were supposed to do with cloth handkerchiefs. Get them all snotty and then give them back to the poor fellow. "Don't you have a Kleenex?"

Mason shook his head. "No, but we do have a washing machine. Just use it."

"I love Tommy. No matter what he's done, I will always love him. He hasn't had an easy life. He got sent off to boarding school when he was a teenager, and I never knew why. I don't think he wanted to go. And I don't think my dad agreed with the decision, but my mother was the law." Now I was really crying. "I can't bear the thought that he might have had something to do with Ellie's death."

Mason hugged me. No one was in the yard and hopefully no one was watching from a window. He held me tight for a minute until I stopped sniffling.

"Look," he said. "I know what it's like to have a brother you can't trust. I didn't tell you how my brother died."

He hesitated, and I stood as quietly beside him as he had stood beside me. If now wasn't the time to tell me more, that was fine.

But Mason was ready to talk. "He was seventeen. I was three years older and away at college. Johnny wasn't a bad kid, but he couldn't stand rules. He had to test everything out for himself, push the limits. He hated school, but he could fix anything and he loved cars. I think that's how he got caught up with the wrong people. There was a strip of old highway near Kennesaw, where kids used to drag race. His buddies supplied the cars. He fixed them and raced them. Then the kids got restless. Maybe they wanted money for drugs. We'll never know. Anyway, Johnny drove the getaway car for a bank heist and was shot and killed before they got out of the parking lot."

"Oh, my God, Mason. I'm so sorry."

"It was twenty-seven years ago," Mason said. "Somehow we all recovered. He was just a stupid kid. A rebel without a cause. A movie he loved by the way."

Mason held me at arm's length for a moment and then he kissed me. A long, slow, gentle kiss. A kiss that pulled me under like a tidal wave. It was a good thing we were in a backyard and not a bedroom. Because I'm not sure what would have happened next. When we came up for air, he held my face in his hands and then he kissed me again. I could feel his arms around me, and what were mine doing? I felt the strength of his back, his rapid breathing and my own. Then we both heard the clang of a cowbell.

We jumped apart and stared up at the porch.

There stood Eddie, cowbell in hand, grinning. "Hope I didn't startle you," she said innocently. "Breakfast is ready." From behind her peeped Lucie.

"Oh, no," I said and turned scarlet.

Lucie tripped down the steps to me, took my hand, and said, "It's okay, Aunt Di. I told you that Detective Garrett had a crush on you. Remember?"

I smiled unhappily. This was not in my game plan. None of it. The timing was all wrong.

Lucie squeezed my hand. "I won't tell anyone. I'm very good at keeping secrets."

I kissed her on the top of her head. "I know you are."

Mason looked almost as uncomfortable as I felt. He didn't seem to know if he should join Lucie and me or keep his distance. Eddie had already disappeared inside. Lucie said she needed to help get the table ready. She scooted ahead of us and didn't glance back.

Mason came up to me and stood beside me. "I'm really sorry," he said. "Not about the kiss. That was wonderful—for me anyway. But I know it was inappropriate. It was something about the way you listened, the way you looked at me. I couldn't help myself. It won't happen again, at least not until this case is solved."

"You didn't do anything I didn't want you to do. It's just more than I can handle right now. The kids, the danger."

"I know. Believe me, it won't happen again."

What came over me was not the sense of relief I expected, but a wave of disappointment and longing. Not happen again? That wasn't what I wanted.

I didn't know it at the time but that moment in the garden was when I fell in love with Mason Garrett.

Mason took my arm and guided me toward the steps. We had only a few minutes before we'd be back inside the house. We both needed to clear our heads, and I needed to find out a few things.

"How do you know all this about my brother—that he did work for Sandler's?"

"From Lurleen's friend Marie Vanderling—before I got pulled from the case. While I'm not sure she told me everything she knows, she did mention that Tommy Brown was a friend of Ellie's and a lawyer who did contract work for the corporation—usually in matters requiring discretion or heavy legal persuasion."

"Hmm. Maybe Lurleen and I should have another lunch with Marie."

"I don't want you anywhere near Sandler's or the people who work there. Promise me you won't do that."

Before I had to give him an answer, Eddie appeared at the back door. If we didn't hurry, breakfast would be cold.

Chapter Eighteen

Everyone else was seated around the farmhouse table when Mason and I joined them. Eddie had done herself proud with lemon and blueberry pancakes, made from scratch, scrambled eggs with heavy cream and a hint of thyme, fresh-squeezed orange juice, which had been Lucie's task, and crisp bacon just the way I liked it. We barely spoke. Even Jason sat quietly munching.

I did my best to focus on breakfast and keep thoughts of Marie Vanderling from my mind. But Marie was our inside man—or woman in this case. I didn't want to go against Mason's wishes by contacting her. I would never do anything to get in the way of his investigation. Except that it wasn't his investigation any longer. And I wasn't an innocent bystander. A childhood friend killed. Her children under my watch. And a brother who just might be involved with all of it.

It was Lurleen who finally broke the silence.

"Ah, *ma chere* Eddie. If I didn't know you two had just met I would have sworn you were Ditie's mother. Never have I seen cooks as perfect as the two of you. I think you may have to adopt her unless Detective Mason has his own ideas."

Eddie smiled and asked for more maple syrup. I turned red and Mason focused on his last bite of pancake. When I could, I shot her a look, but Lurleen just smiled sweetly back at me and twisted her hair into a chignon that she fixed with a clip in the shape of a peacock. "Don't you just love this little bauble," she said to me as if I'd asked her a question. "It was my Aunt Therese who sent this to me not two weeks ago."

"Your Aunt Therese," I said with an evil glint in my eye. "Funny how you've never mentioned her before."

"Silly you. I've talked about her dozens of time. Probably called her Terry. She always hated the name Therese, although I find it quite beautiful. You forgot, with all you've had on your mind."

I gave up. Never would I catch Lurleen in a lie and normally I didn't want to. Her fantasy world gave me as much pleasure as it seemed to give her, and who knew, maybe there was an Aunt Therese. Maybe someday we'd all summer in the south of France. That would be fun, particularly with Mason and Eddie and the kids at my side. I was happy to be as lost in fantasy as Lurleen was.

But not for long. My cell phone rang with a number I didn't recognize. I stepped out of the kitchen to answer it.

"Hi, Ditie. A voice from your past. It's Phil here. I'm down here planning for the Civil War reenactment—the Battle of Atlanta in the summer. I hope we can get together."

I tried to breathe the way you're supposed to when you need to calm down. "Phil, we haven't talked in seven years."

"I know. I know. I've been a lousy friend."

I wanted to say, "You were a lot more than a friend to me," but I kept my mouth shut. I let the silence linger.

"You did get my rose? I didn't sign my name because I wasn't sure how you'd respond."

I remained silent.

"What? You still haven't forgiven me? Maybe you'll be happy to know I'm getting a divorce. I'm actually thinking of moving back here. My father's going to retire, and I might take over his practice."

"I'm not happy about your divorce," I said. "I'm never happy about that, although I know sometimes it's for the best."

"Good Lord, Ditie, you're still the same. Wishing everyone the best."

"I didn't wish you the best, Phil. It took me years to get over you."

"But I never promised you anything, Ditie. I loved you in my own way, but we never talked about a future."

"I know, Phil. You can count yourself blameless. I'm the one who had hopes for the future. So why are you calling me now?"

"I'd like to see you again. No promises, but you never know. You were the one person who got me, all of me. Could we have lunch, dinner?"

"I'm involved with someone right now," I said. It was close enough to the truth to get Phil out of my life.

"Then let's just see each other for old time's sake. I'm glad if you're happy, but I've really missed you. I finally understand what you offered me when I was too stupid to take advantage of it."

"You did hear the part about my being involved with someone, right?"

"Yeah, yeah, but you know me—I never take no for an answer. It's just lunch."

I thought about that. Maybe meeting with Phil would bring me some closure. I'd never loved anyone else so deeply besides my father.

"Okay," I said, knowing it might not be okay.

"Great. I'll call you when I get my schedule straight."

I hung up and Mason joined me in the hallway outside the kitchen.

"Who was that?" Mason asked.

"An old friend. The sender of the rose. He wants to have lunch and I agreed."

"Should I be worried?"

"I don't think so."

"That's probably more honesty than I wanted from you, Ditie. Who is this guy and how do you know him?"

I filled him in on Philip Brockton IV. "He can trace his heritage back to the Civil War and is proud of the fact his great-great-great-grandfather was a colonel in the war. He comes from a line of doctors almost that long. We met during our residencies—his in oncology, mine in pediatrics. He loved books and history and I loved him."

"Why?" Mason asked.

I paused. Why had I loved Phil with all my heart when he loved me only a little? I shook my head. "I don't know why. I'm going to have to sort that out. He was smart and I liked that. He read and talked about books the way my father did." I shrugged and gave up trying to explain what I didn't understand myself.

"Thanks for telling me, Ditie. I'm not happy about it, but I'm glad to know what I'm up against."

"I don't think you're up against anything except a case your boss won't let you solve."

Mason left for work shortly after our conversation. We had a quiet day. In retrospect maybe it was too quiet. The children and I played outside most of the day. Dan hovered nearby. Lurleen was inside, giving herself a spa day—something she offered to share with Lucie, but Lucie wanted to be outside with us. Hermione was in heaven, chasing balls and children to her heart's content. Even the weather was obliging. It was a perfect spring day. It gave me time to catch my breath and I did.

Perhaps Charlie Flack would stay away from us, give up on his quest to get whatever it was that Ellie had hidden away. Maybe the cops had scared him off for good. Maybe he wouldn't figure out where we were living now. It was a lot of wishful thinking, and I knew it was unlikely. But for one day I wanted to believe it was true. I wanted the children and me to have a normal life.

Eddie called us in for lunch—deli sandwiches on home-made bread. Ice cream for dessert. She insisted I take some time for myself after lunch—a nap or a good read. I took her up on it. First with a bath and then an hour to myself. Time to think about something other than the murders.

Of course, what came to mind was Phil.

Why had I loved Phil? Did I love him still? He had my father's intelligence but not his gentleness. What I took for gentleness was actually a passivity, a wish not to rock the boat. He seemed content to be with me, but he was never completely satisfied with who I was. Couldn't I exercise a little more, fix my hair, lose some weight? Why was I always baking? Couldn't I do something more worthwhile with my time? He hurt me in a thousand familiar ways. Always wanting to change me as my mother did.

My mother!

Did I love Phil because he was similar not just to my dad but my mother as well? They say you marry your mother. The thought made me sigh. I'd been running away from my mother most of my life. Had I run straight into her arms when I fell in love with Phil?

I sat up in bed. Now I wasn't about to sleep. I went downstairs to see if I might help with dinner. Dan had taken over the role of kid supervisor. I found Eddie in the kitchen.

"Did you sleep, dear? You must be exhausted from all you've been through."

"I rested. Now I'm ready to help with dinner."

Together Eddie and I searched for the perfect menu—first in old cookbooks and later on the Internet. What would satisfy both the children in our life and the men? Lurleen would be pleased with whatever we came up with. We decided on oven-fried chicken, new potato salad with dill, and grilled asparagus. Eddie and I spent the afternoon together, chatting and chopping, dipping and frying. It was a joy for both of us. Lucie popped her head in and offered to help. We gave her the task of finding a tasty dessert in one of Eddie's cookbooks for kids. She came up with lemon squares and assured us she could do the whole thing on her own. Which she did.

Mason arrived home around six. He'd heard nothing more about Charlie Flack. Flack had apparently disappeared into the woodwork. Maybe he would stay gone. Mason's captain was threatening him with a new assignment in south Georgia, but he would deal with that in the morning. In the meantime, he was quite content to enjoy the sumptuous meal we'd prepared. Lurleen and Dan ooh'd and ahh'd over our efforts. Even Jason asked for more chicken and a second lemon square.

Eddie and I settled in the parlor while the rest of the crew cleaned up. Lucie wanted to help, so we let her. We'd run out of diversions and started talking about the case.

"You are at the center of this, Ditie. What do you think is going on?" Eddie asked.

"I think Ellie was in over her head. She was always looking for a way to strike it rich. Maybe she got involved with the wrong people—Billy Joe, Charlie Flack—and it cost her her life."

"She never gave them what they wanted," Eddie said. "I wonder why not."

"Ellie always thought she could get away with more," I said. "My guess is she either couldn't get the information or, more likely, she was trying to sell it to the highest bidder."

"If she did get it, where is it?" Eddie said.

"That's the question, isn't it? She hid it somewhere. Somewhere that she knew would be safe. Undetectable but safe."

The kids bounced into the room and our conversation ended. Dan, Mason, and Lurleen followed.

We spent half an hour playing charades at Lurleen's insistence. We did titles of children's books. Lurleen relished any opportunity to be dramatic and had us in hysterics as she acted out *Where the Wild Things Are*. Then it was bedtime for all of us.

Mason left early the next morning to sort things out with his captain. The rest of us remained at the kitchen table savoring hot scones and fresh coffee. Minutes later the landline rang.

"Must be Mason," Eddie said. "Probably forgot something." She walked quickly to the phone while the rest of us cleared our dishes.

"Hello. Who is this?" Eddie listened and her face hardened. "Lurleen doesn't live here." She listened some more. "I see. I don't know where she is. I'll try to reach Dr. Brown and see if she knows. Yes, I understand it's urgent. I'll do what I can."

She hung up the phone and looked at Lurleen. "That was Marie Vanderling."

She turned to the children. "Lucie, could you take Jason upstairs and entertain him for a while. I have a trunk full of games in your room. It's in the closet. We'll be up to join you in a few minutes."

"Of course, Miss Eddie," she said. She looked almost as serious as Eddie did, but she didn't ask a single question. "Come on, Jason. I'll be your launch pad for Spider-Man and I'll even be one of your bad guys."

That was all Jason needed. He yelled for Hermione to come and took off up the stairs. Lucie was two steps behind him.

"So," Eddie said, turning to Lurleen. "How is it Marie Vanderling knows where to find you?"

Lurleen's eyes looked like large shiny headlights. "I swear I never said a word to her. Not one word. About the house I mean. I did talk to her a little bit. I mean, she's a friend of mine. She's helped us out. I knew I could trust her. But I never said where we were going. I might have mentioned we were moving to a safer location. But never where. I swear."

Thankfully, she didn't swear in the name of her Aunt Therese.

I studied Lurleen. We all did, and no one said a word.

"Okay, okay," Lurleen said. This time large tears were streaming down her face. "Maybe I did say that Detective Garrett was rescuing us like a knight from the Round Table. And yes I know they were English not French, but I've never been an Anglophobe like some of my relatives. So maybe I did say that. But never where we were going."

"Oh, Lurleen." It was all I could say, and it made Lurleen cry even harder.

"Why didn't she call you on your cell phone?" Eddie asked.

"She probably tried. In all the moves, I didn't bring my charger. It went dead days ago."

Eddie handed Lurleen a box of tissues. "No point crying over what can't be undone. Let's figure out what to do next. Marie sounded desperate. I think you need to call her back. Tell her you and Ditie are staying in a hotel but you're not allowed to say where. I doubt she'll believe that, but it's worth a try. I'll call Mason. Don't make any plans with Marie. Just find out what she needs to tell you and say you'll call her back. Use Ditie's cell phone, so she won't see this number."

I handed Lurleen my phone and sat beside her as she dialed Marie. She put her on speakerphone so we could all hear the conversation.

"Hi, Marie. Mrs. Garrett called Ditie, and she told me you needed to talk to me."

"Where are you? I assumed you'd gone to stay with Detective Garrett, so I tracked down his home number and his mother's." Marie didn't sound like her confident self. Her voice trembled.

"He put us in a hotel under guard. I can't say where. Why did you need to talk to me?"

"I can't discuss this over the phone. I don't know who might be listening. We have to meet. You, me, and Ditie. Please."

Lurleen looked over at Eddie, who motioned that she hang up.

"I'll have to call you back, Marie. Are you safe?"

"I don't know. Please call me soon. Detective Garrett can't come. There's something screwy going on here, and I think the police may be involved. On the wrong side."

She hung up. Eddie called Mason and recapped the conversation. She listened to his response and then gave the phone to Dan.

Dan listened for thirty seconds. "Got it," he said. "I'm on it. I'll keep you posted."

"So?" I said, barely able to stay in my seat.

"You two are to go nowhere near Marie Vanderling." He looked at Lurleen. "You are to call her back and introduce me over the phone. I'll take it from there."

Lurleen took my phone again and redialed.

No answer.

Chapter Nineteen

Lurleen held the phone in her hand as if it might suddenly speak to her. She walked back and forth in the kitchen talking to anyone who would listen. "Marie's in trouble. I know she's in serious trouble. I could hear it in her voice." Eddie took her arm and guided her into the front parlor. The rest of us followed.

"Sit down," Dan said, patting the sofa. "We'll figure out what to do."

Dan tried to call Mason, but he didn't pick up. Lurleen slumped onto the sofa next to him.

"I've made a mess of everything. I've put the kids at risk and Marie as well."

I sat on the other side of her. "I like Marie," I said. "But if she's in trouble, it's trouble of her own making. She likes to know everything, remember? Maybe she found out too much." Or maybe she's in the middle of too much, I wanted to add. But Lurleen was Marie's fast friend. She didn't doubt Marie's honesty, so I kept my doubts to myself.

"Okay," Eddie said. "Enough moping around. I'm setting the alarm, so no one can come or go without letting me know." We nodded our assent.

"We'll have to watch the kids like hawks," I said. "I'll explain to Lucie about the alarm, but keeping track of Jason is going to be a challenge."

"I'll handle that," Lurleen said. "We have a special bond—Jason thinks I'm the Femme Merveilleuse, a French superhero. He'll be happy to spend the day with me. It's the least I can do. I am so, so sorry. And now I'm so worried about Marie."

I patted her hand.

"No crying over spilt milk," Eddie said. "Where does Marie live?"

Lurleen pulled a small leather notebook out of her purse. She wrote out the address, along with Marie's cell number and work number. She ripped out the page and handed it to Eddie who passed it on to Dan.

"You'll have to track her down," Eddie said to Dan. "Do what you can to see if she's at work. Use one of your disguises."

"Disguises?" I asked.

"I do a lot of work on heating and air systems." He smiled. "People are always happy to see me if they think their system might be in trouble."

"I'll keep things safe here," Eddie said. "Mason will call when he can and we'll figure out our next move."

"What shall I do?" I asked.

Eddie stared at me. "I don't suppose you'd like to spend the day baking with Lucie. Take her mind off things, and yours as well."

Lucie. Very-good-at-keeping-secrets Lucie. Was there anything else Lucie might know that she wasn't telling me? "Hmm. I could do that," I said. Baking would give me time to think about our situation. I could think and grill Lucie at the same time. Gently, of course. My supervisor didn't expect me back at work until next week, so time was my own.

Work. It was certainly on the back burner, and I didn't like that. It wasn't that Vic couldn't keep the place running without me. Of course she could. But I missed the place. The work grounded me. It gave me perspective. Then there was the fifteen-year-old who was so distraught. I wondered if the social worker had resolved that situation at home. If I had a second I'd give her a call.

Eddie brought me back to the current situation. "We can't have the kids out of our sight. If Marie figured out where we were, anyone else could as well. Dan, let me hear from you every hour and I'll keep up with Mason if he doesn't call you first." Eddie was clearly command central. I felt sorry for anyone who tried to mess with her.

Lurleen and I went upstairs to find the kids. They were settled on the bed, a card game spread out in front of them. Lucie was teaching Jason the rules.

"Can we talk?" I whispered to Lurleen. I stepped into the hallway and Lurleen followed me.

I stood with my cell phone in one hand.

"Who are you calling?" she asked. "Not Phil Brockton I hope."

I shook my head. "He'll call me if he wants to meet. It's lunch, nothing more."

"Brockton would never call you if he didn't want something from you. This isn't a let's-be-friends invitation. He was never concerned with anyone but himself. I'm surprised you still don't know that."

"I've thought a lot about our relationship. I see him more clearly now, but people do change. I'm not going to chase after him, that's for sure. And lunch is to give me some closure, that's all. I haven't seen or heard from him in seven years."

"Seven years and you still think about him. *Mon Dieu*, I stop thinking about an ex-boyfriend in seven seconds."

"As I said, Lurleen, it's not Phil I'm calling. I had a fifteen-year-old in the clinic the other day, the one I mentioned before. She was hysterical, complaining of stomach pains, aches, everything imaginable. There wasn't anything physically wrong with her that I could find. When I asked about her home situation she burst into tears."

I closed the bedroom door, so the children couldn't hear what I was saying. Lurleen moved closer to me.

"An 'uncle' moved in. He was terrifying her. I did a pregnancy test, and that was negative. But I am worried about her. She wouldn't say he was molesting her but she was too frightened to say much of anything. We have a great social worker, and that's the person I want to call."

I looked at Lurleen. She was trembling. "What is it? Are you sick?"

"No, no, I'm fine. These stories make me sad, that's all. A child in trouble with no one to protect her."

Lurleen didn't look fine. I led her to the bench near the window at the top of the stairs. She let me put my arm around her.

"Please, Ditie, no questions. Not today."

"Not today," I said. "But someday I hope you'll talk to me about your past. Your real past." I held her until she'd regained her composure.

"Do you mind if I sit here while you call?" she asked.

"Not at all." I called the clinic and asked to speak to Cheryl, the social worker. She was out, so I left a message to have her call me when she could. "Well, that's all I can do for now. Are you ready to get the kids?"

"Ready," Lurleen said, putting on her happy face. "Jason will never leave my side."

We opened the bedroom door without knocking and two very guilty-looking children stopped talking. They weren't playing the game. Lucie slid something in her pocket and gave Jason a look.

"What's going on?" I asked Lucie.

"Nothing, Aunt Di," Lucie said and turned red. "Jason didn't want to play by the rules, so I had to talk to him about that."

Jason remained uncharacteristically quiet.

"You must obey me," Lurleen said to Jason. "I am the Femme Merveilleuse. No one can disobey the Femme Merveilleuse." She began tickling Jason, who screamed with delight.

"Come, Lucie," I said. "We have a busy day ahead of us. We have to make enough sweets to satisfy this household and take care of lunch and dinner as well. We are the catering service. Are you up for that?"

Lucie jumped down from the bed. "Of course," she said. "But what about Jason?"

"Lurleen is Jason's sidekick for the day. Don't worry about him."

Lucie whispered something in Jason's ear and left the room with a single stern glance in his direction.

She took my hand and walked slowly downstairs with me. When we got to the kitchen I pulled out a few cookbooks from Eddie's vast collection and put them on the island. Lucie climbed up on a stool and sat quietly beside me. I thumbed through the index looking for a brownie recipe that might rival my own.

"What is it, Luce? You're never this quiet."

Lucie pretended to be interested in a recipe she'd found. "We could make this," she said.

"Lucie, what is it? What did you whisper to Jason?"

Lucie bit her lower lip and concentrated on the recipe.

I took the book out of her hands. "What's going on? You have to tell me."

"You're not my mother! I don't have to tell you anything!"

She jumped down from the stool and ran out of the room. I found her in the giant hallway, hiding behind the massive staircase. There was an open space underneath the stairs—a perfect hiding place for a young girl in trouble.

I sat down on the floor beside her and took her in my arms. "What is it, Luce? Don't you trust me?"

"More than anyone."

"Then tell me. What is it?"

Lucie sat rigid in my arms. In a silent battle with herself—or someone else.

She finally spoke. "Someone might get hurt if I tell."

"Lucie, secrets are never good. Not secrets that threaten someone. Bad people try to get children to be quiet. Please tell me what's going on."

"It's Jason," she said.

"What about Jason?"

"He's seen his dad."

There. It was out. Lucie looked relieved and terrified at the same time.

"What do you mean? I know his dad came over to see your mom with Billy Joe. Is that what you mean?"

"No. Jason has talked to his dad a bunch of times. At school. At your house. His dad knows we're here. Jason has his cell phone. They talk." Lucie reached into the pocket of her jeans and pulled out a cell phone. "This is what I took from him when you came in."

She handed me the phone. "Jason's dad said someone might kill us if we ever said a word."

"Oh, Lucie. We have to tell Eddie and Mason. You understand that, don't you?"

Lucie nodded. "I know."

I started with Eddie. She was sitting in the parlor talking on the phone. When she got off she began speaking before I could.

"That was Mason. He still doesn't know what's going on. The order to take him off the case came from higher up. Nothing his captain could do. Mason's furious, of course. Now he's supposed to go to Albany on a cold case. That could keep him out of town for days." She looked at me. "What is it, Ditie? We'll be okay here, I promise you. And I'm not sure Mason will go on the assignment even if it costs him his job."

"It's not that," I said, "although that's a huge problem." I gave her the phone. "This belongs to Charlie Flack. He's been in touch with Jason all along. I have no doubt he knows where Jason is right now."

Eddie examined the phone and then put it in her pocket. "This changes things," she said. That was all she said for a moment. "I'll get in touch with Mason—with luck, he can trace the phone. We'll make sure every window and door is locked." She used a key to open the gun case at the back of the room, selected a firearm, and slid it into her apron pocket. "We'll be fine."

Lucie had been standing in the doorway throughout the conversation. I motioned her over and she sat between us. "You did the right thing by telling us," Eddie said to her. "Now we can keep you and Jason safe."

I hugged Lucie, and she let out an enormous sigh. She rested her head on my chest, and for a moment I felt she was my eight-year-old daughter. "You don't have to be the adult any longer, Lucie."

Chapter Twenty

Eddie left us sitting on the sofa in the parlor and went into the hallway to call Mason. I could hear the murmur of her voice followed by silence and then more talking. Lucie kept her head on my chest. I realized by her soft, regular breathing that she was asleep. Poor kid. Holding all that inside must have been a dead weight for her. She was so desperate to keep everyone alive she didn't know what to do. I got her comfortable on the sofa, covered her with a soft throw, and joined Eddie in the hall.

"Mason is on his way here. We'll make sure all the windows and doors are locked, and then I'll show you how to set the alarm."

"Are you always this calm?" I asked her as I followed her into the dining room.

"It's the first thing they try to teach you at the academy, and it's one of the last things you actually learn. Like being a doctor I suspect."

We latched each window as we talked.

"Yes," I said. "You graduate after four years of school, and then everyone calls you doctor. But you're a doctor in name only—it's pretty frightening. That first year of residency, your internship year, that's what teaches you to be one. To ask the right questions, to stay calm, to cope."

Eddie motioned me to the kitchen through the butler's pantry and then on to a guest bedroom that also served as her office. It was a beautiful space, added on when the kitchen was expanded I suspected. Cozy, with windows on two sides, a sleigh bed against one wall, and a lovely plantation desk in front of the windows. "My husband designed this space for me before he died. He knew how much I wanted a grand kitchen and a smaller space to call my own."

"It's perfect."

Eddie nodded and finished with the windows as I stood admiring the room.

"Please, don't stop talking," she said. "I've always wondered about life as a doctor. It's something I might have considered if I'd been born in your time and not mine."

"Med school is all about endurance—budgeting your time, trying to remember too much information, but it's nothing compared to the first year after you graduate. That's when you have to make decisions, learn what you don't know, and stay strong. I didn't let myself cry for a year, and then on my weeklong break, it was all I could do. You see too much suffering."

"I can't imagine working with a sick or dying child," Eddie said. "I didn't think I'd recover when my own son died. You don't entirely, but you do learn to cope."

I nodded. I'd seen how crushing it was for a parent to lose a child. It was a pain that never seemed to end. "How did you cope?"

"Time," Eddie said. "Time and friends. I can talk about my son Michael now and remember the good times with him as well as the bad. Someone told me it's like a circle that's been broken. The circle will never be complete again, but over time you can appreciate the part of the circle that remains."

"If you don't mind, I'm going to use that in the future. It may help people."

"Of course, dear. With the loss of my husband and my son, I take nothing for granted. I live every moment to its fullest. Maybe that's why I stay calm. I know I can handle almost anything that's thrown my way." She squeezed my arm. "I see that same toughness in you, although I do wonder . . ." She paused and looked at me.

"What?" I asked.

"It's none of my business."

"You can ask me anything you like," I said.

We kept moving, this time back to the kitchen and the bay of windows that filled the kitchen with light. Eddie dead bolted the door leading to the backyard, as I set to work on the windows.

"I wonder why you aren't married. Never married, Mason said." She looked at me. "I'm sorry, my dear. I'm often accused of being too blunt. In the South, that's not considered a desirable trait."

We both laughed.

"I know. I find it refreshing. I never married because . . ." I couldn't think of how to finish that sentence. "I guess I didn't want to risk losing someone I loved the way I lost my father. It hurt too much. It seemed better not to get attached. To a person or a place."

"But, of course, we do get attached, don't we?" she said, touching my arm. "Forgive me for prying. I want to know everything about everyone. It made me a good cop but an annoying friend." She took her cell phone out of her pocket. "Let me check with Dan and then we'll get the rest of the house secured."

I locked the remaining windows in the kitchen while Eddie made her phone call.

"Dan hasn't found Marie," she said when she clicked off. "He's been to her house and now he's headed to Sandler's."

She took my hand and led me across the hall to a room I'd never entered—a second parlor she called it. It looked like a glimpse into the past, full of antiques. "This is all the furniture from my parents and grandparents. Furniture that we couldn't bear to part with and that never found a good home."

I could find a good home for it, I thought. It was beautiful. A fireplace stood in one corner surrounded by bookshelves and hundreds of books. The room itself was overstuffed with chairs and settees.

"I'm not a hoarder, I promise you. I just couldn't bear to part with what my parents and grandparents so loved."

"I completely understand," I said. We made our way with difficulty to the windows that looked out on the right side of the house. The space outside was narrow and less well-groomed. "It's like a secret garden," I said. "Old rose bushes. An oak tree good for climbing. I hope Jason doesn't discover this."

"Oh, he probably has. The front of the yard is fenced in, but there's a gate leading to this area. We haven't done much with the space. My husband was the real gardener, and this was the project he never got to. I suppose I've left it wild as a memorial to him."

"It looks like someone's been in it," I said, peering out the window. "See the footprints, the trampled earth."

"I can't imagine who that would be," Eddie said, looking where I pointed. "We have a gardener who comes every other week, but I've told him not to bother with this area. Not until we decide what we want to do with it. The footprints look fresh. I'm going to check it out. I'll be back in a minute." She could see the worried look on my face. "I've got my friend," she said, motioning to the pocket that held the gun. "And it's broad daylight."

I waited by the window. Eddie waved at me from outside and I watched as she examined the prints. Then she returned.

"Looks like two different sets. Not work boots. Regular shoes. One around the size of Mason's and one larger. Perhaps Mason and Dan walked out here. That would make sense."

We split up the rooms on the second floor and had everything checked and locked in ten minutes. Lurleen was busy playing I Spy with Jason and understood that her one assignment was to keep him safe. I knew she'd throw herself in front of a bus to do that.

I motioned her into the hallway and let her know the latest on Marie. Jason heard us whispering and joined us in the hall. "You have a secret," Jason said. "When you whisper you have a secret. That's what Mommy says." His lower lip started to quiver.

Lurleen looked at him with her hands on her hips. "You, *mon cher* Jason, or should I say *Monsieur* Spider-Man, must help us protect the household from intruders. That is our mission. I will teach you some moves from my karate class and then we'll be all set."

Jason looked up at her. He mimicked her stance. Earnest face. Hands on hips. "Okay, Fam Mar-"

"-veilluese," Lurleen added.

"Merveilleuse," Jason said as if he actually spoke French. Better French than Lurleen. Even she was shocked. "But I don't need no karate moves. I know karate." He gave a pretty good rendition of someone who actually *did* know karate. Eddie joined us at that point and nodded her approval.

"We'll leave you two at it," Eddie said. "He should never be out of your sight, Lurleen."

"He won't be." I thought she was going to add *Madame Capitaine,* but she didn't.

Mason entered the front door as we came downstairs. He looked grim. "Let me see the phone."

"You're going to hand it over to headquarters?" Eddie asked.

Mason shook his head. "Not right now. I'm taking a few days of sick leave. I've suddenly come down with the flu." Mason was angry, but he clearly wasn't sick.

"What's going on at headquarters?" Eddie asked.

"I wish I knew. Not a word I can trust from anyone. Except that I'm off the case. They don't need me in Albany, and a man can't help it if he gets sick. So I'm here with you."

We heard Lucie stirring in the parlor. She seemed as happy to see Mason as I was. He knelt beside the sofa. "You've been a very brave little girl. I want to ask you some more questions when you're up to it."

Lucie sat up straight, dangled her feet over the edge of the sofa. "I'm ready now."

"Did you know Jason's dad was seeing him?"

Lucie nodded solemnly. "He showed up when no one else was around. Before Mom died, she said I must not tell anyone about him."

"Why did he come?" Mason asked.

"He said we had something he needed. Something small but important. He searched through everything we had, and then he swore at us. Bad words I can't say to you."

"He never found what he wanted?"

Lucie shook her head again. "No. And he always said he would be back."

"Why did he think you had something he wanted?" Mason asked.

"Because it was supposed to be in the Transformer Jason had. It was supposed to be left there. I heard Jason's dad say that to my mom. She said she'd put it somewhere else for safe-keeping. Somewhere nearby, but no one would know where until she saw the money. She said us kids would keep it hidden even though we didn't know what we were doing."

"So she did have whatever it is they wanted," I exclaimed. "Lucie, you have no idea what it was or where it might be hidden?"

Lucie solemnly shook her head.

"When was the last time Jason saw his dad?" Mason asked.

"He came to our window last night."

"What?" Eddie and Mason said together. "That's impossible."

"Someone held the ladder for him. A man, I think. But I couldn't tell for sure. It was too dark."

Eddie and I looked at each other. The footprints were just below the children's room.

Chapter Twenty-one

We sat in the parlor, stunned. Two men had dragged a ladder to the side of the house, and we hadn't noticed? Late-morning light filtered through the two front windows of the parlor. I had a strong urge to pull the curtains and make us invisible to anyone who might be lurking outside.

"How is that possible?" Eddie asked.

"We didn't set the alarm," Mason said.

"But why didn't Hermione bark?" Eddie said.

"She only barks when someone rings the doorbell," I said.

"She was asleep," Lucie added. "I heard her snoring. And Jason's dad wasn't there long. He said he'd be back. He told us to call him when the coast was clear. He said he couldn't call Jason on the phone because he didn't know who might be around to hear it ring."

Mason stood up. "Come on, Mom, we'll have a look outside." He pointed a finger at me. "You stay here with Lucie."

I nodded my assent, but I didn't like the finger pointing. I didn't like it when anyone ordered me about. Eddie and Mason were back in the house in ten minutes.

"We found two sets of footprints. One small. One large. No ladder. Did you see a second person, Lucie?"

Lucie shook her head. "I thought someone was holding the ladder. Jason's dad called to hold it steady, but the other person didn't speak."

"And Charlie Flack said he'd come back when the coast was clear?"

Lucie nodded.

Mason and Eddie were quiet for a moment. I knew what they were thinking. "You want to set a trap for them, don't you?"

"Right," Mason said. "Lucie, you and Jason won't be involved, except to tell one lie. You'll say the coast is clear. Can you do that?"

She nodded like a little soldier being asked to lead the charge out of the bunker. "Yes," she said and reached for the phone.

"Not quite yet, sweetie," Eddie said. "We'll work out the details and then we'll ask you to do that."

Lucie looked relieved.

"For now, do you mind playing with Jason and Lurleen? Not a word to Jason about this, okay?" Mason shook her hand.

I took her to the foot of the stairs and kissed her on the top of her head. "You did the right thing."

She smiled at me. A small, scared smile. "I know. I love you, Aunt Di, no matter what happens."

I hugged her hard. "I love you too. Nothing is going to happen to you or Jason. I made a promise to your mother, and I never break my promises."

I watched Lucie climb slowly up the stairs. She made my heart ache. Is this what being a mother was all about? It was an unfamiliar feeling—like when the Grinch's heart grew two sizes. Painful and powerful.

As I walked into the parlor, I heard Mason on the phone. "We'll see you when you get here."

He looked up at me and patted a seat next to him on the sofa. He could see I had something to say.

"I'm not okay with involving Lucie in this," I said. "No phone call to Flack. No lies. The kid is scared to death. I protect kids. I don't put them on the firing line."

Eddie took my hand. "You do realize the children are in danger whether or not we call Flack directly."

"Of course, but I can't ask her to do this. Lucie's a trouper. She'll do anything we ask her to do, but I won't ask her to do this."

Mason nodded. "It's off the table for now, and maybe it will never come to that. Dan's been busy. He had a long chat with a receptionist at Sandler's. According to the receptionist, Marie Vanderling didn't go into work today and didn't call in. It was totally out of character for her."

"So she's either on the run or she's in trouble," I said.

"That's what it looks like," Mason said. "Dan went through her house pretty carefully and didn't find anything suspicious."

"He broke into her house?" I asked.

"He didn't have to. The back door was unlocked. Dirty dishes were piled in the sink. It's as if she left to go to work and changed her mind. Or someone changed it for her."

I put my head in my hands. "She sounded so frightened on the phone." All I could see was Ellie's face after she'd been shot. Unrecognizable. Horrible. Had this happened to Marie? I couldn't stop myself from shaking. Mason put his arm around me.

"We don't know anything yet," he said, "but we do know that whoever is behind this is getting more brazen. For Charlie Flack to come to the house in the middle of the night, he must be stupid or desperate or both."

"He looked scared to death when I saw him in the car. What happens next?" I asked.

"First off, Dan is going to see what else he can find at Sandler's. According to our very talkative receptionist, all the high-level execs and their staff were called to an emergency meeting. Marie was a no-show. I think we need to get Lurleen involved. She may have some ideas about where Marie went."

"I'll relieve her," I said. "And get the kids to help me with lunch."

"Good."

I went upstairs in time to see Lurleen and Jason rescuing Lucie from the clutches of Hermione, aka *Chien Mauvais*. Hermione was lying on her back being scratched vigorously by Jason and obviously in heaven.

"That's one way to subdue an enemy," I said. "I'm here to get recruits for lunch duty. I need you both." I pointed to Jason and Lucie. "And Mason would like the presence of your company, Lurleen. He's in the parlor."

"*Avec plaisir,*" Lurleen said. "I shall be on my best behavior. You have nothing to fear. He's all yours, *ma chérie.*"

"Thank you. Now come along, kids." We headed downstairs to the kitchen with Lurleen tripping down the steps in front of us. I watched as Eddie closed the door to the parlor after Lurleen entered.

I made a big production out of lunch, getting down pots and pans, planning a menu with Lucie, searching the kitchen for ingredients. I didn't want the kids, especially Jason, to get any ideas about leaving the room. "How about home-made macaroni and cheese? One of my best secret recipes."

"Oh, yes," said Lucie.

"And how about brownies for dessert?"

Jason was more enthusiastic about that.

"To be healthy we'll throw in a fruit salad with my own special topping."

Lunch kept us busy for an hour. Jason grew restless when we had the brownies in the oven. After our third game of twenty questions, Lurleen popped her head into the kitchen. "May I be a sous-chef?" she asked and winked at me.

"Perfect timing. Can you assist Lucie? The brownies should be ready in ten minutes. I'll be back to finish up lunch and we'll eat in fifteen. I didn't hear Dan come back."

Lurleen shook her head. "Still on assignment," she whispered as I wrapped an apron around her. "He's interviewing Barry Hampstead."

The name sounded familiar.

"You know, Ditie, the head of Sandler's mail room. The dear man who's been wanting to marry me for years."

"Isn't that the story with every man you've met?" I asked.

"Oh *chérie,* you are much too kind. I can think of at least two men who never made a proposal. They weren't my type anyway."

I left her with both children seated at the island beside her. She'd come up with some game for them to play—undoubtedly situated in Paris or the south of France.

Everyone was quiet when I entered the parlor and shut the door behind me.

"Apparently Marie kept her private life pretty close to the vest, even with Lurleen," Eddie said. "Lurleen's worried sick, of course, but she doesn't have a clue where Marie might be."

"What do we do now?" I asked.

"Let's see what Dan turns up." Mason stood up. "I'm hungry. I can smell something delicious from the kitchen. Any chance of an early lunch?"

"You smell brownies," I said. "You can set the table if you're so eager to eat."

"*Avec plaisir,*" Mason said, "to borrow one of Lurleen's lines. In the kitchen, Mom?"

Eddie nodded. She walked into the kitchen beside me. "You've already accomplished something I've tried years to pull off—Mason setting the table. Next he'll be doing the dishes."

Lunch was a noisy affair with everyone talking at once.

"I made the brownies, Miss Eddie," Jason exclaimed. "And Lurleen let me eat one before lunch. My mom says no sweets before dinner, but Lurleen said it was okay." Jason got quiet for a moment until Lucie jumped in.

"I helped make the macaroni and cheese," Lucie said. She blushed. "Aunt Di made most of it, but I helped."

"It's delicious," I said. "And the honey topping for the fruit—perfect."

"You are not a modest cook," Mason teased me.

"If something is good, why not say so? And if it doesn't turn out to be tasty, then I'm happy to acknowledge that as well. An experiment gone awry. That's the joy of cooking."

"Don't put that in a book, my dear," Eddie said. "Someone's beaten you to it."

Dan arrived as we were finishing up. He turned off the alarm as he entered the house and then reset it. Lurleen fixed him a heaping plate of food. He worked his way through a second helping before he said he'd had enough. Then he spied the brownies on the counter. "Maybe I have a little room for one of those before we talk." He ate one and then grabbed two more.

Eddie stood up. "If you think you can handle clean-up, I'll take the kids outside." Jason was only too happy to get out of the house, but Lucie shot me a worried look.

I gave her my best *everything will be all right* look and hoped she believed me.

Eddie walked to the security panel in the kitchen and turned off the alarm. "We won't be needing this for the next half hour." Then she slid the dead bolt to the side, opened the door, and ushered the kids outside. Hermione was on Jason's heels, a ball in her mouth. Even Majestic wanted a taste of freedom. She appeared from nowhere, swished her long orange tail in our direction, and left in her Sarah Bernhardt way, ready to find a bird or two she might chase.

Mason and I cleared the table. He put the dishes in the dishwasher, while I scrubbed the pots and Lurleen dried. Dan stood nearby eating more brownies and filling us in on his morning.

Chapter Twenty-two

We finished the dishes as Dan stood beside us, munching and talking. Then we all settled around the kitchen table.

Dan brought the plate of brownies with him, but he didn't offer to share. "The receptionist had a lot to say. I'm not sure why she opened up to me the way she did."

"I know why," Lurleen responded. "You, in that Acme Heating and Air uniform, blue to match your eyes, muscles bulging. She would have talked to you all day. Was she . . . cute?"

Dan knew a trap when he saw one.

"She was okay. I didn't really notice."

Smart boy. He didn't really notice. Right. But Lurleen seemed satisfied.

"She said Marie worked harder than anyone she knew. Marie was there in the morning before the receptionist arrived and still there when she left. If anyone started to give Marie a hard time, she'd give it back to them in spades. Guys high up in the organization or not so high up—it didn't matter."

"I'm not surprised to hear that. We saw that attitude at lunch," I said.

"The receptionist liked working for her. Marie was reliable, fair, spoke to her like she was a real person and not just an extension of the telephone. If she did something wrong, Marie would call her on it immediately, but she never humiliated her. One time Sandler Senior wanted to speak with Marie, and the receptionist told him she was in a meeting. 'Never do that again,' Marie told her. 'If Mr. Sandler calls, I'm always available.'"

Dan looked sadly at the empty plate of what had been a half-dozen brownies.

"I put some away in the freezer. Shall I get them out?"

Dan shook his head and patted his belly. "Watching my weight," he said. "Where was I?"

"Repeating your conversation with the receptionist," Lurleen said, "but I could have told you all that."

Dan continued as if she hadn't spoken. I could see her start to bristle. And then her expression turned to one of sadness.

"She said Marie hadn't seemed like herself in days. Distracted. Secretive. The receptionist had no explanation for Marie's absence, and it obviously worried her."

"*Et moi, ausi. Je suis desolee*," she said. "If I've caused Marie harm, I'll never forgive myself. Never."

For once, Lurleen was not being melodramatic. I knew the feeling. It was the feeling I had when I learned Ellie was dead. "You can't think like that. You didn't make Marie do anything. She prided herself on knowing all the secrets at Sandler's and using them to her advantage. That's a dangerous game to play."

I gave Lurleen a tissue, and she dabbed at her eyes.

"Besides, we don't even know that anything has happened to her."

"Yes, we do," Lurleen said. "We just don't know what."

At that moment my cell phone rang. We both glanced at the number, hoping it might be Marie's. I didn't recognize the number, but Lurleen did.

"It's Phil Brockton," she said much too loudly.

"How'd you know that?" I asked.

"I'm an accountant," Lurleen said. "Or I used to be. Numbers are a part of my brain. I'm surprised he even owns a phone."

When Mason gave her a questioning look, she continued.

"Phil Brockton is the guy who sent Ditie the rose. The guy who's down here so he can play Civil War games. Everything is all about the eighteen hundreds. And I mean everything. His office is probably an antebellum mansion with gas lighting."

"He lives in New York," I said.

"So what?" Lurleen asked.

"Antebellum isn't really the style in Manhattan."

"I'll bet you a nickel he's got a Civil War museum somewhere in his house or office. You know it's the truth."

"Are you done?" I asked. By this time, Phil had gone to voice mail. I stepped into the hall to get the message.

It was Phil all right. "Hi, Ditie. We need to set a date for lunch. Soon."

Everything was urgent with Phil and always on his schedule.

I sighed and called him back. He started talking immediately. "I stopped by your house and then your office. No one seems to know where you are. Your house looks like no one's been there for weeks. Your grass needs cutting. I saw weeds around the roses. That's not like you, Ditie. Where are you and what's going on?"

I'd never known Phil to take an interest in what I was doing. I guess a less than manicured yard bothered him. Normally, it would bother me as well.

"I'm okay, if that's what you're asking." Of course, it wasn't what Phil was asking. He just didn't like his perfectly controlled world to seem out of order. "I've been busy and I'm staying with friends right now. I can't do lunch at this point."

Phil was quiet for a heartbeat. "But I have to see you," he said. "Everything has changed. My wife has left me. She couldn't handle my outside commitments. She wanted me to turn my life around just for her. You'd never ask me to do that."

I wouldn't have seven years ago, and I wouldn't now. But for very different reasons. "I know the Civil War reenactments are your passion, Phil. I know they keep you sane when you see too much real death and dying in the work you do. But I'm not married to you. I don't have to stitch the official patches on your uniform with specially spun thread or help you get your gear together when you're off to Gettysburg or Yorktown. I'm sure that could get old. And what about your children? Do they get to see enough of you?"

"No children, Ditie. We never had time for that. Tiffany got on that kick as well. Her biological clock was about to explode. Now was the time for children. Now or never. So I said never. And she said bye."

Phil sounded as if he were talking about an outdated television set. Time for a new model. And perhaps the new model was supposed to be me. Someone who wouldn't demand too much of him.

"I have to see you before I go back to New York. You said we'd have lunch. I'm not asking for anything more."

"Things are complicated, Phil. You can't just show up in my life after seven years and expect me to come running after you."

"I'm not asking you to do that. I need to see you. I'm—I'm confused. You could always ground me. I need your help. I need you."

The magic words. If Tommy were in the room, he'd be shaking his head. "Here you go again." Instead, it was Lurleen standing beside me. Phil was talking loudly enough for Lurleen to hear every word. *Don't do it*, she mouthed.

I held the phone away from my ear and tried to shoo Lurleen back into the kitchen, but she stayed at my side—just moving her head from side to side, her wavy hair following in slow motion. *No, no, no*, she continued to mouth.

"Phil, I can't do anything right now. I'm in the middle of something. If you went to my work, which I wish you hadn't, then you know I'm off for the rest of the week. You'll have to call me later."

Phil turned cold. "If that's the way you want it. I always thought I could count on you." Then he hung up.

"Good girl," Lurleen said. "Except for the 'call me later' part."

We reentered the kitchen where Mason and Dan were waiting for us.

"Anything I should know?" Mason asked.

I shook my head.

Lurleen patted Mason's arm. "Nothing to worry about, *cher ami*."

Mason nodded at Dan, who continued with his exploits at Sandler's. "I spoke with Barry Hampstead. That guy has a real crush on you, Lurleen."

"Don't be silly. Barry loves having a crush on people. He's just lonely. Did he have some information?"

"Apparently everyone at Sandler's is worried about a major shake-up in the organization. Rumors are flying. The organization is losing its share of the market. Kathleen Sandler was always assumed to be next in line, but people are starting to doubt that. She and the old man have sent some nasty e-mails to one another. You'd think people would learn that e-mails are always public information. A board of directors meeting is scheduled for the end of the week. Someone's on the way out, according to Hampstead. His guess is that it's Kathleen. Nothing concrete, but he'll keep his eyes and ears open. He said to give you his best regards."

Lurleen smiled sweetly, and then she stopped smiling.

"Why didn't I think of this before. I know Kathleen Sandler. We were mah-jongg partners. I dropped out after a few months. Nothing French about the game, and everyone would get so excited but not in a good way. She kept after me for a while, begging me to come back. Said I brought a lovely European sophistication to the game. Maybe I could give her a call."

"It might be dangerous," I said. "If she's embroiled in this, you could be walking into trouble."

Lurleen smiled. "The idea of Kathleen being part of something illegal is impossible. She's as straight as . . . as you, Ditie."

"It might help," Mason said. "If you could arrange to meet her in a public place, a restaurant, Dan or I could be nearby. First sign of trouble, we'll get you out of there."

"Ah, a secret agent," Lurleen said. "Right up my alley." She flicked her red hair, so that it fell over one eye.

"Easy," Mason said. "One interview and a few questions. That's all."

"*Bien sur.* But how will I reach her? My cell phone is dead. She won't pick up a number she doesn't know."

"You got your phone?" Dan asked. He reached in his pocket. "I've got a universal charger."

Lurleen smiled at him. "You certainly do."

"I'll leave you to it," Mason said. "Ditie and I will be out back with the kids."

We barely made it to the back porch before he stopped to question me. "Anything going on with this Phil Brockton guy?"

I shook my head.

"I'm asking because you shouldn't be going anywhere on your own. It's too dangerous."

I smiled. "So if I invite him over here you're fine with that?"

"You know you can't let anyone know where you are." He rubbed his bald head. "Oh, I get it. You're making fun of me."

"Never," I said. "I just wondered if you had a more personal reason for not wanting Phil around."

"Maybe I do."

At that point the kids accosted us. Jason took Mason's hand, and Lucie took mine.

Lucie's eyes were sparkling and her face was flushed. "We had so much fun," she said. "Hide and seek in this big, big yard."

I smiled a thank-you to Eddie as we walked into the kitchen. She followed behind with Hermione and Majestic at her side.

Once inside, she got water for the kids and animals. "It's getting warm out there. In the summer we'll get the sprinklers going and really have fun."

Eddie was talking about the future—a future that included the kids and no more fear. It couldn't come soon enough for me.

Mason whispered something to her, and she told Jason he needed a bath upstairs and after that she'd read to him.

"Can you read me about Superman?" Jason asked.

"Mason, where are the old comics you and Michael loved?"

"I'm sure they're in the closet, Mom, with the games. You never get rid of anything. We got tired of them, but you said they might be valuable one day."

"And see, I was right. Jason will enjoy them. I'll read you one as soon as you finish with your bath," she said, taking him by the hand.

Lucie knew she'd been left behind for a reason. "You want me to call Jason's dad, don't you?" she said.

"Just the opposite," I said.

"Hopefully, you'll never have to do that," Mason said. "But I do want to know if you have any more ideas about what Charlie Flack wants or where it might be hidden."

Lucie was quiet, lost in thought. "I know it's something small. Because it was supposed to be in the Transformer, and I know my mom had a lot of hiding places. She would hide money in the sole of her shoe or in the freezer. But I don't know where she hid this thing."

Lucie looked worn out.

"I'll take you upstairs, sweetie. Maybe you can take a nap with Jason."

"I'm too old for a nap," Lucie said, rubbing her eyes.

"Then maybe you can keep an eye on him for me." I took her hand and led her up the stairs. Jason was in the bath, so Lucie and I sat on the bed looking at the comics Eddie had found. They were mostly old Superman comics, but one of them was Wonder Woman.

"I wonder if this one belonged to Eddie," I said.

Lucie picked it up, fascinated. She snuggled up beside me. I lay back on the pillow and discovered Lucie's monkey underneath it. I pulled him out and settled him between us. Lucie cuddled him with one arm and with the other held the comic book.

"Read it to me," I said.

Lucie started reading. I closed my eyes and could hear Ellie's voice. I was back in Iowa, helping Ellie with her math, listening to her stories. Wonder Woman had to save the world, of course—this time from a threat of world domination. She had to find a tiny key before the bad men did, hidden somewhere, that could turn on a machine that would take over people's minds. A single mastermind would control the world. A hidden key. A machine. A mastermind. Something small enough to fit in the Transformer compartment. Important enough to kill for. Where would Ellie have hidden it?

Chapter Twenty-three

Eddie and Jason emerged from the bathroom. I'm not sure how Eddie managed to keep an eye on Jason in the bath and still give him his privacy, but apparently she'd pulled it off. Jason jumped on the bed in a fresh T-shirt and shorts, eager for a story. Lucie and I made room for him.

"Superman!" Jason said. "Look. There are so many Superman books. One, two, three . . ." He stopped counting when he got to ten. "Can we read them all, Miss Eddie?"

"Yes, but for now we'll read just one. Do you know any of the words, Jason?"

"Superman," Jason said proudly. He pointed at the picture and the name.

"Lucie, can you read to Jason, so Eddie and I can talk?" I asked.

"Sure," she said. She could barely keep her eyes open, and I was pretty certain in a minute or two they would both be sound asleep.

Eddie and I stood in the hallway listening to the murmur of Lucie's voice. In a little while everything was quiet. Eddie peeked in the room.

"They're both asleep. Jason is covered in Superman comics, and Lucie is hugging Wonder Woman, my old favorite." She closed the door to the bedroom and stood beside me near the window looking out on the front yard. A bush of knockout red roses was blooming along the low-lying fence. The grass was a luxurious green. Everything looked peaceful and in its right place. Eddie brought me back to reality.

"Charlie Flack and whoever he's working with seem convinced the kids have something they want. They're willing to take any risk to find it."

I nodded. "Small enough to fit in the compartment of the Transformer, even though it never made it there apparently."

"Yes," Eddie said. "And related to corporate espionage. Some information that could be turned into a lot of money."

I turned away from the window toward Eddie. "Charlie was a biochemist. He worked in the new product division before he got fired. And Marie talked about a new product soon to be released. A game changer. Are we looking for the secret formula, details about the product? All that data could be stored on a—"

"A flash drive," Eddie finished for me. "That's what we're looking for—a flash drive."

"Or a memory card," I suggested. "They could be even smaller than a flash drive. Easier to hide."

Of course, we couldn't know for sure. But it all made sense. Something small enough to be stored in a Transformer action figure. Something to do with the new product Sandler's was getting ready to unveil. Something worth thousands, if not millions, of dollars to the right buyer. Something valuable enough to kill for.

"We have to tell Mason, and then we have to go through everything the kids own," I said. "Ellie was clever. She could have hidden it anywhere."

We were halfway down the stairs when we heard Lurleen scream.

We raced to the parlor. I was surprised the kids weren't on our heels. Apparently the doors in this old house were solid enough to block out the sound of a woman's scream.

Lurleen lay on the sofa, one hand over her head. She looked exactly like a film star from a silent movie who'd just received shocking news. I could see she was breathing and in no physical distress. Dan was kneeling at her side rubbing one hand.

Mason grabbed me as I entered the room. "Lurleen got in touch with Kathleen Sandler. She was on speakerphone, so we could hear the entire conversation. They agreed to meet for a drink after work. Then Ms. Sandler called back to say she couldn't come—there'd been an emergency—an explosion in a lab. Some people were hurt, maybe killed. That's when Lurleen dropped the phone and screamed. She's convinced Marie was in the lab and died in the explosion."

"Is there any reason to think that?" I asked.

"None that I could figure out. She kept murmuring that she knew something terrible had happened to Marie and now she knew what it was. Intuition, she said."

I went over to Lurleen. She looked up at me. "She's dead. I know she's dead."

"Why do you say that, Lurleen?"

She sat up with difficulty. "I just know it. The way I know sometimes who's calling when my cell phone rings before I look at the number and answer."

At that moment her cell phone did ring. Let it be Marie, I thought. But it was Kathleen.

"We must have gotten disconnected," she said, still on speakerphone. "I thought I heard a scream and then the phone went dead. Are you all right?"

Lurleen managed a noncommittal yes.

"The lab explosion wasn't an explosion at all. Someone tried to break into the new product lab with a small explosive device. Must have been desperate to think they could pull it off in the middle of the day. Knocked out a guard, but he's recovering. They didn't get in but they did get away. Probably hurt themselves more than they hurt the door."

Now Lurleen was on her feet. "I'm so glad. Not about the break-in, just that no one was hurt. Can we still meet, *chérie*?"

"No one's called me *chérie* in a long time. I've missed you, Lurleen. And I definitely need a drink. Give me an hour to finish up here."

Lurleen hung up the phone and practically danced around the room. "Marie didn't die in an explosion." Then she stopped. "But we still don't know where she is. And she's definitely in trouble."

Mason turned to Dan. "Call Grady ER. See if anyone's turned up with hand burns. Then try the other hospitals."

"On it," Dan said. "Mind if I use your office, Eddie?"

"Be my guest." Dan disappeared down the hallway.

"Are you up for this interview, Lurleen?" Mason asked.

"Of course. You'll need to give us time for a few drinks. Once Kathleen has had a couple of martinis, she gets a lot more talkative."

"What's her relationship to Billy Joe?" Mason asked.

"Cousins. She'll be devastated about his death, of course, but they never got along. He was the black sheep of the family and Kathleen is—all white. Old-man Sandler loves her to death. He's been grooming her to take over the company."

"But Dan said there were nasty e-mails between them, that she might be on her way out," I said.

"Kathleen stood up to the old man. She's every bit as tough as he is, but together they run the company. He wouldn't kick her out. Now I must get ready to see my old friend." Lurleen left the room with a flourish. It appeared she had completely recovered from her near-death experience, or more accurately, the imagined near-death experience of her friend Marie.

Eddie stood up. "I'm going to check on the kids." I started to join her. "You stay here, Ditie. I can handle it."

I sat down again next to Mason. "Any chance I can come along?"

Mason hesitated. "You could be my date. That would give me some cover. But if there's a problem, you'll have to get out of there fast. Understood? Dan and I will be focused on Lurleen and Kathleen Sandler."

"Got it. But why do you think there could be trouble?"

"We have no idea who might be watching them, and despite what Lurleen thinks, we don't know if Kathleen could be involved."

Eddie came down a minute later. "The kids are still sound asleep." She sat down across from us. "Ditie and I have been talking, and I think we know what Flack and the others want. A memory card or a flash drive. Easy to hide."

Mason smiled and nodded his agreement. "It could contain all the information needed about the new product. But where did Ellie manage to hide it?"

"Lucie said her mother hid money in her shoes and in the freezer. I suppose you checked all of Ellie's clothing," I said. "And I'm sure you combed through her apartment."

"I was involved with the apartment search. If there was anything there, we would have found it. I know they looked through her clothes, but now that we know what we're looking for, we can do it again. Of course, I'm off the case, so I can't do anything officially. But maybe I can get the word out."

"Ditie and I will go over everything the kids own," Eddie said.

At that moment, Mason's cell went off. "It's my captain," he said glancing at the number. "Maybe he's come to his senses."

Chapter Twenty-four

Mason took the call in the kitchen. He returned a minute later.

"It was my captain all right," Mason said. "He wanted to know how I was doing. More likely, he wanted to know *what* I was doing. Then he warned me again about getting involved in something that was strictly off limits. Wanted my guarantee I'd stay out of it. It could cost me my job, he said, if I interfered. I told him I was just a sick man trying to recover. There were a lot of lies going back and forth." Mason looked disgusted.

"Does this change your plans?" Eddie asked.

"Nope."

Dan came into the parlor to catch the end of the conversation. "A guy did turn up in the ER with minor hand burns," he said. "He told them his name was Mark something and disappeared as soon as they finished with him."

"Mark. You think it was Charlie Flack?" I said.

Both Dan and Mason nodded. Lurleen reappeared in a pencil skirt and silk blouse. "Work attire," she said and twirled slowly so we could all admire her.

I ran upstairs to change out of jeans and into my own work attire and to check on the kids—still asleep. Before we left, I checked with Mason about leaving one person alone with the kids.

"My mother could guard the Hope Diamond. No one's going to get into this house on her watch. I promise you that."

Eddie patted my hand. "They're safe with me," she said.

Mason told Lurleen what information he wanted, and she assured him that would be no problem—she could get information from an onion.

"I think you mean blood from a turnip," I offered.

"That too. But turnip is such an unromantic word. And blood is so—well—*degoutant*. Anyway, I could get a mute man to break his silence."

"I know that's right," Dan said, squeezing her hand.

Lurleen drove in her car. We followed behind in Mason's. The bar was in Buckhead and already busy. It was unlikely we'd hear any of their conversation. An attractive woman sat on a barstool finishing a martini. She was a natural blond, slender, understated, probably in her early forties.

Lurleen rushed up to her, hugged her, and settled onto the stool beside her. We chose a dark corner, close enough to be of help if needed and far enough away to be unobtrusive. The conversation lasted an hour, through two more martinis each, and got more and more raucous by the end. A couple of men tried to hit on the girls, something that made Dan clutch his Coke. I wondered how much information Lurleen was actually getting in the midst of so much laughter.

A lot as it turned out.

Lurleen and Kathleen left first. We paid our tab and found Lurleen outside the bar waving at Kathleen as she drove away in her sky-blue Lamborghini, top down.

"Wow," Dan said.

"*Merci,* Dan," Lurleen said. "I always try to look my best."

Dan blushed. "I was talking about the car, but you look hot too."

This time Lurleen blushed, and not with pleasure. "Okay, so I am just your *cheval qui travaille*."

"No, I don't see you as my workhorse," Dan said, trying hard to get his foot out of his mouth. "I see you as a beautiful, good-hearted, very smart woman."

"All right then. I forgive you. Now, Detective Garrett, do you want to hear what I've learned?"

"I'm all ears, but let's go someplace a little more private." We headed for a coffee shop across the street and found a spot outside, away from people.

I made a quick call to Eddie. The kids were fine, playing Lurleen's Notre Dame Chutes and Ladders. I could hear a certain weariness in Eddie's tone.

"We'll be home soon. I promise."

"I will cut to the chase," Lurleen said. "Isn't that how you men like it?"

Mason nodded. "I may ask you for some more detail, but start with the high points."

"Well, a big power shake-up is going on at Sandler's as Barry suspected. Top-level management are under fire for some mishaps with security and finances. It started with an attempted computer hacking regarding the new product." Lurleen gave a meaningful look in Mason's direction. "It was

Kathleen who called the Cyber Crimes Unit and got Detective Schmidt involved. Her grandfather was furious—he didn't want some cop he didn't know getting into Sandler's business. When Schmidt got killed, Sandler Senior said he was handling the internal situation and he wanted her to stay out of it. Kathleen didn't like that. It was as much her company as his. She suspected someone high up might be involved in corporate espionage. Kathleen claims she doesn't know who it is."

"Do you think she's lying?" Mason asked.

"I don't know," Lurleen said. "She's usually pretty tight-lipped about the company—got that from Sandler Senior. I'm not sure if she was spinning me a story or just so worried she had to vent."

I jumped in. "You said she was a straight arrow. Did something change your mind?"

"I'm not sure. I really don't know her all that well, yet she was willing to tell me everything. Apparently the company is in some financial trouble. Hard to believe with all the Sandler Sodas people drink worldwide, but that seems to be the situation. Someone may be skimming off the top or intent on destroying the company from within. Needless to say everyone is on edge. Internal security is doing all they can. And they've brought in people from outside. Unnamed people from unnamed agencies. How is that for intrigue!"

"It's good for intrigue but a little short on IDs," Mason said. "Did she mention anyone she suspected besides the ones we know about?"

"She recognized Ellie's name as someone who flirted with corporate husbands and got sacked because of it. She knew Ellie was close with Billy Joe and that he was up to no good—as usual. I mentioned a few other people, including Marie Vanderling. She said Marie moved along the top level of the corporate ladder and gathered information to be used to her best advantage."

"You mean like using it to blackmail people?" I asked.

"She never said that exactly, but she was worried about Marie's disappearance. Not so much for her safety, but Kathleen wondered if she'd left with a lot of secrets and money. And then there was another name I mentioned." Lurleen paused.

I knew what she was about to say. "You asked about Tommy, didn't you?"

"Yes."

"And what did she say?"

Lurleen was silent for a moment, sipping her coffee. She glanced around to make sure no one was within hearing range, but the other tables were empty. "Kathleen said she'd heard Tommy's name from time to time and met him once or twice. He got called in whenever there were sensitive personnel matters at the firm. He was good at being discreet and good at getting people to leave of their own accord. Sandler's has managed to keep a low profile in terms of scandals thanks in large part to your brother, Ditie."

That didn't sound too incriminating. "So maybe he's one of the good guys here," I said. "Involved in finding out who's doing what with this corporate espionage idea. Searching for a memory card perhaps. The way we are."

Dan looked at Mason and then at me. "Memory card? What are you talking about?"

"It's a theory Eddie and I came up with. We don't have any proof that it exists, but it would explain everything, including Ellie's behavior. Charlie Flack and Billy Joe Sandler wanted something from her. Something very valuable and small enough to fit in the compartment of the Transformer. Given Charlie Flack's background in new product development, it makes sense they could be trying to get information about Sandler's next big product. A memory card could contain all the information they needed to sell to the highest bidder."

"A miniSD. Easily hidden," Dan said. "It might be exactly what we're looking for. But why get the kids involved?"

"Ellie couldn't keep it with her," I said. "She couldn't leave it in her terrible apartment. In her mind, it would be safe with the kids. They wouldn't know they had anything of value—she wouldn't tell them obviously. The Transformer might have been the first plan. And then when Ellie got greedy, she came up with something better."

"Or worse," Lurleen said.

"We've searched every place Ellie has been," Dan said.

"We haven't searched the kids," I said.

"We have to get back to them," Lurleen said. "I'm having a bad feeling."

I grabbed my cell phone and called Eddie again. "We're fine," she assured me. "But if you're done, I could use some help."

"On our way," I said.

Dan and Lurleen jumped into her Citroën. I wasn't sure how Dan fit his large frame into that tiny car, but he managed it. We were seconds behind in Mason's Jaguar.

When we arrived at the house fifteen minutes later, no one greeted us. No one came to the door when Mason rang. He used his key, entered, and found the alarm still on. He turned it off and then started yelling.

Chapter Twenty-five

The house was silent. Dan entered right behind Mason. He motioned for us to stay back. Lurleen and I stood by the opened front door. After a few seconds that felt like hours we heard a noise from the basement. Both Dan and Mason drew their guns.

"Outside," Mason shouted at us. "And stay down."

Lurleen and I backed up. We crouched on the porch beside the door where we could see everything but run if we had to.

Footsteps pounded up the basement stairs and no one breathed. Then we heard Eddie's voice.

"We're all right," she said, as she popped her head out from behind the basement door, a pistol in her right hand. "I had to make sure it was you. Someone tried to break in five minutes ago. Did you see anyone on the road?"

"No one," Mason said. "But we came the back way. Did you see who it was?"

"Later," Eddie said, motioning to the children.

Lucie was holding on tightly to Jason's right hand, and Eddie had an iron grip on Jason's left. I ran up to them and squeezed Lucie's free hand. I put an arm around her. She was trembling.

We gathered in the kitchen. I watched Mason as he scanned the backyard through the kitchen windows. Eddie hadn't let go of Jason, and I held on to Lucie. We sat at one end of the wooden table. Lucie looked stricken. Jason was chattering away to Dan.

"We heard the bad men," he said. "They pounded on the door and Eddie said be quiet as mice and I was. But I had my cape, so I wanted to go get them. But Eddie said no and made us hide in the basement like hide-and-seek. And Lucie said be quiet. So we hid and then you came." Jason ran out of breath and stopped to gulp air. "I can help you get them, Uncle Dan."

"I know you can," Dan said. "But you did the right thing. Whatever Eddie says do, you do. Eddie is the top commander—you got that?"

Jason nodded. "Yes, boss." He gave Dan a mock salute, and I had a tiny sinking feeling. Was my innocent little boy getting a bit cheeky? *My* boy. That word again.

I took Lucie over to the sink and asked if she wanted a drink of water. She looked pale. "Did you see anything?" I asked her.

Lucie shook her head. "We heard someone knocking. Miss Eddie told us to stand by the door near the basement, out of sight. She told me to go to the basement and lock the door if anyone tried to break in."

Lucie started to shiver and I knelt down beside her. "You don't have to tell me anymore right now if you don't want to."

"I want to tell you. The knocking got really loud. I peeked out and saw Miss Eddie walk closer to the door. She had something in her hand. I think it was a gun. The knocking stopped. Eddie waited and then she came back to us. We went to the basement." Lucie paused. "I wish Miss Eddie had been there to protect my mom."

I knelt down beside her. "I do too," I said. Lucie hugged me long and hard—like a little girl desperate for a safe place to be.

Dan was on his feet. "We must have interrupted them. Why didn't they break into the house? Especially if they thought the house was empty."

"I saw them through the leaded glass," Eddie said. "Not clearly enough to identify them. But I wouldn't rule out that they saw me and maybe what I was carrying. I stayed long enough to see them move away from the door. Then I went for the kids."

"You take the front yard," Mason said to Dan. "I'll take the back. We'll see if any of the neighbors saw anything. Be discreet—we're not on duty—just checking on our neighborhood."

While they were gone I asked Lucie to help me and Eddie with dinner. Lurleen offered to take Jason upstairs to play. Of all of us, Jason was the one who seemed to be the least concerned about what had happened. He lived in a world of good guys defeating bad guys, so a real-world adventure didn't faze him.

"You are strong for a girl," he said to Eddie. "Like Wonder Woman. And I was Superman, right, Ms. Eddie?"

"You were indeed." She gave him a peck on the cheek, and he scooted off happily with Lurleen. "Miss Eddie is as strong as you," he said to her.

She smiled. "We'll have to find a name for her. I'm *Femme Merveilleuse*. She can be . . ."

"Grandma Merveilleuse," Jason said.

"I heard that," Eddie called, "and I accept."

I asked Lucie what she might like to eat for dinner, and she said she wasn't hungry.

"It was pretty scary, wasn't it, honey?"

Lucie nodded. "Like when the bad men came to our house. They didn't knock. They just came in, and they got madder and madder at my mom." Lucie started to cry. "William grabbed my mom's arm. 'Don't play around with us,' he said. 'You'll regret it.' And my mom said she wasn't playing. What they wanted took time to get. She was working on it. If only I'd told someone, I could have protected her."

"Lucie, none of this is your fault. None of it. Your mom got involved with some bad people. There was nothing you could do." I held her and let her sob. When she was done, I took her to the bathroom and washed her face with a wet towel. She washed her hands, and we went back to the kitchen to help Eddie.

"I think we'll keep it simple," Eddie said. "Do you have a good pasta recipe?"

"I have a great pasta recipe," I said, "if you have artichoke hearts, angel hair, and pine nuts."

Eddie pulled jars and pasta from her walk-in pantry. "Good," she said. "You and Lucie work on the main dish, and I'll handle the salad. I've got some homemade sourdough rolls in the freezer. I'll get them out."

"You make your own sourdough?" I asked. "I've never mastered that."

"Then we'll have a good time, the three of us. I have starter left over. I got it when I did a bread-baking class in California. My husband loved to spoil me with trips to exotic places for cooking classes."

"Does it make you sad," Lucie asked, "that he died?"

Eddie sat at the table for a moment and motioned Lucie over to her. She pulled a chair out beside her, and Lucie sat down. "It used to make me sad all the time," she said. "I'd cry and cry. Then a little bit at a time, it got better. I'd remember all the fun we had together. And remembering that made me smile. Now I only get sad every once in a while. Mostly I think about how much I loved him, and how he would be glad to know I was happy. And I am happy, Lucie. You will be too one day. Not right now, but one day."

Lucie nodded. Her lower lip quivered, but she managed a tiny smile.

"Now let's get this dinner together before the boys get back," Eddie said.

The men were back before we had quite finished. "No one saw anything," Dan said. "You saw two men?"

Eddie nodded. "It was two people for sure. I couldn't see them well enough to identify them through the frosted glass. And, of course, I have no idea if someone else was waiting in the car."

We finished up the pasta, stirring the tomatoes, olives, pine nuts, and artichoke hearts in with the angel hair. "Yum," Mason said, leaning over me, so he could see what I was doing. Eddie had the salad on the table and was taking the rolls out of the oven as Lurleen and Jason rushed into the room.

"I thought I smelled something delicious," Lurleen said. "And I thought Jason and I better hurry before Dan managed to eat it all."

"I'm not sure I'm the one with the biggest appetite around here," he said to Lurleen.

"Let's not argue about eating," Eddie said. "Let's enjoy the food before it gets cold."

Despite Lucie's claim she wasn't hungry, she helped herself to seconds on pasta. Between mouthfuls, we talked about everything except the attempted break-in. For dessert we had ice cream and chocolate sauce.

"You kids need to stay here for a while," Mason said. "My mom never makes food like this when it's just the two of us."

"That isn't true, and you know it," Eddie said. "For that statement, you are on KP duty."

Dan and Lurleen offered to help while I took the kids upstairs to get them ready for bed. I decided the kids would sleep with me that night. We'd all sleep a little easier.

I urged Jason out of his cape.

"I need it," he said, "in the night. For the bad men."

"Look, we'll put it right here on the bedpost, where you can grab it. And I think we'll sleep with a night light—that okay with you two?"

"I'm no baby," Jason said. "Mommy says night lights are for little boys. I'm big now."

"You are. I think the night light is for me."

"You scared of the dark, Aunt Di?" Jason asked.

"No, but I'd like to see where the two of you are, just for tonight."

I tucked both of them into bed. "You sleep with your locket, Lucie? Or shall I put it on my nightstand?"

Lucie fingered it tenderly. "I don't like to take it off, ever. It's the last thing Mommy gave to me. Right before—you know—right before we came to stay with you."

"Really? I thought you had it for years."

"Mommy said I wasn't old enough and then suddenly she changed her mind."

Something clicked in my brain.

"Lucie, may I look at your locket for a minute?" I unfastened it from her neck, opened it up to the pictures inside, and gently poked around the edges. Her father's picture came loose, and I pried it away from the locket. Behind it was a tiny, flat object. Shiny. What I imagined a memory card might look like.

Chapter Twenty-six

I held the tiny object between my thumb and index finger and studied it. Could this really be what everyone was searching for? I think I half expected it to talk to me. Lucie and Jason stared at me wide eyed.

"You broke Lucie's necklace," Jason said indignantly. "Careful! Careful! Careful!"

I could hear Ellie admonishing him, and it made me want to cry. I also wanted to shake her. How could she have put her children at risk in this way?

"The necklace is fine. See, Jason?" I closed it up and showed him. "We've found something really important and I have to show it to Detective Garrett. Is that all right with you, Lucie?"

"Yes. But what is it?"

"This little object may have a lot of information on it. It might solve the mystery of what happened to your mother."

"It will say who hurt her?" Lucie asked.

"Probably not. But it might tell us *why* they hurt her."

Jason stayed very still during this conversation. He grabbed a piece of the sheet, rubbed it against his cheek. "I want my mommy," he said. Lucie and I hugged him tight.

"It's time to do something," I said and stood up. "We'll all go downstairs, give this to Detective Garrett, and have some hot chocolate. How does that sound?"

"Okay," Jason said and took my hand. "Can I give it to 'tective Garrett?"

I glanced over at Lucie. "Okay with you, Luce? After all, it was found in your locket."

"Yes," Lucie said. "Jason's five. He's a big boy now. He'll be very careful with it."

Jason beamed.

We walked downstairs together. I'd put the memory card on a tissue and carried it like it was the Holy Grail. We found everyone seated in the parlor, planning strategy I suspected. They stopped talking as we entered. I opened up Jason's hand and put the tissue with the tiny object in his palm. "Jason has something to give you."

Jason walked painfully, slowly toward Mason, hand outstretched, eyes never wavering from his treasure.

Mason put on a glove and took it from him equally carefully. "You found this where?" Mason asked me.

"Lucie's locket. The perfect hiding place."

Eddie, Mason, Lurleen, and Dan fussed over the kids while I made hot chocolate. The adults got a little Kahlua added. It had been a long day.

By the time I got back to the parlor with my tray of hot chocolate, Dan was on his computer, finding a way into the memory chip.

"Ah," he said a moment later. "It's all here. The formula for the new product. It's going to be called the Sandler Shake."

We stared over his shoulder as he talked through what he was finding.

"It's a new vanilla milk product, like a milkshake. Shelf life a year or more. No refrigeration needed. It represents a new direction for Sandler's. Actually has significant nutritional value. According to the marketing plan, it will turn Sandler's around. A blockbuster in the making. Millions of dollars in estimated sales in the first five years."

Eddie had heard enough. "I'll take the kids upstairs. You all can finish this without me."

I nodded gratefully at her, hugged the kids, and watched as they walked hand in hand up the stairs.

"All this money for a milkshake?" I asked.

"A milkshake that requires no refrigeration. As important as the product is, it may be the container that is the truly innovative part of this. You just shake it up and activate the can. The shake gets cool, creamy, delicious. At least that's what the marketing strategists claim." Dan was reading from the computer screen. "Revolutionary. Tasty. Good for you."

"So this was enough to cause the death of two people?" I asked.

"You left out Schmiddy," Mason said. "He must have been on to what was going on. That's why he was shot. Not a random drive-by but a calculated murder. And somehow his notes were destroyed."

"This looks big," Dan said. "Plenty of companies are coming up with more nutritional products, but a container that gets cold when you shake it? That's a secret formula worth having. And it's all here. I don't know how Ellie managed to get so much information."

"She had to be working with someone on the inside," Mason said.

Lurleen jumped in. "Kathleen Sandler talked about money skimming, leaks, a lot going on. Maybe this memory card was the way out for someone within the organization. Grab a bundle of money by selling the information to a rival company and escape to some place safe to spend it."

"An insider like Marie Vanderling," I suggested.

"Oh, no," Lurleen said. "Not Marie."

"Kathleen said she wanted to force Marie into an early retirement," Mason said. "Maybe Marie didn't like that idea."

"Everyone is a suspect," I said. "Even my brother."

Lurleen shook her head. "It's not Marie. Marie has been my friend for fifteen years."

"People change," I said. "They get desperate. They fall in with the wrong folks."

Lurleen kept shaking her head. Her glorious curls caught the waning sun. "Not Marie. You heard how frightened she sounded. Scared to death. She's running from someone."

"Or *to* someone." Why was I arguing with Lurleen? I wanted her to stand her ground and convince me that people could be trusted. If Marie wasn't involved in something bad, maybe my brother wasn't either.

"I'm sorry, Lurleen." I grabbed her hand. "This whole thing has unnerved me."

Mason looked at both of us. "We're a step closer to finding out what's going on and who's behind it. This is the evidence we've needed. I'll have to take it to my captain tomorrow."

"You want me to take it?" I asked. "Since you're officially off the case."

"We'll go together. Can you make a copy of all this, Dan?"

"Already done."

"Get some sleep," Mason said to Lurleen and me. "Dan and I will look out for things tonight."

"You mean in case Charlie Flack or whoever tries to break in again?" I asked.

Mason nodded. "This is what they want," he said, nodding at the card now enclosed in a clear plastic bag, "and the information is priceless."

I didn't think I'd sleep that night. I was too keyed up. We'd found what Charlie and the others wanted. If we could just get it to the police, maybe the kids would be safe. That is, if the police could be trusted. Mason and

Dan had planted a lot of doubts in my mind. Who were the good guys? I needed to think, which meant I needed to bake.

First I needed to make sure the kids were okay. Lurleen and I walked quietly up the stairs and found Eddie standing outside the children's room. "They're fine," she said.

"Mason has sent us off to bed," I said. "But I'm not sleepy. I'm going to do some baking if that's all right with you."

"Be my guest," Eddie said. "I'd join you but I'm bushed. Fending off criminals isn't quite as easy for me as it used to be when I was younger." She gave Lurleen and me a kiss on the cheek and disappeared into her bedroom across the hall.

We glanced in the children's room. The night light was on and both children were sound asleep in the middle of the very large bed.

"I'm also a little tired," Lurleen said. "But if you need a sous-chef, I'll get my *vent second* in a minute or two."

"No need for a second wind. Would you mind sleeping with the children tonight? I'll join you later."

"Of course, *chérie*. I will sleep on the far side and leave the side near the door for you. *A bientot.*"

"*A bientot.*"

Mason was none too pleased about my plans to bake, until he realized it might mean some hot-out-of-the-oven cookies to be consumed.

"What sounds good?" I asked them.

"Make whatever you want," Dan said, "and we will come."

It sounded like a good plan since I was wide awake, and they would be up all night guarding the house and the memory card. I thought about a few projects I had in mind. Finding the best ginger cookie was one. Not the crisps but the big chewy molasses ones. I poked through Eddie's cookbooks and the computer in her office to come up with something.

While I was there, I thought I might just spend a few minutes looking for news on Sandler's. Would there be anything online about the new product? Or about financial difficulties? Nothing. Lurleen was the true guru of the Internet, but she was sound asleep. I'd see what she could dig up tomorrow. Sandler had some good PR folks and a strong clamp down on the news media. No word of any problems. While Detective Schmidt's and Billy Joe Sandler's deaths had made the news, there was no association with problems at the company. Schmidt's death was said to be the result of a drive-by shooting, still under investigation. Billy Joe was said to have died in a car crash. End of story.

I printed out a couple of recipes for ginger molasses cookies and set them on a stand Eddie had for recipes and cookbooks. If I combined them, adding a little more of this and a little less of that, I might just come up with the perfect mix. It took twenty minutes to get the first batch in the oven. Now I had ten minutes to think.

Ellie had found the information everyone wanted. She'd even found a way to smuggle it out of Sandler's without being detected. So why hadn't she given it to Billy Joe and Charlie Flack as she initially intended? Why did she put them off and get herself killed in the process? Had she gotten a better offer from someone else? A better offer would mean more money— that's always what Ellie wanted.

I looked in the oven. The cookies were almost ready. Another minute or two.

Ellie never understood the danger she was in until it was too late. Was that what had happened this time? Did she go off to meet her killer thinking he—or she—was going to give her money and not a bullet in the head? Poor Ellie. And poor Lucie and Jason. Ellie was too smart and too stupid for her own good.

Time to get the cookies out. The smell was enticing enough to lure Dan into the kitchen.

"Give them a minute to cool," I said, waving away his hand. "I'll bring a plate out with coffee in five minutes."

I ripped open a paper bag and laid the cookies on top to cool, slipped another two trays into the oven, and sat again on the stool to wait while the coffee brewed and the cookies cooled.

Did Ellie have any sense of right and wrong? That made me think of Tommy. Where was Tommy in this mix? He'd seen Ellie, that's for sure, but he didn't mention it to me. Were they working together? How could it be I knew so little about either of them? I could tell I was getting tired.

I poured the coffee. None for me or I really would be up all night. Mason and Dan came in as I was putting a dozen cookies on a plate.

"We'll eat in here," Mason said. "You don't have to wait on us. We'll even do the dishes when you're done. That will keep us alert."

I sat down with them and nibbled on one cookie. It was as good as I hoped. Unlike Phil, the recipe was a keeper. I smiled at my own joke.

"What's the smile about?" Mason asked.

"It's a long story," I said. "Mostly it's about being pleased with how the cookies came out. What do you think?"

"Good enough," he said, grabbing the last cookie as Dan was reaching for it.

I got the last batch out of the oven, scooped them onto the paper, and turned off the oven.

"If I can trust you boys to put what you don't eat into a plastic container, I'll head for bed. Let them cool completely before you put them away."

"Understood," Dan said, giving me a mock salute.

"Did you learn that from Jason?"

"He's a great kid, isn't he?" Mason said. "And so is Lucie."

"Ellie was a good mother," I said, "even though she did some really stupid things."

I suddenly felt like crying. Such a terrible loss. I left the kitchen before I got started. Walking slowly up the stairs, I could cry as much as I wanted to. Privately. I drew a bath and soaked and cried until I was finally ready for sleep. I slipped into bed beside Jason. He handed me one of his action figures and rolled over to sleep on his other side.

I slept soundly. So soundly I heard nothing in the night.

In the morning, Eddie shook me awake. She whispered in my ear. "Where are they?"

I sat upright, stared at the children beside me. "They're here. They're fine."

"No. No. Where are Dan and Mason?"

Chapter Twenty-seven

I gave Eddie a blank look and climbed out of bed. No one else stirred. It was still dark outside and the bedside clock said 6:10 a.m. She motioned me into the hallway and closed the bedroom door before either of us spoke. I realized I wasn't breathing.

"What do you mean? They're both gone?"

"Mason's car isn't in the driveway. They're not here. No note. Nothing."

I tried to keep my voice steady. "Any sign of a struggle?"

"No," Eddie said. "No struggle. Just gone."

At that point, I went into doctor mode, trying to diagnose a difficult case. No emotion. Just the facts.

"They never would have let anyone into the house," I said.

"No. They must have seen something. Followed someone outside. That's the only explanation. Dan's cell phone is in the parlor. Mason may have his, but he isn't answering it."

"And the memory card? Gone as well?"

Eddie shook her head. "Mason and I have a hiding place for valuable objects. I checked it, and the memory card is still there. Dan's laptop is in the parlor. Nothing seems to have disappeared but the two of them."

"You called the police?" I asked as I followed Eddie downstairs. She led me into the kitchen and motioned to a chair as she set about making coffee.

"Not yet. The alarm is still set, and it never went off," Eddie said. "Mason had the presence of mind to do that—turn it off and on again. So it isn't as if they were grabbed unaware." She sat down beside me. "I need to think like a cop. No struggle. No alarm sounding. Both men gone. And we have no idea when this all might have happened. Did you hear anything last night after you went to bed?"

I shook my head. "I left them in the kitchen around eleven." I looked around the room and spotted a plastic container with half a dozen cookies in it. "They had time to finish off most of the cookies and clean the kitchen."

"I didn't hear anything either," Eddie said. "But something woke me up early. Maybe a door closing. That's it. I heard the front door close. That's what got me up. That would have been around six. I went downstairs, checked outside, and then came to wake you."

"If anyone had broken in they would have set off the alarm."

"Right," Eddie said.

"So they must have seen something outside."

"I can't believe they both would have left the house. If that were the case Mason would have yelled for me. They'd never leave us unprotected. It's more likely one of them left to check something out and the other followed later. Someone reset the alarm, and Mason's car is gone."

"Dan's car?" I asked.

"In the garage."

"Maybe Dan saw something suspicious outside and got grabbed by someone when he was checking it out. And Mason had to follow." I sighed. "He reset the alarm, but didn't have enough time to call you."

That made sense. Of course, there were a dozen other scenarios that probably also made sense. I couldn't think of a single scenario in which they voluntarily left. There would have been a note or a call to Eddie. They obviously had to react in a hurry. Maybe they saw someone prowling and jumped in Mason's car to chase him. "When do we notify the police?"

"We give them another ten minutes and then we call. Time for Dan or Mason to reach us. After all, we still have the memory card."

Ten minutes. Long enough for someone to be killed. I didn't say that out loud, but Eddie responded.

"I know," she said. "I'll make a sweep of the yard. Don't worry. I have my gun. Set the alarm when I'm gone and don't open the door unless you can see it's me and I'm alone. The best vantage point is the window on the upstairs landing."

Eddie left. I set the alarm and ran upstairs to the landing. I watched her search the front yard and then disappear along the road, which curved around the side of the house. I couldn't see what she was doing back there without entering the kids' room, so I stayed at my post and counted the minutes. They stretched into what felt like an eternity. I looked at my watch. Eddie had been gone seven minutes. How long did I give her before I called the police myself? Something bumped my legs and I put a hand over my mouth to keep from screaming.

It was Majestic. Mewing at me. Hungry no doubt. I picked him up and stroked him and then went back to staring at empty space in the front yard. Majestic wouldn't settle in my arms. He insisted on jumping down. Paced around me and then away from me—toward the kids' room. I noticed for the first time the door was ajar. I'd closed it tightly.

I walked over to the door and looked inside. The bed lay mussed. And empty, except for Hermione, who was snoring peacefully in the middle of it. I'd read a book once where half the people disappeared one day. No one ever knew why. This time I did scream.

Chapter Twenty-eight

My scream stopped midway as I clamped a hand over my mouth. The bathroom door opened slowly, and Lurleen appeared as two terrified children looked out from behind it. She ran up to me and patted me as if she wanted to make sure it was really me.

"I heard what Eddie whispered," Lurleen said. "And then I heard someone running up the stairs, so I grabbed the kids and we hid in the bathroom. I had no idea it was you."

I got down on my knees and beckoned the kids to me. Hermione got there first and licked me all over. "I'm okay," I said to her, and to the kids.

Lucie was crying like she couldn't stop. Jason was biting his lip. "Big boys don't cry," he stammered. Another unnecessary message from Ellie.

"Big boys do cry," I said. "And big girls too." Now I had managed to traumatize the kids along with myself. "I got scared when I couldn't find you, but we're all fine now."

"I thought . . . I thought the men got you like they got Mommy," Lucie sobbed.

"I know, honey. I'm so sorry to scare you like that."

"I need my cape," Jason said.

I grabbed it from the bedpost and tied it around his neck.

"I sleep with my cape," Jason said.

"Okay from now on." I sat on the bed hugging both of them until our heart rates had settled and the tears had stopped. "You all get dressed and I'll meet you downstairs for breakfast." Lurleen went to her room to get dressed, and I left the kids to resume my post at the window. Miraculously, I saw Eddie backing away from the front porch, staring up at the window with her hand shielding her eyes against the porch light. I rushed downstairs, turned off the alarm, and let her in.

"Where were you?" I said. "I waited and waited. Then I couldn't find the kids. They're fine. I panicked. I'm sorry. I stirred up everyone."

Eddie hugged me the way I hugged the kids. The way my mother could never hug anyone but Tommy. Eddie didn't let go until I was ready.

"I was gone longer than I expected to be," she said. "I found tire marks and wanted to see where they were headed. Two sets. Down toward the main road. One of them Mason's—I know the kind of tires he has. I'm sorry I worried you. I'm going to call the police. How much do we tell the kids?"

"Let me think about that while I get breakfast started."

"Keep it simple, dear. I'm not sure any of us will have much of an appetite."

I nodded. I'd brought an untouched canister of home-made granola to Lurleen's, to Tommy's, and now to Eddie's. It was time it got eaten. As I set the table I thought about what to tell the kids about Mason and Dan. I was used to telling parents bad news, and children as well. The kids usually handled it far better than their parents.

Lurleen, Lucie, and Jason were downstairs in ten minutes. They sat at the table as Eddie and I served up a breakfast of granola, yogurt, and fruit.

What I decided to do was tell them the truth and what we were doing about it. I made it sound like Mason was chasing the bad guys and the police were going to help.

"What about Uncle Dan?" Jason asked. "Is he chasing the bad guys?"

Lurleen stepped in. "You know Uncle Dan. He has to be in the middle of the action. He probably has the bad guys pinned down somewhere and is waiting for Mason and the police to come."

I squeezed her hand under the table. I realized what a great actress Lurleen could be when the circumstances called for it.

She looked over at me and tried to smile. Lucie caught the glance. She got up from the table, gave Lurleen a pat on the shoulder, and started clearing the table. "It will be all right," she whispered as she took Lurleen's untouched bowl. Lucie stood beside me at the sink. I rinsed and she loaded the dishwasher. Eddie took Jason and Hermione outside for a little exercise. It was light now and promising to be a glorious day.

"You can go outside with Eddie," I said.

"No, Aunt Di, I want to stay with you."

"You're a brave girl, Lucie, and you've been through a lot."

Lucie looked up at me. "It will be all right, won't it, Aunt Di?"

"It will be all right, sweetie. Whatever happens, we'll handle it together."

Lucie took my hand when we finished with the dishes. "I love you Aunt Di."

"I love you too."

Lurleen was just where we'd left her—at the table staring into her cup of tea. We sat on either side of her, determined to cheer her up. Lucie spoke first. "Lurleen, could you tell us the story about your old boyfriend Andre, the one who gave you the jeweled tiara and then took it back when you wouldn't marry him?"

I saw a tiny sparkle in Lurleen's eyes.

"That's one I haven't heard," I said.

"Really?" Lurleen said with a sly smile. "I'm sure I've told you about Andre a dozen times. Sometimes I think you don't listen to me. Very well, if you really want to hear it. I had just turned eighteen and I was visiting my aunt in Paris. Eighteen in France is quite old, old enough to marry, to do a lot of things." She looked over Lucie's head at me, and I shook my head ever so slightly. "I mean things like date without an escort, that sort of thing."

Maybe Lurleen was right. Maybe I didn't always listen to her. Her lilting voice faded into the background. Why hadn't we heard from Mason and Dan? It was one thing to run off without telling us, but it was something else altogether not to call by now, two hours later. It wasn't like either one of them. They had to be in trouble. No forced entry. No sign of a struggle. Just whisked away. Without the memory card. That fact made it sound more like a chase than an assault. If someone had attacked them, wouldn't they have demanded the memory card and wouldn't we have heard something in the house? My thoughts were interrupted by a clamor on the back porch.

Jason burst into the kitchen, a ball and bat in his hands. Hermione and Eddie came in panting behind him.

"I hitted it a mile," he said to me. "Didn't I, Miss Eddie? Hermione had to run and run to find it. Didn't I hit it far, Miss Eddie?"

"Almost out of our yard," she said and smiled. "Now I need to have a chat with Ditie."

Lurleen offered to take the kids upstairs. "Did I ever tell you about my adventures in the Black Forest of France?" she asked. "About how I became an expert archer?"

"Archer?" Jason asked.

"Like Robin Hood," I said. "Shooting arrows."

"Robin Hood?" Jason said.

"I'll take it from here," Lurleen said, giving me a patronizing look. Suddenly she was the expert on little boys.

Eddie waited until we heard the upstairs bedroom door close. "The police will be here soon," she said to me. "Mason's captain—Dave Blakely—is coming. I've told him what happened."

Captain Blakely came with two patrolmen. He sent them outside to examine the area.

"We have an APB out for Mason's car," Blakely said. "Now tell me again what happened."

Eddie told the story succinctly, in a way that suggested Mason's primary concern was protecting me and the children. She didn't mention the memory card.

Blakely didn't push for more information, but Eddie did. "What is this all about? Why have you left Mason in the dark?"

"Has to be that way right now. This is way over my head and yours."

Blakely left fifteen minutes later. He said the patrolmen would keep an eye on the house but that we shouldn't go anywhere without letting him know.

Eddie and I sat huddled on the couch in the parlor.

"Where would we go?" Eddie said. Wrinkles I'd never seen before on her face now looked deeply etched. "Why wasn't Blakely more worried about what was going on?" she asked. "I've known Dave for years. He and Mason go way back. Why did he act so casual about the whole thing?"

I shook my head. "Someone will call."

The police officers knocked on the front door to announce they were leaving. Captain Blakely had an urgent assignment for them.

"About the case?" Eddie asked.

"Something else," one of them said, "but we'll be back and check in with you later on."

"Check in with us?" Eddie was incredulous. "Two men are missing—one of them a detective—and you'll check in with us?"

"I'm really sorry, Mrs. Garrett. Those are our orders."

She closed the door with enough force to let them know what she thought of their orders. Then she joined me in the parlor. "Something is terribly wrong," she said. "And I don't mean just about Mason and Dan. Something is wrong in the police department."

"I'll going to call Tommy," I said. "He's somewhere in this loop."

I reached for my phone, but before I could dial, Lurleen burst into the parlor, phone in hand. "It's Marie. She's alive. She has news."

Chapter Twenty-nine

Lurleen closed the parlor door and held the phone in her hand. She punched in some numbers and waited. "Marie's gone again," she said. "I can't reach her back, but she gave me information. Are the police still here?" Lurleen looked around the room frantically as if a cop might be hiding behind a door somewhere.

"They left," Eddie said.

"Good. Marie said I was not to talk to you if the police were still around."

I motioned for Lurleen to sit down on the sofa, but she was too wound up for that. "What did Marie say?" I asked.

"Dan is with them. They're holed up on West Paces. Marie's boyfriend's house." Lurleen started pacing. I stopped her so I could hear every word. "Is Dan all right?"

"Yes, thank God." She smiled and then caught herself. She looked at Eddie, who was standing as still as a statue by the fireplace. "They don't know a thing about Mason. I'm sorry."

"Who are 'they'?" I asked. "And who is Marie's boyfriend?"

"They are Tommy and . . . Mr. Sandler Senior. Mr. Sandler is Marie's boyfriend."

"Tommy? And Mr. Sandler?" Eddie jumped in. "Isn't Mr. Sandler too old to be involved with Marie? He took over the company when I was in my twenties. It made the news because he was such a young man and it all happened so quickly. His father was forced out—that's what the tabloids said. Early Alzheimer's. But that was forty years ago."

"He's old enough to be Marie's sugar daddy, if that's what you mean," Lurleen said. "Late seventies but looks like he's sixty. Plenty of hair. Gets it styled every week I suspect at that very exclusive salon Stefan's. He's trim, rides his bike to work when he can. He's no slouch, and he's not about to let his business be destroyed. He'll stop at nothing to save it."

"You're suggesting murder?" I asked.

Lurleen didn't answer me.

"What's Tommy's involvement? What is going on?" Now I was pacing beside her. I grabbed my cell to call Tommy.

"Wait," she said. "There's more. They let me speak to Dan. They won't let him leave but they haven't harmed him. Marie says they have him in protective custody. So he doesn't get hurt or in the way."

"What does that mean?" I asked.

"Marie said they are very close to identifying the mastermind behind all of it, but they couldn't have a private investigator stirring up the waters. She said if they hadn't stopped Dan, he might have gotten himself killed."

"You believe that?" Eddie asked.

"I don't know what to believe. I know Dan's all right for now," she said, looking at both of us.

"What's Tommy's role in all this?" I asked.

"I didn't talk to Tommy. I don't know. Marie just said he was there, as if he were a part of the whole thing. Helping Mr. Sandler I assumed." Lurleen abruptly sat down, as if the weight of all the information had suddenly made her tired. "There's something more. I told the children to stay upstairs. I didn't want them to hear any of this, except the part about Dan being okay."

Eddie opened the door to the parlor. "We'll hear them if they come down." She positioned herself near the door so she could see the stairs. She nodded at Lurleen to continue. I took a seat next to her.

"Marie is certain she knows who killed Ellie and Billy Joe. She said they were waiting for Charlie Flack to supply them with the proof they needed to arrest someone. She said it all to me in a code we used when we didn't want the execs to know we were talking about them. We'd talk about a Mr. Fisher or Mr. Frye whenever we had gossip to share. Every exec had a nickname. I'm not sure why she had to use a code with me, unless she didn't want Dan to know. Or Mr. Sandler. Maybe she didn't think Mr. Sandler could handle it until he saw the evidence with his own eyes."

"Lurleen, we don't have time for this," I said. "Who is it?"

"It's Fairchild. Maybe I should say Ms. Fairchild. It's Kathleen Sandler."

Chapter Thirty

The three of us were silent. We could hear the first drops of rain outside. We were in for a typical afternoon storm. The drops of rain turned into a torrential downpour and the room darkened. I was the first to speak. "Kathleen Sandler killed Ellie and her own cousin?"

"Or more likely had them killed," Lurleen said.

"I thought you said Kathleen was a straight arrow," Eddie said.

"I thought she was. But I don't know her as well as Marie does. And I did wonder why she was opening up to me the way she did over drinks. Now I wonder if that was all a setup. Feeding me the information she wanted me to believe. I know Kathleen is tough. If she wants something, she gets it, like her grandfather."

"But what is it she wants?" Eddie asked. "She's next in line to take over the company. It's her family legacy. Why would she want to destroy it?"

"You heard the rumor," Lurleen said. "That she and the old man weren't getting along, that she was about to be ousted."

"I'm calling Tommy," I said. "I'll make him tell me what's going on." His cell went immediately to voice mail. "Tommy, call me back." I tried not to yell.

The next thing we heard were footsteps running down the stairs. Lucie poked her head into the parlor. "I'm sorry, Aunt Di. Jason got so scared I couldn't keep him in the room."

"Not scared," Jason hollered. "Need to 'tect you. I'm Superman."

He was trembling. I took his hand. "We do need you to protect us. You did the right thing, Lucie. We have to stick together."

I looked at the windows in the parlor. Locked but the drapes were open. We were ten feet from the ground. The sky was dark outside, and the rain hadn't let up. "Did you hear the thunder?" I asked Jason.

Jason nodded.

I took him on my lap. "I used to get so scared of the thunder and lightning. My dad told me it was God bowling. Every time the skies lit up, it meant God had made a strike. That's when you knock down all the bowling pins." The memory of my dad made me smile, and the story seemed to comfort Jason.

"Is my mommy playing bowling with God?" he asked.

"Maybe so," I said. Jason cuddled with me for a minute and let me stroke his head. Then he jumped down and ran over to Lurleen. "Can you teach me to bowl, Lurleen? Like we did at my party?"

"Of course, *mon cher* Jason."

"You won't believe this," Eddie said. "But I used to be on the police bowling league. Our team won three years in a row."

"We have no trouble believing that," Lurleen said.

Eddie smiled. "I think I have my old jersey somewhere. And I know I have a kids' set of pins and a rubber bowling ball. My boys loved to play when they were little. Try the closet with the toy chest, Lurleen. I'll search in the second parlor."

I took Lucie away to the sink where I could talk to her privately. "Lucie, big stuff is going on right now. We have to talk to a lot of people. I'll need your help. You might hear some things that scare you, but I want you to help keep Jason occupied. Can you do that?"

Lucie stood up as straight as a bread stick. "You know I can, Aunt Di. And I'm not scared. We'll all take care of each other."

"Good girl, Luce. We'll all take care of each other."

We heard Eddie call upstairs to Lurleen. "No luck. How about you?"

"No luck," Lurleen called down. "But I have another plan."

Moments later, Lurleen appeared in the kitchen with a large unopened suitcase. Jason was at her side.

"I was saving this for a rainy day," she said. "And here we have a very rainy day." She opened the suitcase and pulled out what looked like linoleum squares. They locked together and formed a giant game board, painted with famous buildings from around the world. She began spreading them around the kitchen floor and out into the hall. Then she pulled out cardboard dolls in the likeness of Lurleen, me and the kids, Dan and Mason.

"I didn't have time to make one for you, Eddie, but I'll work on it," Lurleen said.

"When did you do this?" I asked.

"You know I can't sit still. And I don't need much sleep."

"I don't play with dolls," Jason said.

"I know, I know, *mon cher*. But these are no ordinary paper dolls." She pulled hers out for our inspection. It was made of pressboard with articulated arms and legs, dressed, of course, to the hilt with a silk scarf wrapped around doll-Lurleen's neck. The hair was auburn curls made of shiny ribbon.

"Michaels," she said before I could ask where she found all the material. "A store opened up in midtown. Lucky us."

She pulled me out next. I was rounded with cotton ball stuffing and Brillo Pad hair. I gave her a look.

"See what you're holding?" she said to stop me from fixating on my hair. "See the little rolling pin, the apron with your name on it, the doctor's bag. I even put a stethoscope around your neck."

Lucie took the doll from her. "It's soft like you, Aunt Di. The face is beautiful just like yours."

I squished it. It was soft like me. The face was carefully painted and lovely.

Jason couldn't stay away when Lurleen pulled out his doll. A real superhero. He was Spider-Man and Superman combined. Lurleen had made him bigger than all the other dolls.

Jason picked up the doll. "It's big like me," he said. "You're little, Aunt Di, and I'm big." He took the doll over to mine and compared sizes. He began marching the figure around the room, diving it off the table ledge, zooming around Majestic, who got out of the way in a hurry.

Lucie held her doll in both hands. She was gorgeous, with long blond hair made of shimmering yarn, a princess dress that was bejeweled. The doll held a book in one hand, an art pad in the other. "Oh, Lurleen," she said.

Lurleen beamed.

I left my doll in the company of Lucie, who promised to take good care of it, and stood beside Eddie.

"I called Captain Blakely and filled him in," she whispered. "The police are on their way to Sandler's house. We should know something soon."

Nothing to do but wait. Again.

I studied the board. On it were various places in Paris. The Eiffel Tower. The Champs-Élysée, two cafes, a boulangerie. The spinner pointed north, south, east, and west.

"If you get tired of Paris, I have other board pieces for other cities. Want to know the name of the game?" Lurleen asked, clearly bursting to tell us. "It's Where in the World Is Lurleen du Trois? Or as I like to say, *Ou se trouve Lurleen du Trois?* When it's someone else's turn the name changes to them."

"Oh," I said. "That old game that was on TV—*Where in the World Is Carmen San Diego?*"

"*Exactement.* I imagine a place I want to be, somewhere on the board. And you have to figure out where it is."

Interesting rules.

"You spin the spinner and move the number of spaces in the direction shown and ask me a question, like 'Are you closer or farther from me?' or 'Is it a place where you eat something?' or whatever you like."

Lucie went first. We all started at the Charles de Gaulle airport. She spun five south and moved in that direction. "Are you at a place where you drink coffee?" she asked.

"*Non,*" Lurleen said. "Good guess."

We helped Jason go next. He could read the number of spaces and we helped with the direction. "Do you need Superman to find you?" he asked.

"*Mais oui,*" said Lurleen. "I will give you a little clue. I am very high up."

Lucie looked over the board and gasped. She whispered something to Jason.

"Are you in the awful tower?" Jason said.

"Yes, yes," Lurleen said. "The Eiffel Tower. Here." She plopped her doll on the Eiffel Tower square and Jason swooped his doll in to rescue her. "Your turn next, Ditie," Lurleen said.

Just then my cell phone rang. I left them to it. Lucie would play for me until I got back.

I went into the hall to take the call, praying it was Mason. It wasn't. It was Phil Brockton.

"I know you said you'd call me about lunch," he said. "But I'm free tomorrow."

"I'm sorry, Phil, but tomorrow won't work for me."

Phil was apparently speechless. He wasn't used to being turned down—especially by me.

"What's happened to you, Ditie?" he finally asked.

"Life happened."

"For me too. That's why I'm desperate to see you. I'm a changed man. I know how good you were for me. I can't leave without seeing you again."

"I'm sorry, Phil. I'm not on your schedule anymore. I've got some real problems here, and I can't leave right now."

"What kind of problems? Maybe I can help. I've got a lot of connections in Atlanta. What do you need?"

This was a first. Phil asking to help me. For a moment I felt hopeful. Then I remembered Tommy. Willing to be there for me unless it interfered with plans of his own. But Phil wasn't Tommy. He deserved a chance to show he'd changed. I sat on the first step of the stairs.

"You know anything about Sandler's Sodas?" I asked.

"Sure. Employs half of Atlanta, including my dad."

"What are you talking about?"

"My dad is the concierge doc for the Sandler family."

"Unbelievable."

"Which part? My dad's getting ready to retire. He switched to the concierge business a few years ago. Now he has a few clients who pay him a healthy stipend for being available whenever they want him. It's a good business. I might take over his practice."

"Wouldn't that cramp your style in terms of reenactments?"

"I'd be part of a group, of course. We'd cover for the patients we had. No problem. Smaller numbers of better paying clients. You should think about it."

"No one in the refugee clinic has money for an operation like that."

"Oh, yeah, I forgot. You're still the do-gooder, aren't you, Ditie?"

That jarred me. Was I really a do-gooder when I'd missed so much work? What about the teenager Beza I was so worried about? I hadn't given her a second thought in days.

"Not such a do-gooder," I said. To be honest with myself, I always chose a low-cost clinic wherever I lived. Partly to provide good care for the poor. But as much because it was easy to get into and out of those clinics when I felt it was time to move on.

"So what does Sandler's have to do with your problems?" Phil asked.

"You heard about Billy Joe's death?"

"Yeah," he said. "Sad."

"Does your dad know how he died? How he really died?"

"What do you mean? He died in a car crash. It's public knowledge he was into drugs."

"He was shot in the head before he ever went over that embankment."

"What in the world are you talking about, Ditie?"

"Just what I said. There are problems at Sandler's, and for complicated reasons I'm involved. My kids are in danger."

I heard a gulp of air on the other end of the line. "Your kids?"

"No, no. Not my kids. A friend of mine's. She was murdered like Billy Joe—a shot to the back of the head. She used to work at Sandler's."

"I'm sorry to hear all that. I don't know any more about Sandler's than you do."

"I bet your dad does."

"Are you asking me something?"

"I wondered if your dad ever mentioned anything about what was going on at Sandler's. Maybe Sandler Senior or Kathleen Sandler said something."

"You know I can't say anything about that, even if I knew, which I don't. My dad keeps his professional life where it belongs. In the office. He's a stickler for protocol."

"Like you," I said. "It's one thing I've always admired about you, Phil. You always kept that line straight. No discussion of your patients." Phil kept all his lines straight. There was his work life, his Civil War reenactor's life, his home life. All in their compartments. Never intersecting.

"I'm not asking you to divulge anything about health issues among the Sandlers."

"That's good because I won't."

"As far as I know there aren't any health issues," I said.

Phil was quiet.

Had I touched a nerve? Something I didn't know about? Were there health issues in the family? "Why so quiet?"

"I probably shouldn't have said as much as I did about Billy Joe," he said. "Except all you have to do is read the newspaper to realize Billy Joe had his problems with drugs and alcohol."

This conversation was going nowhere. "Look, I'm sorry about lunch. If things were different, I would see you. But I can't right now. I've got to watch out for the children."

Phil didn't press me. "I've got to go back to New York soon. If you come up for air, call me. If I don't hear from you, I'll write. You're not about to make another move, are you?"

"Another move?"

"Out of Atlanta. On to greener pastures."

"No," I said, and realized that was true. "I'm not thinking of moving right now." Funny. I'd had that thought a week ago, but it was nowhere in my mind now.

"Good, then we'll talk later."

Phil hung up. I stared at the phone for a moment and gave the clinic a call. Vic was available.

"We're okay here," she said. "Do you know when you'll be back?"

"Soon, I hope. Do you have a minute? I wondered if there'd been any follow-up on the fifteen-year-old I was worried about, the one in the home with the 'new uncle.'"

"Good timing. I just spoke with the caseworker. The uncle has left the home, and we have a follow-up scheduled with the girl next week. Hopefully, you'll be back by then. If so, we'll switch her over to you."

"Thank you. I know I've been unreliable. I'll do everything I can to make it up to you."

"Don't worry. It's the nature of our work. Predictable chaos. We're managing."

I hung up the phone and saw Eddie waiting for me in her office. She looked at me expectantly.

"Who was that?" she asked. "Mason? Tommy?"

"Neither one I'm afraid. It was an old friend, and then I checked in with the clinic."

"Do they need you back?" she asked. "If so, we can manage."

"I'm not going anywhere," I said. "How are you holding up?"

For a moment Eddie let down her guard. "It's hard," she said. "The longer we hear nothing, the more worried I get."

"I'm calling Tommy again."

This time he answered.

"Thank God," I said. "Where are you, Tommy? What's going on?"

"Easy, Mabel. You sound hysterical. I don't have a lot of time. Are you alone?"

"Why do you care?"

"Just answer me." Tommy's veneer was cracking. "I need the memory card and I know you have it."

"Where are you? Are you with Marie and Mr. Sandler?"

"Who told you that?"

"Is Dan there? Mason?" My veneer had cracked a long time ago. "Tommy, what's going on?"

Silence.

"Are you there? Talk to me."

"You're in danger. If you don't give the card to me, then someone else will get it from you. Is that clear? You don't know who you're dealing with. Everyone will be safe if you give the card to me. I'm coming over. Don't call the cops or someone will get hurt."

"Tommy, I don't even know you anymore."

"You never did. Get the card."

Click.

I turned to Eddie. "Did you hear any part of that?"

"Not enough," she said.

"Tommy's coming over here. He warned me not to call the cops or someone would get hurt."

"You get the kids and Lurleen upstairs," Eddie said. "I'll get my gun."

Chapter Thirty-one

Eddie and I found Lurleen in the hallway. The game had spilled out of the kitchen and out of France. They were now in England, and Lurleen was educating them about Big Ben. Once again, Jason had rescued her—this time from the clock tower before it struck midnight and she might have plummeted to her death.

"You are my savior," her doll said to Jason's.

"Your turn, Lucie," I said and gave her a nod. She understood perfectly.

"Let me see where I want to be," she said examining the board. "Okay, Jason, spin the dial."

I pulled Lurleen aside and told her what was happening. "I'm a sharpshooter," Lurleen whispered back.

"Since when?" I asked.

"Since I almost married Gerard from the south of France. Very into hunting. You should take the kids, and I'll stand with Eddie. I promise I won't shoot to kill, just wound your brother in some vulnerable part of his body."

This was no time to argue. We moved the kids and the game upstairs. Lucie went into action mode, settling Jason on the floor of their bedroom with the tile pieces. I explained to both of them that no matter what happened, they were to stay in the room. Lurleen or I would be with them. I nodded at Lurleen.

"For now, you stay here. He's my brother. I'll deal with him."

I ran downstairs to join Eddie. She was in the parlor staring out the front window. "You know I had to call Captain Blakely," she said.

I nodded.

She filled me in. No one was at Sandler's house other than the house staff when the police arrived. The staff confirmed that Sandler, Marie Vanderling, and another individual had left shortly before the police arrived. No sign of Mason.

"Blakely promised to send two men over here to apprehend Tommy when he showed up."

Nothing happened in the next hour, the next two hours. No officers came. Eddie called Blakely again. He said his men were tied up, but he'd send a patrol car as soon as he could.

Where was Tommy? I gave Lurleen a break and tried to keep the kids entertained. We played hide-and-seek upstairs, superheroes, anything to keep them occupied. I left Lucie reading to Jason and tried to contact Tommy with no success. He was done talking to me apparently.

By midafternoon, Jason was exhausted enough to take a nap. Lucie stayed with him while Lurleen and I hovered nearby in the foyer at the top of the stairs. No Tommy.

That was where we were when Mason came stumbling up the front drive. The rain had stopped, and the sun was peeking out behind white fluffy clouds.

Lurleen spotted him before I did from the window on the landing. She yelled for Eddie and ran down the stairs. Lucie stuck her head out of the bedroom and I assured her everything was fine. Then I raced down the stairs to the opened front door.

Eddie stood there with one arm around Mason's waist. We helped her take him to the parlor where he sank onto the sofa. He was drenched.

"What happened?" Eddie asked.

Mason struggled to speak. "My car . . . I'm okay . . . where is Dan?"

"Dan's all right," I said. "Lie still. I have to see if you're hurt." I asked Lurleen to grab my medical bag from the downstairs coat closet. I checked him over. He was scraped and battered but seemed to be otherwise intact. No obvious broken bones. Of course, I couldn't check for internal injuries. "We have to get you to the hospital," I said. I called Piedmont Hospital over Mason's protests and spoke with an ER doc I'd known since med school.

"An ambulance is on the way," I announced at the end of the conversation.

We made Mason comfortable on the sofa. Eddie washed his face and hands. We helped him out of his wet clothes and into new dry ones. Most of the injuries appeared to be on the exposed surfaces of his body. When he was settled, he started to revive and asked to sit up.

I shook my head. "Lie still and tell us what happened to you."

Chapter Thirty-two

Mason struggled to get comfortable, but I could see by the look on his face he was in pain every time he moved. He was determined to sit up. Eddie and I helped him, and he seemed to breathe more easily in a sitting position.

I went over to the parlor door to close it, and there stood Lucie and Jason, hand in hand in the hallway. We hadn't heard them come downstairs. "You look like little mice," I said. "Come on in." Their color didn't look much better than Mason's. "It's okay. Mason had an accident but he's all right. We're going to send him to the hospital to get checked out."

Mason managed a smile.

Very delicately, Lucie touched his hand.

Jason gave him the tiny action figure he held in his left hand. "You can take my little Spider-Man to the doctor's office. Mommy always lets me take him with me to the doctor. She says Spider-Man never cries. So I never cry, even when I get a shot." He looked about ready to cry now. Mason thanked him. I hugged Jason, and Lurleen put an arm around each kid as she led them back upstairs.

Eddie and I remained at Mason's side.

"I'm all right," he said. "I walked half a mile to get here."

"Your color is better." Suddenly all the emotion I'd been afraid to feel washed over me. "We're so relieved you're safe. You're back here with us."

I looked over at Eddie. She'd teared up. "Thank God," she said.

"I got off easy. It's just my ribs. I think I bruised them in the accident. I was pushed off the road like Billy Joe."

"Only Billy Joe was dead when he got pushed off the road," I said. "Shot in the head. Captain Blakely didn't tell you the truth."

"I know. Dan told me what really happened. Blakely hasn't been honest with me about a lot of things." Mason shifted on the couch and winced in pain. "Where is Dan?"

"Lurleen spoke to him a few hours ago," I said. "He was at Sandler's house with Marie Vanderling. They wouldn't let him leave, but he wasn't harmed. Marie said they wanted him out of the way for his own good."

Eddie draped a throw over his legs. "The police checked out Sandler's home and didn't find him. They'd moved on apparently."

"Who are 'they'?"

"Marie Vanderling and Mr. Sandler Senior," I said. "And Tommy."

"So Tommy is involved. And Mr. Sandler?"

"It's hard to sort the good guys out from the bad," I said. "Marie said they were about to capture the mastermind, and she was sure it was Kathleen Sandler. She said they were afraid Dan would mess things up before they got the evidence they needed and maybe get himself killed in the process."

Mason rubbed his bald head. "None of it quite fits."

"Why did you leave without telling us?" Eddie asked.

"I didn't have time to call you. I'm sorry, Mom. I know you were worried sick about me." Mason shifted on the couch to look at his mother. He tried hard not to show her he was in pain. "Dan heard something. He took his gun and went outside. I watched from the window but it was too dark to see where he went. A car with no lights was parked at the edge of the drive. It took off ten seconds later." Mason coughed and grabbed his side. He stopped speaking for a moment to catch his breath. "That's when I set the alarm and left the house. I was sure they'd grabbed him, so I jumped in the Jaguar. I almost caught up with them, when another car sideswiped me, and I ended up in Nancy Creek." Mason rubbed his bruised cheek. "It's wasn't an effective way to kill someone if that's what they intended. The embankment is fifteen feet at most. I think whoever did it wanted to scare me or put me out of action for a while. It worked. I don't know how long I was out, but I spent most of the day trying to get myself out of the car. It's totaled."

"So you were knocked unconscious?" I asked.

Mason nodded.

"No one saw you?" I asked while I examined his head. No visible lumps. No cuts or lacerations.

"My car was buried in the overgrowth."

I told Mason the rest of what we knew, including Tommy's demand that I give him the card. "Then he never showed up." Suddenly I got scared for Tommy. What if something had happened to him?

Eddie saw me blanch. "Don't jump to any conclusions." Before she could say more, we heard someone ring the doorbell.

It was Dave Blakely.

"What the hell happened to you?" Blakely asked when he entered the parlor and saw Mason on the couch.

"Nice to see you too, Captain."

"We have an APB out for your car."

"You'll find it in Nancy Creek, half a mile from here. Someone ran me off the road. And Dan is being held hostage at Sandler's mansion."

"Not any more. No one's there now." Blakely took a chair across from Mason. "It's time you know what's going on."

"Past time, I'd say."

At that moment the EMTs arrived and pounded on the door. Once we let them in, they took over. They questioned Mason about what had happened, took his vital signs, and moved him to the gurney. As they were about to leave with a protesting Mason, Blakely asked for a minute with the patient. When they resisted, he flashed his badge.

"Thirty seconds," one of them said as they moved reluctantly into the hall. Blakely closed the door.

"I'll keep it brief. Mr. Sandler called in the police after Billy Joe was killed. He wanted things kept as quiet as possible. The police chief and he go way back. That's why you got pulled."

Mason nodded. "I knew it wasn't you who pulled me off."

"Sandler was determined to handle the whole thing without getting the press involved, and the chief went along with him. Sandler brought in Tom Brown to help identify the mastermind of a corporate espionage scheme—it had to be someone who knew the business and knew what the new product would be worth to the right bidder. Before Billy Joe got killed, Sandler knew his grandson was involved, but Billy Joe wasn't smart enough to be the mastermind. That's where Eleanor Winston came in. Brown got her involved. She was to offer to help Billy Joe and his mysterious boss pull off stealing the information."

"So you're saying my brother was working for Mr. Sandler and not against him?"

"Yes. Tom Brown is on our side."

"And Ellie was too."

"She started out on the right side before everything went south."

At that point one of the EMTs stuck his head into the parlor. "We have to get this man to the hospital."

Blakely stood up.

I asked if I could ride in the ambulance.

"No, ma'am. We're taking him to Piedmont Hospital. You can see him there."

Eddie, Blakely, and I remained silent until the EMTs left. Then I told Blakely about my conversation with Tommy. "He threatened to come here for the memory card but he never showed up."

"You have the card?" Blakely said. He sounded incredulous. And something else I couldn't quite name.

Eddie disappeared for a moment and returned with the card. "Dan has a copy on his computer."

"I'll take them both."

For the first time I noticed that Blakely was alone. Eddie appeared to have the same realization.

"Where's your backup?" she asked.

"I don't need backup for this."

Eddie nodded. She saw Blakely eye the laptop on the table beside the sofa. "That's my Mac," she said. "Let me get you Dan's." She hurried out of the room and returned moments later with a Toshiba.

She closed the door on Blakely before either of us spoke.

"You don't trust him?"

Eddie shook her head. "He came here alone. How do we know his story is the truth? Marie said she was scared of the police. I'm just not sure about Dave anymore."

"He'll discover you gave him the wrong computer."

"He might not check it. He's got what he wants. And I've still got contacts on the police force. I'm going to make some phone calls."

I left Eddie with her cell phone in hand and hurried upstairs.

Lurleen poked her head out of the bedroom. "Is the coast clear? Is everything all right?"

"I'm not sure about that. But we're alone for now."

"Any news about Dan?" Lurleen asked. Her lip quivered.

I held her hand. "He'll be all right," I said. "He's tough and he's smart."

Lurleen nodded but the look in her soft, hazel eyes said she didn't believe a word I was saying.

Chapter Thirty-three

Lurleen pulled herself together the way I imagine people do when they have to go on stage. She made two staccato whistles that sounded like birdcalls. Lucie responded with one of her own. Then the kids exploded from the bedroom.

"It's our code," Lurleen whispered to me. "You'd think we were just two birds talking to each other, wouldn't you?"

I nodded. "Two birds that got locked up in a 1905 farmhouse."

Jason and Lucie skipped down the stairs. We followed behind. Lurleen had managed to calm their fears and make them feel safe. I wished I could do the same for her.

"Did you hear me, Aunt Di?" Lucie asked at the bottom of the stairs. "Lurleen taught me to sound like a mockingbird."

"I did hear you. Where did you learn that, Lurleen?" I was almost afraid to ask.

"Oh, you know. Another beau. Let's see. Not Maurice. Not Simon." She furrowed her brow in mock concentration. "No, it was Arneau. More the bookish type. Loved his birds. And me, of course."

Lucie giggled. "Why didn't you marry him, Lurleen?"

She knelt down beside her. "He never made my heart tingle," she said.

"You mean like Detective Garrett does for Aunt Ditie and Uncle Dan does for you?"

"*Exactement.*"

"Where is Uncle Dan?" Jason asked.

For just a moment, I thought Lurleen might lose it. She turned away. "I hope he'll be on his way home soon," I said.

"And Detective Garrett?" Lucie asked, peering into the empty parlor.

"He's being checked out at the hospital," Eddie said, "but he's going to be fine. I think you can start calling him Mason. Now, who's ready to make dinner?"

"I am," Lucie said.

"Me too," I said. I took Lucie's hand and headed for the kitchen, two steps behind Eddie.

"Well, Jason, that leaves you and me," Lurleen said. "Maybe it's time I told you about the days I worked as an undercover agent for the French police."

"Under the covers?" Jason said. "You stayed in bed?"

"Not exactly."

That was the last we heard from the two of them as they tromped back upstairs. Once this was all over, we were going to play outside for at least a week. Go camping or to the beach. Once this was finally over.

I got Lucie set up at the sink peeling carrots, and I was rummaging through the refrigerator when Eddie poked her head into the kitchen.

"Can I have a word?" she asked. I looked at Lucie and she nodded back at me.

Eddie took me into the parlor. "It's about Dave Blakely. I reached my contacts. They couldn't or wouldn't tell me much. They claimed they didn't know where Blakely was. Thought he was on leave. We're on our own."

My cell rang. It was the ER doc I'd spoken to earlier. I'd asked him to ring me once he'd examined Mason. "Detective Garrett is doing fine," he said. "Looks like he has a slight concussion and some bruised ribs. We're keeping him overnight for observation."

"Thanks for looking after him. Can I talk to him?"

"Sure."

A moment later Mason was on the line. "I'm good. Any word from Dan?"

"Not yet. I'd like to see you but I think I need to stay with the kids."

"Don't come. Just get me out of here tomorrow morning as early as you can."

"Will do."

I didn't tell Mason about our current situation. I was afraid if I did, he'd leave the hospital against medical advice and come home. I turned to Eddie. "What do we do now? Do you think Tommy will still come?"

"I don't know, but we'll get prepared," Eddie said, showing me the gun she had in a flat holster, hidden in the pocket of her slacks. "We still don't know where Charlie Flack is or how he fits into the espionage scheme. Does Lurleen actually know how to shoot a gun?"

"I wouldn't count on it, but I *would* count on her ability to protect and hide the kids if it comes to that."

"Do you know how to shoot?"

"I learned at my mother's insistence. Tommy's the real ace. But if you have a rifle, I can use it."

"Good. First we feed the kids and get them settled. Then you and I will keep a vigil tonight."

We heard Lucie singing "Alouette" and joined her in the kitchen. I helped her make pineapple coleslaw while Eddie cooked hamburgers and sweet potato fries. She turned on the radio to a sixties rock-and-roll station, and we were dancing by the time Lurleen and Jason joined us. Jason made a face when he heard the music, but Lurleen had him doing twists and turns until he was breathless with laughter.

We ate every bit of food, including some molasses cookies for dessert. Cleanup was an assembly line, and then I got the kids ready for bed. Eddie must have explained the plan to Lurleen because she came up twenty minutes later to take over her post.

"I'm gonna sleep with you guys, okay?" she said. "I get lonely in that big bed and I want to have a sleepover."

"A sleepover?" Lucie asked.

"You know, where your friends come and spend the night."

Lucie shook her head.

"Well, you'll have your first one now," I said. I kissed the kids. "I'll leave you to it but no talking after nine p.m."

"*Oui, maman,*" Lurleen said. "If we don't make too much noise, she'll never know," I heard her whisper as I left.

I found Eddie downstairs. "What do you think we're waiting for? Captain Blakely has the memory card. Aren't they done with us?"

"I don't know," Eddie said, "but I want to be prepared."

I made another attempt to reach Tommy. No answer.

We pulled the shades in the kitchen, checked the doors and windows one more time, and decided we'd station ourselves in the parlor. Eddie brought me a rifle from the gun cabinet and loaded it. She settled in the oversized stuffed chair. I lay on the sofa. We talked softly, as if we were in a library.

"What do you think is going on?" I asked. "Is Blakely corrupt?"

"I've known Dave for ten years. I don't want to think anything bad about him. But how did he get here so fast? Why didn't he have anyone with him? Mason said he's changed since he got a divorce two years ago. He's a lot more cynical about life and seems to have financial worries."

"And Tommy? Do you think Tommy's involved in this?" I asked.

"If we believe Blakely, then Tommy's trying to sort things out."

"That's a big if," I said. "For all we know, they're both on the wrong side."

"I'm sorry, dear, but you could be right about that."

We grew silent. I grabbed a magazine to read and Eddie took up her knitting. Every time I dozed off I woke up to find Eddie sitting up straight in her chair, unspooling more yarn.

At two a.m. we heard it. A scraping sound. From the back of the house? On the porch?

Eddie held her gun two-handed in front of her and headed through the kitchen to the back door. She pulled back the edge of the curtain on the door as she turned on the porch light. There stood Tommy and Dan.

She lowered her gun and motioned for me to turn off the alarm. I put the rifle down and did what she asked. When she opened the door, Tommy and Dan burst into the room. I rushed up to Tommy, but he backed away. Eddie put the safety on her gun and lowered it as Dan tried to motion behind him. A moment later, from the shadows, came Charlie Flack. He had a gun pointed at all of us.

"Put the gun down," he said to Eddie. She placed it on the counter. "Look," he said, "I don't want to hurt anyone. Just get me the memory card and the computer, and we'll be out of here."

Tommy stepped away from me. "Do what he says, Mabel, so no one gets hurt."

"Captain Blakely has the memory card," Eddie said calmly.

"Then get me the damn computer," Charlie yelled. "He said he made a copy." Charlie motioned to Dan.

"Do it," Dan said.

I went to the parlor, got the computer, and brought it back.

"Show me it's there," Charlie ordered. "Now." He nudged Dan with the gun.

At that moment, Jason burst into the kitchen.

"Daddy, I heard you. I knew it was you. I couldn't sleep. I knew you'd come."

I scooped him up before he could run to his father.

"Damn," Charlie shouted. "Get my kid out of here."

Lurleen stood in the doorframe of the kitchen.

"I'm sorry," she said to me. "He was too fast for me."

I handed him off to Lurleen and she backed away.

"No, no." Jason wriggled out of her grasp. "I want my daddy." He was on his father before any of us could stop him. He hugged his leg and pulled at his arm to be picked up. Charlie kept his gun and his focus on the rest of us. Jason seemed oblivious to anything but his father. "Daddy, you came back for me."

I made a move toward Jason, but Charlie had already peeled his son off him. He used him as a shield as he grabbed the computer. Then he pushed his son toward us as he ran out the back door.

Tommy and Dan ran after him.

I picked a sobbing Jason up from the floor. "It's okay," I said. "It's okay." I took him to the parlor, while Eddie called the police.

I sat with Jason on the sofa until he quieted. His body was rigid with pain.

"Daddy didn't say nothing to me."

"I know, Jason. I'm sorry."

"He didn't want me."

There wasn't much I could say to that, so I held him tight and rocked him. But Jason was too angry to sit still. He jumped off my lap. "Daddy is a bad guy. Like Mommy said." He ran around the room, swooping his cape. "Daddy had a gun. I saw it. Daddy hurts people."

"We don't know that, Jason," I said. I remembered how frightened Charlie Flack was when he had me in the car. "Your daddy's scared. Really scared. Sometimes being scared makes people do bad things."

Jason wasn't listening. "I'm Superman. I'll get Daddy. I'll take him to jail."

Eddie and Dan joined us in the parlor. "Tommy and Flack are long gone," Dan said. "They left in the same car. I'm sorry, Ditie."

I nodded.

Lurleen rushed to Dan. "Are you all right? Are you really all right?"

"I'm fine."

For five minutes, we said nothing. Lurleen examined every inch of Dan to make sure no limbs were missing. I got Jason to curl up beside me, and when he was asleep, I carried him upstairs.

Lucie had somehow managed to sleep through the whole encounter. She stirred slightly as I settled Jason into the bed next to her. I stayed with both of them until I heard the sound of heavy breathing. Their breathing settled me, and I could have watched them all night. But not this night.

I left the door open and crept downstairs. Dan was ending a conversation I wanted to hear. Lurleen was hovering over him.

"I'm putting him to bed," Lurleen said. "Eddie can fill you in, and I'll look after the kids."

"Thanks."

We heard them walk slowly up the stairs. I turned to Eddie. She looked exhausted.

"It's still a confusing story," she said. "Dan spotted a car outside the house early in the morning. Marie Vanderling was sitting in the passenger seat. When he questioned her, she said she had to talk to Lurleen. When he started to look around for the driver, someone stuck a gun in his back and put a chloroformed cloth over his face. That's the last he remembers until he woke up at Sandler's house tied up. Sandler said they wanted him out of the way before he messed things up. They monitored the call he made to us, and then they left him tied up in an upstairs closet. He heard the police but couldn't get to them. When the police left, Tommy found him and untied him. Charlie Flack appeared from nowhere and brought him to our house."

"So Tommy is involved," I said.

"Flack had the gun. Dan still doesn't know if it was aimed at Tommy or not. Tommy was focused on getting Flack to settle down. Flack was intent on getting the memory card. Before it was too late, he said."

I was sitting on the edge of the sofa. "Maybe our part is over," I said and leaned back into the cushions. "We don't have any more information. It's all been taken. The police have the card. Flack has the computer."

"The police don't have the card," Eddie said. "I went up the food chain. Blakely hasn't shown up at headquarters. No one can find him."

We saw the lights of the police car before we heard their knock. Two officers showed up at the door. "A neighbor heard a commotion," one of them said.

"We did have a break-in, but the perpetrators are gone. Dan Devalle is upstairs. He was held hostage but he's back and safe. Captain Blakely knows all about it."

The first officer looked at the other. "Let me make a call." He went outside and returned a minute later. "Captain Blakely says we can follow up in the morning since no one's hurt."

"Thank you," Eddie said. She showed them out. "Something's not right," she said. "No one knows where Blakely is, but these two reach him immediately. And Blakely says they don't need to investigate tonight."

Eddie and I stayed put for the rest of the night with our guns close by. I dozed and woke with every unexpected sound. In the morning, we both showered before the kids got up and tried to look as if we hadn't been awake all night. The guns were locked up in the gun cabinet before Lurleen and Lucie came down. Eddie took care of breakfast, while I checked on when I could pick up Mason.

Dan slept until eight. I found Jason curled up in bed beside Lurleen and still asleep. As I stood there, Jason opened his eyes, smiled at me, and then closed them again. Maybe the night before would seem like a bad dream.

I picked up Mason around nine, and he looked a lot better than the last time I'd seen him. He tried to hug me, but his ribs were too sore. His concussion might leave him confused for a few days, but he had no internal injuries. A lucky man.

Mason wasn't ready to take it easy. Neither was Dan. Eddie fixed bagels for both of them, and we sat around the kitchen table as they ate. We kept the conversation light. Jason didn't say anything about the night before. Had he really forgotten it?

I got him to sit on my lap. "How did you sleep last night, Jason?"

"I had a bad dream. Lurleen said it was just a bad dream."

Lurleen looked at me and shrugged.

We'd have a talk about what really happened later. For now, I didn't want to upset Jason. Lurleen offered to take the kids out back for a bird-watching expedition. Once they left, the rest of us shared what information we had.

"So all our evidence is gone," Mason said.

"Maybe now the kids will be safe," I said. "We don't have anything else to give them."

"You sure about that?" Mason asked.

"What do you mean?" I could feel my heart rate pick up.

Chapter Thirty-four

Eddie gathered up the empty plates from breakfast and took them to the sink. She was still close enough to hear everything we discussed. Dan and I sat glued to the kitchen table.

Mason looked at me. "We don't know who's behind all of this." His gray eyes were a shade too dark for my liking. "It's possible the kids know more than they realize or that someone may think they do."

"Like maybe they could identify the mastermind," I said. "But Lucie said she never saw the third person."

"I wonder if the person in charge believes that."

"So they may still be in danger," I said.

"Yes. I've had a lot of time to think. You don't get much sleep in a hospital."

"That's for sure. What have you come up with?"

"A number of suspects, police included."

"Captain Blakely?" I asked.

"Yes. Blakely for one. Dave's an old friend. But what's he doing taking the memory card that no one at headquarters seems to know about?"

"He didn't deliver the card to the chief, that's what you're saying?"

"I'm still persona non grata, so I can't say for sure. But I did have some visitors last night from the department. They said the chief and Sandler are frantic to find the card and it hasn't turned up."

"But why keep you out of it now? They can't suspect you of being involved." I hesitated. "It's Tommy. They think he's involved, don't they?"

"Maybe."

"Should I try him again?"

"Don't bother. You won't reach him. He and Charlie Flack are long gone. That would be my guess."

"And the bad guys have the information? But surely, it won't do them much good at this point."

"My guess is they have a buyer lined up and a way to remain protected. Or they plan to leave the country." Mason looked discouraged.

"That could be good for the kids," I said.

"Could be."

"And what about Kathleen Sandler? Has anyone followed up with her?" Eddie asked.

"You're asking the wrong man. I'm now officially on sick leave for a week. But I don't feel sick."

"You don't know how sick you are when you have a concussion," I said. "You might not be thinking clearly for a while. But perhaps the five of us can think clearly."

Mason nodded. "I'm not about to let this drop."

"Whatever you say we do, boss. I'm with you," Dan said.

Eddie poured Dan and Mason another cup of coffee. "I'm in all the way. You know that."

"That would be my mother," Mason said. He spoke to me but he was smiling at Eddie. "Never leaves an investigation until it goes down. If it takes twenty-four hours or twenty-four years, my mom is on it."

"You know this could cost you your job, Mason," Eddie said. "The job you love."

"I'm not sure I still love it."

The kids and Lurleen ran in from the backyard. "*De l'eau, de l'eau,*" Lurleen cried, running to the faucet. I pulled out three glasses from the cupboard, filled them with ice, and handed them to Lurleen. She poured the water and handed each child a large glass.

"We ended up playing softball. You may not realize it but your son Jason has a mean slipper of a pitch."

"Slider, Lurleen, slider," Dan corrected.

No one corrected the "son" part, but I could see the funny look on Jason's face. I took his hand and knelt down beside him. "Your mom is always your mom, Jason. But I can be a substitute mom, kind of like a substitute hitter. You okay with that?"

Jason nodded. "You won't go away like Mom?"

"No," I said. "I'm not going anywhere."

Lucie sidled up beside me and took my other hand. She looked so small standing beside me. Just a little girl trying hard to act grown-up, to not be a burden, to not show how much she missed her mother.

"Now, I see some individuals who need a bath," I said. "And I don't mean Hermione."

Lucie giggled and rubbed at the mud that was covering her shorts. She stopped smiling when she saw they were ripped. "I'm sorry. I've made a mess of things. Money doesn't grow on trees."

Eddie took a look at the tear. "That, dear one, is easily mended. I'll show you how to do it." She looked at me. "I'll handle the baths."

She took the kids upstairs and we didn't see them again for half an hour. Long enough for the four of us to come up with a plan.

We reviewed everything we knew. Dan was the biggest help. He'd been in the middle of most of it.

"Marie Vanderling and Sandler are definitely partners," Dan said.

"Partners like business?" I asked. "Or partners like lovers?"

"I don't know for sure. They were all over each other, but I couldn't tell if one of them might be playing the other. They didn't keep me around long enough to find out."

"Who knocked you out?" Mason asked.

"I'm not sure. Sandler said they had to do it to keep me quiet. The investigation was winding down and he couldn't take any chances. That's why they tied me up, or so they said."

"Marie was involved in that part?" Lurleen asked.

"Marie seemed to be involved in all of it," Dan said.

Lurleen looked upset. "Marie has been telling me about this mysterious boyfriend of hers. I thought she'd have better taste."

"You saw Tommy?" I asked.

"The only time I saw Tommy was when he untied me and Charlie Flack showed up."

"They seemed to know each other? As if they were working together?" I asked.

"Flack had a gun and was talking trash. He was waving it at Tommy. 'You got me into this. You're going to get me out. I'm not gonna die with a bullet in my head.' Then he started waving the gun at me. Tommy told him to settle down and ordered me to drive to your place."

"Hmm," Mason said. "We have plenty of suspects. Marie and Sandler. Tommy and Charlie Flack. Dave Blakely. And Kathleen Sandler. How does it fit?"

"In med school, you're trained to list all the possibilities but look for the simplest diagnosis that explains all the symptoms. If it walks like a duck and quacks like a duck it's probably a duck. This quacks like a business in trouble with a game-changing product that could turn the company around. Who would want to keep that from happening and why?"

"It's one giant puzzle," Lurleen said. "I do love puzzles." She settled herself next to Dan. "I can tell you one thing. Marie would never be involved in murder. Never. I don't know about Sandler. In his youth, he was ruthless. Loyalty, like mafia loyalty, has always been his thing."

"And Kathleen Sandler?" I asked. "How does she feel about loyalty?"

"She was schooled at the old man's knee, that's for sure. The same steel runs through her," Lurleen said. "That's why the old man was grooming her to take over. But killing her own cousin?"

"The Tudors did it all the time," I said. "The Sandlers are a kind of US royalty. Maybe the same rules of human nature apply."

"I like your idea," Mason said to me. "Keep it simple. According to Dave, it was all part of a sting operation. With Billy Joe at the core and someone higher up pulling the strings. Of course, we don't know how much of Dave's story is the truth."

"Billy Joe loved money and always wanted more. He thought he was smart," Lurleen said. "No matter what the evidence showed. I remember Marie telling me that Sandler had had enough. Billy Joe was being cut off. That was more than a year ago."

Mason shifted on the sofa, put his hand against his ribs, and grimaced. "Detective Schmidt must have figured something out. That's why he got shot. And someone cleared out his notes. That had to be someone within the police department."

We heard skittering down the stairs before we saw two squeaky clean children.

"Don't you two look well-scrubbed," I said.

Jason made a face. "She's going to wash my cape!"

The "she" was Eddie. "You can help me do it, Jason," she said. "Superman would never run around with a dirty cape."

That seemed to make an impression on him. "Can I do it myself?"

Eddie nodded.

"Can I help?" Lucie asked.

The three of them disappeared into the basement with a basket full of dirty clothes.

"I would guess that gives us another five minutes to talk," I said. "Where do Tommy and the police come in?"

"The chief has helped Sandler out in the past," Mason said. "I know that. I've seen it happen. If Tommy is the deal maker, then it may be he got brought in to help. Just the way Dave said."

"Are you saying that to make me feel better?" I asked.

"It could be true."

I let out a breath. "I hope you're right. And Captain Blakely?"

"What do you think, boss?" Dan asked. "Has he gone rogue?"

"I don't know. If it was all a sting operation, then why didn't he give the memory card to the chief? He's seemed different lately, desperate for money. I gave him a loan two months ago, but I can't see him killing Schmiddy. And whoever killed Schmidt did the same to Eleanor and Billy Joe." Mason stood up. "We have a lot of theories and not many facts. It's time the chief and I have a talk. I'm going to police headquarters. You stay here, Dan."

Chapter Thirty-five

We followed Mason out the front door and stood on the wraparound front porch. It was another perfect spring day. It lightened all of our moods a little. Except for Mason's.

Mason was all business. "I'll need to take your car, Dan."

"Fine, I'll stay put."

"I want all of you to stay put," Mason said. He stared hard at Lurleen and me.

Lurleen nodded but didn't make eye contact. I looked at her, but she kept her eyes glued to the ground.

"What was that all about?" I asked her later.

"Nothing."

Lurleen's "nothings" have always made me uneasy. Like when a two-year-old gets too quiet and you know he's up to something. "What are you planning to do, Lurleen?"

She primped her hair. "I'm going stir-crazy," she said. "I might need to take my little car out for a drive. Look at the weather. Don't you need to get out of here?"

"Where are you planning to go, Lurleen?"

Lurleen shrugged. She could be very annoying when she chose to be.

"What are you up to? You want to find Marie? To see Kathleen? I let Ellie walk out on me. I'm not letting you do that. We could still be in danger. Don't you realize that? Let Mason see what's going on." I felt myself getting more agitated. "Lurleen, you're my best friend. Don't make me worry about you. We stick together."

She took my hand. "I'm sorry, *chérie*. I know how strong you are and I forget that even you may have a *point a casse*."

"Yes, Lurleen, I do have a breaking point."

"Perhaps we both need a little ride in the country," Lurleen said. "Dan and Eddie can watch the kids, although God knows they need a break as well."

Once Lurleen had planted the seed, I couldn't let go of it. To get out of the house. Nothing sounded better. I broached the subject with Eddie privately, and later with Dan. Eddie understood, but Dan refused to budge on the issue.

"The boss said we stick together. That's what we do."

He was right, of course. I helped Eddie make dinner along with the kids. We chose something elaborate enough to occupy our time and something the kids could help with—no-knead bread with meatloaf and green beans. Lurleen said she needed a rest and disappeared upstairs. Dan played with the kids. We heard nothing from Mason until dinner was on the table. Then we heard him unlock the front door. The kids jumped up from the table and rushed to meet him. Eddie went to turn off the alarm and discovered it wasn't on.

"That's not like me," she said, frowning. "I was so sure I set it."

"Never mind, I've got news," he said. "And I'm starving."

Mason gave Eddie a hug and sat down at the table. Lurleen was still upstairs. I called up to announce that dinner was on the table. No answer.

"She's either sulking or in the bathtub," I said. "When she's really upset she drowns her sorrows in a bubble bath. We wouldn't let her leave the house."

"All that may be behind us," Mason said. "I finally got to see the chief. He had the memory card and thanked me for my help in locating it. Sandler and Tommy were in the room with him."

I held my breath.

Eddie looked at both of us and stood up. "I think I'll take the kids outside for a special picnic." She looked at Lucie and Jason. "Would you like that? This is going to be boring adult talk, and I for one need to have some fun. Grab your plates and we'll sit on the porch."

Neither one of them argued. You didn't argue with Eddie. They'd learned that some time ago. Jason was always happy to be on the move. "Can Hermione come?" he asked.

"Of course," I said.

Lucie stood up more slowly and I gave her a quick hug. "I'll tell you everything you need to know after dinner," I whispered to her. "I promise."

Once we heard them settled at the table on the back porch, I closed the door and Mason continued.

"It's been an elaborate manhunt, according to the chief. I got pulled off because of you, Ditie. Tommy said he couldn't do his work if you were involved, that I was too close to you."

"His work?" I asked.

"Tommy has been Sandler's man throughout most of the operation. Sandler got wind of something brewing in his company. First he blamed it on Billy Joe. Then he realized it was more than that. He learned that someone in his organization was trying to sabotage the company, starting with the hacking incident."

Mason paused to catch his breath and take a bite of meatloaf. "Fantastic," he said with a nod in my direction. I nodded back at him. It was a great recipe.

"Go on," Dan said between mouthfuls.

"When Kathleen got the police involved and Schmiddy was killed, Sandler wanted to go underground. He wanted Tommy to help put the sting operation in place. Tommy had helped Ellie get a job at Sandler. She owed him. He helped her connect with Billy Joe under the pretense she wanted a big-money deal and heard he had some scheme going."

"So Ellie was doing the right thing," I said. "No wonder Tommy was so upset by her death. He got her involved."

"And she got Charlie Flack involved," Mason continued. "They needed a technical expert, and Charlie was it. He'd worked on a prototype of the new product, and he felt as if the company owed him something. He didn't know it was all a setup. He was in for the money and a chance to get back with Ellie. When Ellie was killed and then Billy Joe, all Flack wanted was out, but Sandler wouldn't allow it. Sandler needed to know who was betraying him at the top."

"Tommy was supposed to figure that out?" I said.

"He'd done it before for Sandler. Apparently your brother has a way of getting people to trust him and tell him everything he wants to know."

"He certainly manipulated me often enough when we were kids," I said.

"A smooth operator. That's what Sandler needed," Mason said. "Tommy thought he had Ellie on his side. She was to go along with things until the person at the top of the pyramid could be identified. But Ellie got killed before she could give Tommy the information. No one knows if she switched camps thinking she could make more money or if someone found out what she was up to."

"Oh, Ellie." I'd probably never know the answer to that. Had her greed led to her death or had she really been trying to do the right thing?

"When Billy Joe died, Sandler and the chief brought Blakely on board and took me off the case."

"So Blakely is also on the right side," I said.

"Yes. Tommy thought that if Blakely acted like a renegade, ready to sell the memory card to the highest bidder, he could find out what Tommy didn't know—who the person at the top was."

"Did he succeed?" Dan asked.

"He did." Mason wasn't big on drama, but even he couldn't pass up the moment. He paused to take a bite of meatloaf.

"Come on," Dan and I said together.

"Lurleen won't want to hear this," he said. "I'm glad she's upstairs. It was Marie Vanderling. It broke Sandler's heart apparently."

"She's in custody?" Dan asked.

"Nope. Disappeared. I think Sandler let her get away."

"Wow. Everything tied up with a bow," I said.

"Pretty much."

"But she couldn't have done the killings herself," I said.

"Why, because she's a woman?" Mason asked.

Before I could respond, Dan jumped in. "What about Schmiddy?"

"Same murderer. Had to be. Blakely got Schmiddy's notes and delivered them to the chief. Cleared the file, so no one else would interrupt their plan."

"And who pushed you off the road?" I asked.

"Charlie Flack, according to Sandler."

"So is it really over?" I asked.

"I don't think Marie or Charlie Flack are going to come back to find you or the kids," Mason said.

"Thank God." I stood up to carry dishes to the sink. Mason and Dan joined me.

"We'll handle this," Mason said to me. "Why don't you let Lurleen know the news. It would be better if she hears it from you. I'll tell my mom. Then I think we should celebrate."

"Let's go out for ice cream. Dairy Queen," I called back as I headed upstairs.

I knocked on Lurleen's door. No response. "Lurleen, I know you're in there. This is no time to sulk. I'm coming in."

I gave her five seconds and entered. No Lurleen. Instead, there was a note.

I'm sorry. I couldn't stay cooped up any longer. I had to escape. I went down the back stairs and turned off the alarm. I must talk to Marie. Be back soon.

I didn't panic right away. Marie Vanderling was undoubtedly long gone. Or was she? Did Lurleen know where Marie was?

I ran downstairs and told Mason what Lurleen had done. Then I grabbed my cell and texted Lurleen: *Call us immediately. The case is solved. Don't go near Marie.*

Maybe that would get her attention. Five minutes later, my cell rang. It was Lurleen.

"What are you talking about?" Lurleen asked. "The case is solved?"

I explained to her what Mason had found out.

"But I'm here with Marie. In a hotel. She's scared for her life. She isn't the murderer."

Chapter Thirty-six

I put Lurleen on speakerphone so Mason could hear. "Where are you, Lurleen? What hotel?"

"I can't tell you that. Marie doesn't trust anyone, including the police. I have to stay with her."

"Listen to me carefully, Lurleen. You have to get out of there. Now. Use any excuse. Just get out of there."

"I want to do what you say, but I can't leave Marie."

"All right. Then we're coming to you."

"No." For the first time in her life, Lurleen hung up on me.

"Come on." I grabbed Mason and pulled him upstairs. "I'm sure Marie called her for help. And if I know Lurleen, we'll find the address somewhere in her room." If Lurleen was on the phone, she was always doodling or writing down information so she wouldn't forget it. It was there near the tub. A smudged and damp piece of paper with a picture of crackers and a car along with the name Amy Serandon. "Crackers and a car," I said. "It's the Ritz Carlton under that name. But which Ritz?"

"The one downtown, closest to the airport, I bet," Mason said. "I'll call it in for both locations. We'll head downtown. Take your car?"

"Of course." It had just been returned to me, newly washed and cleared of any evidence that Charlie Flack had ever been inside it.

We arrived at the downtown location but not before the police got there. And not before Marie had disappeared again. We found Lurleen sitting alone in the suite, eating See's candy.

"She's not guilty, you know," she said to us and the policeman. The policeman deferred to Mason, who asked for time alone with Lurleen.

"She's not acting like an innocent person, Lurleen. Where is she?"

"I don't know. She wouldn't tell me where she was headed. She didn't want to get me in trouble."

"And who's helping her leave town?" Mason asked. "Someone has to be."

"She wouldn't tell me that either."

That's the way the conversation went. Lurleen refused to say anything except that Marie was being falsely accused of crimes she didn't commit.

"What about Kathleen Sandler?" Lurleen asked when Mason was done with his interrogation. "Why aren't you talking to her?"

"We will. She's out of town currently. It looks like we have the facts, Lurleen. Much as you don't like them."

"I don't like them and I don't believe them. Marie is a scapegoat."

"If she is, then she's in danger," Mason said. "The real murderer, if it isn't Marie, won't let her survive to tell her side of the story."

That got Lurleen's attention. "Ah, *mon dieu*, you're right, of course." She stood up, grabbed her knockoff Chanel purse. "I'll take you to her."

We followed Marie in her yellow Citroën through downtown Atlanta and onto I-75/85 headed for the airport. She turned off on Riverdale Drive. She pulled into a gas station and began to pump gas. We drove to a second pump. Marie appeared from the small office and climbed into Lurleen's car. It was there Mason confronted her. She made an attempt to leave, but Mason held the passenger door shut.

"How could you?" Marie said to Lurleen.

"For your safety," Lurleen said. "I had no choice."

Marie turned on Lurleen. "You've ruined everything. Everything."

Mason radioed for a police car. I watched Lurleen's face melt into a river of despair as two officers arrived to take Marie to the station.

Chapter Thirty-seven

I took Lurleen home in my Toyota. Mason followed in her Citroën. She didn't speak to me on the long ride home. When we pulled up in the driveway to Eddie's house, she climbed out of the car stony faced. Mason pulled in behind us and joined me in the driveway. It was beginning to get dark, but we could both see the fury outlined on Lurleen's face. She finally broke her silence when Lucie and Jason ran up to her. They were playing near the big magnolia in the front yard.

"Oh, Lurleen," Lucie squealed. "You're back. Are you okay?"

"Of course, *ma chérie*. Never worry about Lurleen. She can take care of herself."

Lucie took her hand. "Are you all right?"

"Of course." She saw the worried look on Lucie's face. "I'm sorry if I frightened you. I never want to do that." She headed inside with two children running beside her. Dan opened the door for her. She raised one eyebrow. "Did you have some part in this?"

"In this?" he asked innocently.

"You know perfectly well what I mean."

He didn't respond with words. Instead, he put his arms around her and lifted her off her feet. Then he kissed her. A big mushy kiss, as Jason would have described it. She couldn't seem to help herself. She responded to the kiss, and with Dan at least it seemed that all was forgiven.

Mason and I watched them disappear inside. Then we settled ourselves on two rocking chairs on the porch. Eddie came outside to join us.

"Where's the truth?" I asked. "Is Marie guilty or is it Kathleen? Mr. Sandler is all about family. Would he protect Kathleen and throw Marie under the bus?"

"My guess is no one throws Marie under the bus," Mason said. "I need to hear what Marie has to say. I'm going downtown. I'll call you when I know more."

"We're not under protective custody anymore?" Eddie asked. "We're free to come and go?"

"They picked up Kathleen Sandler at the airport. Charlie Flack is still missing. But we have nothing he wants."

"Apparently that includes his son," I said.

Mason looked sad. "I'm sorry about what Jason had to witness. And Lucie as well. Anyway, from the safety standpoint, I'd say you're free to move around as you wish."

"Good. I have some business to take care of," I said.

"Tonight?" Mason asked. "Can't it wait until morning?"

I shook my head.

"Tommy?" Eddie asked.

"Yeah, Tommy." I looked over at Eddie. "I'll let you know when I'm on my way back home."

"Good," Eddie said. "Take your time. I'll put the kids to bed."

Mason nodded his goodbye. He was halfway down the drive, eager to act like a detective again. I'm sure he hoped he could get in on both the interview with Marie Vanderling and the one with Kathleen Sandler. "I'm borrowing your car, Mom."

Eddie entered the house and reemerged with a set of keys. She threw them to Mason.

"How did Lurleen manage to drive her car out of the driveway without any of us noticing?" Mason asked.

"There wasn't room for Lurleen's car here," I said. "She parked it down the street."

I watched as Mason maneuvered Eddie's Ford Focus out of the garage and around my car.

"I'm next," I said once Mason was gone.

"Fine." She turned toward me as I gathered up my purse and keys. "Take care and remember he is your brother."

"You mean the blood is thicker than water idea?"

"Something like that. Let him have his say. He sounds like a hero."

"My brother always sounds like a hero."

I followed Eddie into the house, told the kids I had to run an errand, and left before I had to answer any questions.

It felt good to be in my reliable car once more—by myself. The night was dark, no moon yet, and I couldn't help checking the back seat to make sure Charlie Flack wasn't waiting for me. Then I headed for Tommy's condo. I didn't call first. It was early for Tommy to be out celebrating. With luck I'd catch him at home.

Chapter Thirty-eight

I spent the ten-minute drive to Tommy's wondering what I would say to him and what he would say to me. The change in scenery was dramatic. I left a quiet neighborhood for the bustle of Buckhead, with its bars, fine restaurants, lights. Oddly, that was what struck me the most. All the lights, the glitz. It suited Tommy to a T. He could hide behind the lights, the glitter, so that no one, least of all his sister, ever knew who he really was.

I should have felt relieved driving to Tommy's and instead I felt uneasy. The murders felt so neatly solved. It was just the murderers that didn't quite fit. Was Marie really a killer? Lurleen had such faith in her, and Lurleen was good at sizing people up. Was it Kathleen? Maybe Tommy could enlighten me. Would he be as full of himself as usual? The man who saved Sandler's single-handedly. With Tommy it would always be single-handedly. So what? This meeting had more to do with me. To clear the air. To understand what happened. To apologize for the mistrust I had of him. I sighed. Was that mistrust really gone?

I drove slowly down the long drive to Tommy's thirty-floor building that overlooked Phipps Plaza, a shopping mall that was too rich for my blood. I announced myself to the disembodied voice that asked my business. "I'm Mabel Brown, here to see Tommy Brown."

"Please enter. The valet will park you." The gate swung slowly open and I drove to the circular drive. A valet opened the car door for me. "Welcome, Dr. Brown."

I entered the art deco lobby and once again admired the furniture, the fireplace, the twenty-foot ceilings. Oscar was still on duty. "Dr. Brown," he said. "How nice to see you. I believe Mr. Brown is out."

"Do you think I could wait in his condo?" I asked.

Oscar hesitated. This was not protocol. "I think that will be all right. After all, you stayed with him for a while. I don't think he'd object."

I smiled. I guess Oscar didn't know Tommy as well as he thought he did. Someone in his apartment and Tommy not object? That would be a first.

I entered the elevator for the south tower and Oscar sent me up to the tenth floor. The door opened to the foyer. I still had the key Tommy had given me, so I let myself in after I knocked first to make sure he wasn't home.

A light was on in the bedroom. The rest of the apartment was blackout dark, curtains pulled shut across enormous windows. I called out again. "Tommy? Tommy, it's Mabel."

No answer.

I walked to the bedroom and looked inside. He wasn't there. I sat on the bed. Suddenly I was exhausted. Too much had happened. I lay down on a gold damask coverlet and listened for Tommy's return. Silence. I let my eyes drift around the elegant room. It was scrupulously clean and nicely appointed— meaning Tommy had hired the best interior decorator in town. He'd paid a pretty penny for an antique highboy and an eighteenth-century secretary. Everything was tucked away. One saw only what Tommy wanted you to see. Except . . . what was that near the closet? I sat up to get a better look.

My umbrella. The umbrella my father had made just for me with the linden tree grip. The one I had lent to Ellie the day she died. Tommy hadn't even tried to hide it. It was leaning against the wall in the corner of the room. I crouched down beside it to get a better look, but I didn't touch it.

My heart crumpled. Oh, Tommy. What have you done?

It took me a minute before I could call Mason. He didn't pick up, so I left a message. That I'd found the umbrella but hadn't found Tommy. That I was waiting for Tommy in his condo.

Mason called me back a few minutes later. The sound of the phone ringing was deafening. "You need to leave the apartment now," Mason said. "Get out of there and call me when you're safely outside. I'm sending someone over but leave now."

"What are you talking about?"

"Leave now!"

Mason had never been curt with me before. I hung up the phone, grabbed the umbrella, and headed for the front door. I heard something before I saw the gray outline of a man on the sofa in the living room.

"Why such a rush, my dear? I see you found the umbrella. Come sit with me."

It wasn't Tommy's voice.

Chapter Thirty-nine

The man clicked on the lamp next to him. His gray hair caught the light. He could only be one person. A man I'd never met. A man I knew only by reputation.

"You're Mr. Sandler," I said.

He nodded. "A pleasure to meet you," he said. "Although perhaps not in these circumstances." He motioned me over to sit across from him. I could see the glint of a small weapon in his right hand.

I walked slowly to the chair he indicated. "Please don't be fooled by my age. I'm a very good shot. Detective Schmidt, your friend Eleanor, and my grandson found that out the hard way."

I sank into the chair. "You killed Billy Joe, your own grandson?"

"No choice," he said. "In the same way I have no choice but to kill your brother and I'm sorry to say you as well. You do provide me with a simple way to make it look as if the two of you struggled over a gun. You learned Tommy killed your dear friend and he had to stop you from taking the umbrella to the police. Nice touch, don't you think?"

"So you brought the umbrella here? To incriminate Tommy."

Sandler nodded. "I knew Tommy wouldn't be home for a while. I sent him out to celebrate. And we both know how much Tommy likes to celebrate. Plenty of time to plant it and wait for Tommy's return."

"How did you get in without Oscar seeing you?"

"Tommy kindly gave me access to the parking garage and a key to the back elevator, so I could come over without being noticed. He asked me to keep his gun while you were staying here. He was very accommodating, my dear, but then I was paying him a hefty sum to help me out of a difficult situation."

"But why do anything more? The case is sewn up. The police think they have their murderer."

"The case *was* sewn up. Until you meddled with it. Marie was on her way to Ecuador, where she expected me to join her. Unfortunately, she was going to have a plane accident on the way. Engine trouble."

"Marie didn't kill anyone? She didn't know what you had done?"

"Of course not. Marie wouldn't hurt a fly. Unless of course the fly was my granddaughter Kathleen. She bought the story that Kathleen was behind all of it, something we couldn't prove. Marie loved me, but I couldn't be sure she'd keep her mouth shut during an interrogation. Not with Kathleen in another room testifying."

"And Tommy?"

"Tommy's a clever boy. He might put things together. I couldn't have that. Now he'll make the perfect murderer. Going after his own sister. It's his gun I'm holding."

We heard the elevator at the same time. Sandler motioned me to be still and turned off the light.

"What the hell?" Tommy yelled as he entered. "The door's unlocked. Where are you, Mabel? Oscar said he let you up."

"Watch out, Tommy!" I screamed and hooked the handle of the umbrella over Sandler's outstretched arm.

There was a shot in the dark.

Chapter Forty

"It's Sandler," I screamed as I ducked behind the chair. "He has your gun."

As if to prove my point, two more shots were fired.

Tommy hadn't said a word. Was he hurt? Killed? I had no way of knowing. I inched my way in the general direction of the foyer. My eyes were getting accustomed to the darkness and I could see furniture and Sandler's outline. That meant Sandler could see me.

I saw him creeping toward the foyer, more intent on finding Tommy than me. Then I saw another form. This one not moving. Crumpled at the foot of the open door.

Oh, my God. Tommy. That's when I made a running tackle at the back of Sandler's body. We fell together into the doorframe leading from the apartment into the foyer. I heard something crack and I saw Sandler's hand go limp. The hand holding the gun. It dropped with a smack on the tile in the entrance hall.

I climbed off Sandler, grabbed the gun, and pointed it at him. He moaned and twitched. I kept the gun pointed at him as I turned on an overhead light in the foyer. Then I moved to Tommy. With my free hand I felt for a pulse. Strong. He opened his eyes as I searched for his wounds.

He tried to sit up and sank back down again. "My shoulder," he said.

There was a round hole in his left shoulder with a small amount of blood oozing from it.

"You'll be all right," I said. "Lie still. I'll call for help."

I could see both men clearly. Tommy slumped against the wall beside the door. Sandler on the floor, his head against the doorframe. He'd stopped moving. His eyes were open. He looked dead, but I'd seen too many movies where the bad guy acted dead and then sprang into action. I wasn't going to touch him until I had some protection. I called 911 and waited.

Seconds later I heard the mechanical hum of the elevator. And then the ding as the door opened. Three armed policemen burst into the foyer, their guns drawn. I motioned them to Sandler.

They took a look at him. Felt for a pulse. "He's dead, miss. See the back of his head?"

I looked at the blood forming a halo around Sandler's head. I saw his eyes looking toward heaven. The only time those eyes would have looked in that direction.

"How did you get here so fast?" I asked.

"Detective Garrett called. He's on his way."

Oscar poked his head out of the elevator. He looked ashen. "Someone in the next apartment heard shots, and before I could call the police, they arrived." He looked at Tommy. Then he looked at me holding a gun.

"It's all right, Oscar," Tommy said. "My sister saved my life. Again."

I looked at him. "What do you mean by again?"

Tommy smiled a wan smile. "We'll talk when I feel better."

Chapter Forty-one

The paramedics arrived and took over. I watched as they ministered to Tommy and took him away on a gurney.

"You all right, miss?" One of the officers came over to remove the gun I still held in my hand. He escorted me to a sofa in the living room.

"Tommy will be furious if I mess up his sofa," I said. "Better take me to the kitchen. I may be bloody."

"Huh? You got hit?"

I realized then I was not all right. I wasn't thinking clearly. "I'm fine, I promise you. I didn't get hit. I'm a doctor. Tommy's sister."

"Tommy? The young man with the shoulder wound?"

"Yes."

"If you're up to it I'll take your statement," he said.

At that moment we both heard the hum of the elevator and the click as it opened. Mason entered the apartment and found me in the living room. "I'll take the statement, officer. Officer Hernandez, isn't it?"

"Yes, sir." He beamed at the recognition and left the room.

Mason picked me up and hugged me until I couldn't breathe. Then he set me gently back down in the chair. "Oh, my God, Ditie. I heard it was a 187 and all I could think about was what if I lost you. Don't ever do that to me again."

"A 187?"

"A homicide."

"I will do my best never to do that again." Idle words given what happened to me a few months later, but that's a different story.

Mason listened as I told him about Sandler's confession. "That's in line with what we heard from Marie and Kathleen. Marie didn't know Sandler was guilty of anything except trying to help her escape, but she had her doubts. She was supposed to supply Sandler with an alibi for the time Billy Joe was killed.

"Kathleen Sandler was a different story. She broke down. Not as tough as she looks. She's been worried about her grandfather for the past two years—afraid he was slipping into dementia like his father. He was making bad decisions, spending money inappropriately."

"Phil Brockton's dad is a concierge doc for the Sandler family—available at their beck and call. Phil almost let something slip about the health of one of them. I assumed it was Billy Joe, but I'll bet it was about Sandler Senior. Phil's dad probably knew Sandler was deteriorating."

"Maybe so. But Sandler was determined to keep the reins and wouldn't listen to reason. Kathleen was planning to replace him."

"And he got word of it?" I said.

"Your brother was supposed to convince him it was for the good of the company. Some kind of miracle worker, your brother. But even he couldn't get Sandler to play nice. Kathleen never said her grandfather was behind the killings or the espionage—the loyalty issue—but I think she knew it was him. The chief of police didn't want to believe it either, but he heard the interviews. He'd seen Sandler change over the years."

Mason looked at me and apparently saw how exhausted I was. "I'll take you home, and then we'll go to the hospital to check on Tommy."

"My house, please," I said. "I don't want the kids to see me like this."

We left the kitchen and walked around the police tape that marked off most of the apartment. Mason got me home in twenty minutes. I showered and changed. It was good to be in my own house, poking through my own closet for something to wear. By the time we got to the hospital, Tommy was about to go into surgery.

They said I could have a few minutes with him. They were waiting on a CT scan. Mason left us alone.

I took Tommy's hand, and he squeezed it. "Thanks, Mabel," he said.

"You're welcome. You had me scared. I wasn't always sure which side you were on."

"I know," Tommy said. "You've had a lot of reasons to mistrust me. And you never really knew who I was."

"You said that before. What do you mean by that?"

"You never knew why Mother sent me away, did you?"

I shook my head. "I assumed she thought you were hanging around with the wrong crowd."

Tommy smiled. "The wrong crowd to our mother were guys like me. The other boys who didn't quite fit into an Iowa farming community."

"Guys like you?" Pieces fell into place. Tommy would pretend to be whatever our mother wanted him to be—the kid who loved to hunt, the kid who would do whatever our mother wanted him to do. But he hid most of himself from her and from the rest of us. Tommy would disappear for hours. I assumed he was in the woods with his friends but maybe he was somewhere else. He dated girls, like Ellie, but never seemed to care much about them.

"Yes," Tommy said. "I'm gay. Mother couldn't stand that. She sent me away to get straightened out." He laughed bitterly. "Just made me more bent I'm afraid. And a little craftier at hiding it."

"You never told me. You couldn't think I'd care?"

Tommy shook his head. "I got so used to keeping secrets, I didn't get around to telling you the truth. We were never that close, you know. Mother saw to that as well. I wrote you from boarding school, and you never wrote me back. You didn't get my letters, did you?"

I shook my head. "I thought you left us for a new life and wanted nothing to do with me."

"All I ever wanted was your approval," Tommy said. "I think that bothered Mother as well. It was one reason she was so hard on you. I was supposed to be the man of the family. The one who would always stand by her. And only her. I was supposed to make up for Dad's softness."

"Tommy, I'm sorry."

"It doesn't matter anymore. Thank God for that."

"Do you have someone?" I asked.

"I thought I did. But that all went south. I caught him in a gay bar playing up to some young dude. You remember the morning I came in beat up? That's what that was all about. I was drunk, and I lost it to a guy twice my size."

"Oh, Tommy. But you're a hero now."

Tommy shook his head. "That's not all it's cracked up to be. Sandler called me in to work his scam for him. I knew it didn't feel right, but I couldn't put my finger on what was wrong. I didn't want to know. That's the truth. When Ellie got murdered, everything changed for me. I got her involved in this, and it cost her her life. Then Billy Joe died, and Charlie freaked out. It was all I could do to keep him in line.

"All along, Sandler kept saying we were so close to finding the mastermind. What he meant was he was so close to having it all. Walking away with the product information he could sell to the highest bidder anonymously while he kept his hands clean and framed someone else. Then he'd go after his competitor, take him to court, and save his new product. He'd look like the star—keep his power, his company, and his money. I knew how his mind worked. I just didn't want to see it. So, Ditie, I'm no hero. If I were, Ellie would still be alive."

"I'm not sure about that, Tommy," I said. "I loved Ellie, but she was always after the money. Did she decide she'd go for the highest bidder instead of staying with your plan?"

"I don't know. The people who could tell us are dead."

"Where is Charlie Flack?" I asked.

"In police custody. For his own good. He's gotten immunity for his testimony. He knew it was Sandler in the end and kept that to himself. He was terrified he'd be the next one killed."

The nurse stuck his head in the room. "Time to get you to surgery," he said.

I kissed Tommy on the cheek, and he didn't flinch.

Two nurses entered the room and asked me to leave. I watched from the doorway as they gave Tommy a sedative through his IV and helped him onto the gurney.

I found Mason in the small waiting room off the surgical wing. He handed me a cup of coffee.

"You have time to stay with me?" I asked.

"Yes. They understand it's a family matter, and I have to stay."

We talked about the case, the kids.

"I still don't understand," I said. "How could Sandler take the company he loved and sell a secret to the highest bidder?"

"He was a desperate man," Mason said. "And a bitter one. The board was ready to replace him, and he wasn't ready to go. It was always more about him than the company. It crushed Kathleen to learn the truth."

"Why did he get the chief of police involved?" I asked.

"A foolish move. Sandler was arrogant. Thought he could manipulate the chief. They were old friends. He thought he could limit the number of police involved and feed them the information he wanted them to have. That was one reason I was taken off the case. I might cause trouble for Sandler."

Suddenly, I could barely keep my eyes open. Mason saw it and stopped talking. He put his arm around me and I rested my head on his shoulder. Some time later, he nudged me awake. A surgeon was standing in front of me.

"Dr. Brown?"

I nodded.

"Your brother came through surgery fine. No complications and remarkably little damage. He'll be back in his room in forty-five minutes or so."

I thanked him and told Mason to get back to work.

"It's six o'clock in the morning," he said.

I looked at my watch. We'd been in the waiting room most of the night.

"Still, you must have a million things to handle. And I'll bet you and your captain have a lot of catching up to do. I'm fine now. Lurleen can bring me home."

Reluctantly he left me there. I waited half an hour, and then I called Lurleen. She picked up on the first ring.

"I have been so worried, *chérie*. Mason called us, but still I was so worried. Are you all right?"

"I'm good, Lurleen, and Tommy's going to be fine."

"I'm so relieved. Now to know Tommy's okay, well, life is perfect. I will bake a cake to celebrate."

"Maybe I should bake the cake. I have a great recipe for a strawberry one. Lucie can help. Is she there?"

"Hanging by the phone."

Lurleen handed me over to Lucie.

"Hi, sweetheart. I'll be coming home soon. Are you and Jason okay?"

"Oh, yes. Now that I'm talking to you."

"Good. We'll have a lot of baking to do when I get back. Maybe Lurleen can pick me up in an hour and bring you and Jason with her. We'll stop off at a store and get what we need."

"Okay, but Jason has plans. Uncle Dan promised to teach him how to play football today."

"Fine. Then it will just be us girls."

I went up to see Tommy in his room. He was groggy but conscious.

"I never told you about saving my life before, did I?" he managed to say.

"No, you never did."

"Mother found all the stuff I'd stolen from Mr. Pinchley's pharmacy. I did it just to prove I could. Mother was going to beat me within an inch of my life, and then you appeared. You said you'd taken all of it to give to your friends. You'd hidden it in my room, and you were really sorry. You were too old to get a beating, so Mother marched you over to Mr. Pinchley's and you had to work there for free on the weekends until school let out."

"I'd forgotten that."

"Well, I didn't. I never stole another thing. Ever." He drifted off.

I kissed him goodbye and promised to take him home when he was released the following morning. Then I waited for Lurleen and Lucie at the ER entrance to Piedmont Hospital.

Chapter Forty-two

We stayed at Eddie's one more night.

I called Vic to let her know I'd be back at work the next day.

"We've missed you," she said. "And the teenager you worried about—Beza—seems to be doing well. All her blood work came back within normal limits. No hidden infections. Her complaints were just what you suspected—psychological, based on problems at home. And it seems the problem uncle has left the house. She has an appointment for tomorrow, so you can see for yourself."

"I feel as if I've been gone a month," I said.

"Only a few days actually. We'll be glad to have you back and in one piece. Are you sure you're ready?"

"The sooner the kids and I get into our normal routine, the better. I'm glad I still have a job!"

"As long as you want it," Victoria assured me. "I hope for a long time."

Lurleen was standing beside me as I hung up the phone.

"All's well in the clinic," I said. "The girl I was worried about seems to be out of danger. The 'uncle' is gone. I'll see her tomorrow."

Lurleen looked almost as relieved as I felt. "I'm glad for her. A lot of kids aren't so lucky."

"Sometimes I get the feeling you're talking about yourself, Lurleen. I hope you'll tell me about that one day."

"Maybe . . . someday. If I ever tell anyone, it will be you."

We hugged and turned our attention to the grand celebration we'd planned for the evening. My strawberry cake was a big hit. Lurleen and I filled it with prizes wrapped in wax paper, so it became a fortune-telling cake. That was Lurleen's idea. She and I carefully marked each piece of cake so that everyone got the right fortune, and then we warned people to find the fortune before they started eating the cake.

Jason unwrapped a tiny superhero action figure—I didn't know they made them that small. He would do heroic things when he grew up. Lucie, a tiny book. She would be a best-selling author. Dan got a dime. He'd be rich. Mason unwrapped a shiny penny for good luck.

"I've had plenty of that already," he said, looking at me.

We gave Eddie a small plastic dog. She'd fallen in love with Hermione. I promised that Lucie, Jason, and I would go with her to the pound to pick out a dog just for her. I selected the prize for Lurleen as she did for me. Hers was a tiny plastic globe, meaning she would travel the world. And what did Lurleen get for me? A miniature family, of course. A boy, a girl, a mother, and a father. All carefully wrapped in wax paper. It made me cry.

When the kids were asleep, we talked once more about the case. There was one loose end bothering me. What was all the fuss about the Transformer? What did it have to do with anything?

"I can answer that," Lurleen said with a broad smile. She glanced at Mason.

"Be my guest."

"Sandler was all about security. Employees were checked and double checked coming and going. Ellie could never have sneaked a memory card out of there. But her son Jason could. For all his paranoia, Sandler never thought to check the children from day care. They were free to come and go with toys and backpacks. Occasionally, security might check a backpack or two, but a secret compartment in an action figure? No way."

"A masterful deduction," Mason said, "and right on target."

Lurleen beamed. She turned to Dan. "Maybe I can help you on a case sometime."

Dan looked less than happy. "I'm kind of a loner when it comes to work."

"Well then, I guess it will just be you and me, Ditie. I'll keep my eyes open for someone who needs our help."

"Right now I think we have our hands full," I said. "I'm going to need your help taking care of Jason and Lucie."

"Of course. *Bien sur*," Lurleen said. "But if something should fall in my lap, I'll let you know."

We drank champagne to celebrate the end of harrowing times and made an early night of it.

Eddie had the children up at seven—fed and dressed by the time I came downstairs. Their backpacks stood ready by the door along with a small suitcase for each child.

"I found these in the attic," Eddie assured me. "This way the children can come for a visit whenever they like."

I had my own suitcase in hand. Lurleen and Dan promised to come back and pick up the rest of our stuff. We were good to go by seven thirty.

I teared up as we left Eddie's house.

She smiled indulgently. "I'm not that far away, my dear. Twenty minutes? We'll see each other all the time."

Once we were in the car I couldn't wait to get home.

I couldn't stop smiling when I saw my house again. The magnolia was beginning to blossom. My neighbor had cut the lawn, and while the tulips were past their prime, the roses were beginning to blossom. Hermione had to sniff every corner of the yard. Even breakfast couldn't entice her inside. As for Majestic, she sidled into the house but lost it when she saw her old toys. She ran around like a crazy animal, bouncing her stuffed mouse all over the living room.

The kids put their suitcases in their room, gathered up their book bags, and waited by the door.

"You both look eager for school," I said.

Jason made a face, but I knew he'd missed his friends. Lucie smiled up at me. "Third grade is a very important year," she said.

"It is, and I bet Michael has missed you."

Lucie blushed.

"I won't tease you about Michael if you don't tease me about Mason. Deal?"

"Deal."

I dropped the kids off at school and arrived at the clinic a little before nine. Vic gave me a hug.

"So glad to have you back," she said. "Everything is settled?"

"Everything is settled. The kids are safe, and the bad guys are gone."

"Good. It's been a madhouse here. Beza came in early. You ready to see her?"

"More than ready."

I went to the first exam room and found Beza seated on the examination table. "Do you need to examine me today, Dr. Brown?"

"Not today. This is a wellness check. Are you well?"

Beza gave me a dazzling smile, white teeth against her beautiful coffee brown skin. "Yes. I am."

"Where is the uncle you worried about?"

"He has gone back to Nigeria. He said there is no opportunity here for a man like him."

"He's right. Is there opportunity for the rest of the family here?"

"My mother and father work in a 7-Eleven near our home. I wanted to work there too, but they insist I stay in school. We manage."

"Good. Your brothers and sisters are well? How many are there—four, I think?"

"Four. All in school. All well."

The good visit started my day off perfectly, and the rest of the day disappeared before I knew it.

When I picked the kids up in aftercare, they were bubbling over with news. Especially Lucie.

"Miss Langston said she didn't know how she managed without me. And you know, Aunt Ditie, I could do all the work. Almost like I hadn't missed any school at all. And even Michael said hi to me. And my friend Amanda wanted to know everything that happened." Lucie was quiet for a second.

"What?" I asked.

"Do you think Amanda could come home with me one day after school?"

"Of course. If she comes on a Friday, she could come for a sleepover."

"A sleepover?" Lucie's eyes widened. "Could we have popcorn and watch movies and stay up past my bedtime?"

"Absolutely."

"I want a sleepover too," Jason said.

"You and I will have our own fun, I promise. And maybe Lucie will let us all watch a movie together."

That seemed to satisfy him. He was an easy boy to please. He ran after Hermione, who rolled over on the floor so he could scratch her belly.

Lurleen and Dan came for dinner that evening, along with Mason, who brought pizza and salad for all of us.

Lurleen was as happy to be settled into her house as I was in mine. "Bring the kids over whenever you want. Dan wants to have a lot of cookouts this summer." It seemed that Dan's lease was up the end of the month, and Lurleen's house was certainly big enough for two.

My house was full of the warmth that only children can bring. Children and baking. I taught the kids how to make bread and even Jason got into the art of kneading, as long as it didn't go on forever.

Phil called me one last time after I moved back home. He was in New York but promised to get in touch when he was heading south for the Battle of Atlanta reenactment. I warned him I might be too busy to see him then. Or ever, I thought.

In exchange for his testimony, Charlie Flack was released without charges. He was the cornerstone of the district attorney's case. He came over for a few visits before he left for California where he had a job lined up with a biochemical research firm.

Kathleen Sandler, the new head of Sandler's Sodas, decided she could give him a decent recommendation. After all, it was his preliminary work that had led to the phenomenal new product. She also thought it would be good to have him on the other side of the continent. Charlie, for his part, assured all of us he had learned his lesson. He could be content with a simple life. He told me he wasn't suited for a life of crime—there was an understatement.

Though Jason was afraid of him at first, they gradually worked things out. Charlie played ball with him and showed him some chemistry experiments. By the time he left, Charlie had one of Jason's favorite action figures for safekeeping. There was no talk of Jason living with Charlie, and I decided to let sleeping dogs lie.

Life quieted in a way I couldn't have imagined. After a few weeks, I managed to get in touch with Ellie's mother, who told me she'd found a home and a husband in Costa Rica. She wouldn't be coming back to the US anytime soon, but if I wanted to bring the children down for a visit, she'd be delighted to see us. Since the children had only seen their grandmother on two occasions, I didn't rush to buy airline tickets.

It felt wonderful to be settled in with Hermione, Majestic, and the kids. I had a formal foster care arrangement with the Division of Family and Children Services. It didn't hurt that I knew the head of the agency well. I arranged my hours at the refugee clinic so I could take the children to school and pick them up in the afternoon. Lurleen was delighted to look after them if I had to stay late and on Saturday morning while I worked.

What had changed the most was me. I stopped thinking about my next move. There wasn't going to be a next move. Atlanta was my permanent home. The home where I'd raise my children. *My* children. What a magical ring that had to it.

And Mason? What would happen with Mason? We'd been to war together, but I wasn't sure how we'd do in peacetime. We'd have to see. That didn't mean Mason wasn't at our house most nights for supper because he was.

Ditie's Sampler of Best Recipes

Ditie is a collector and not an inventor.

She doesn't create new recipes, but she searches for the best of everything.

She doesn't mind doctoring recipes (pun intended) until they taste just right.

When she can she attributes the recipe to the person who created it.

Enjoy!

Best Chocolate Chip Cookies

Chocolate chip cookies should be a mainstay of any baker. They are quick, easy, and delicious. The recipe doesn't really matter. I use the one on the package of the semisweet chocolate chips.

The secret is in the baking. If you want cookies that are soft, chewy, and melt in your mouth (as I do) decrease the suggested baking time by one to two minutes. The cookies will look underdone but when they cool, they will be perfect.

Mexican Chocolate Cake

If you love chocolate, pecans, and cake, this is the recipe for you. Even if you're not sure you love all those things, this magnificent cake will convince you.

Servings: 10–12

Difficulty: Moderate. This is more time consuming than difficult but worth the effort.

Cake Ingredients

1 stick margarine (1/2 cup)

1/2 cup vegetable oil

2 squares unsweetened chocolate or 4 tablespoons unsweetened cocoa

1 cup water

2 cups unsifted all-purpose flour

1 teaspoon baking soda

2 cups sugar

1/2 cup sour milk (place 1 1/2 teaspoon vinegar in 1/2 measuring cup. Fill with milk.)

2 eggs, beaten

1 teaspoon cinnamon

1 teaspoon vanilla extract

Instructions

1. Preheat oven to 350 degrees.
2. Combine margarine, oil, chocolate, and water in a saucepan and heat until chocolate is melted.
3. Combine flour, baking soda, sugar, milk, cinnamon, and vanilla in a large bowl.
4. Combine both mixtures.
5. Pour batter into a greased 12 by 18 inch pan or two greased and floured round cake pans.
6. Bake 20–25 minutes or until done.
7. Five minutes before cake is done, make frosting. (I usually start the frosting when I pull the cake out of the oven. I like to use the cake rounds even though it makes the cake a little trickier to frost.)

Icing Ingredients
1 stick margarine (1/2 cup)
2 squares unsweetened chocolate
6 tablespoons milk
1 package confectioner's sugar
1 teaspoon vanilla extract
1/2 cup chopped pecans

Instructions
1. Combine margarine, chocolate, and milk in saucepan and heat until bubbles form around edge.
2. Remove from heat.
3. Add confectioner's sugar, vanilla, and pecans.
4. Beat.
5. Ice cake while still warm. (Pan cake can be iced immediately. Cake rounds will need 10 minutes so they slip out easily from the pans.)

Summer Pasta
From my colleague Salley Jessee, MD.
Children and adults love this light dinner, no matter what the season.

Servings: 4–6
Difficulty: Easy

Ingredients
2 tablespoons olive oil
1/3 cup pine nuts
2 garlic cloves, minced
2 large tomatoes, seeded and diced (preferably fresh ripe)
16 ounce jar marinated artichoke hearts, drained and quartered
10 pitted Kalamata olives, sliced
1/3 cup chopped fresh basil
2 teaspoons fresh oregano (or 1/2 teaspoon dried)
Salt and pepper to taste
8–10 ounces capellini cooked according to directions
Grated fresh parmigiana cheese (don't even think about canned!!)

Instructions
1. Heat oil in skillet. Add pine nuts and garlic and sauté until the pine nuts and garlic are light brown. (Be careful not to brown the pine nuts as they will taste burned.)
2. Stir in the tomatoes, artichoke hearts, olives, basil, and oregano and heat through.
3. Season to taste.
4. While the sauce is heating, cook the capellini and drain.
5. Pour the sauce over the pasta and serve with the freshly grated parmigiana.
6. Serve with a fresh green salad and bread.

Best Barbecue Meatloaf
(Don't be put off by the name)
This is a fabulous, easy recipe from *Cooking Light*

Servings: *Cooking Light* would say six. I would say three to four.
Difficulty: Easy

Ingredients
1 1/2 pounds ground beef, extra lean (raw)
1/2 cup dried breadcrumbs
1/2 cup chopped onion
1/2 cup barbecue sauce, divided
1 tablespoon prepared mustard
1 1/2 teaspoons chili powder
1 teaspoon garlic powder
1/2 teaspoon salt
1/2 teaspoon freshly ground black pepper
2 large egg whites
Cooking spray

Instructions
1. Preheat oven to 350 degrees.
2. Combine the beef, breadcrumbs, and onion, 1 tablespoon barbecue sauce, and remaining ingredients except cooking spray in a large bowl. (If cooking is a sensual experience for you, mix it up with clean fingers.)
3. Shape meat mixture into a 9 by 5 inch loaf on a broiler pan coated with cooking spray. (I use a cookie tray and it works fine.) Spread the remaining barbecue sauce over top of the meat loaf.
4. Bake at 350 degrees for 1 hour or until a thermometer registers 160 degrees. Let stand 10 minutes. Cut loaf into 12 slices. (Yield according to *Cooking Light* is 6 servings, two slices each. It's so good we usually eat more than that at a sitting.)
5. I often double the recipe and freeze one loaf after cooking.

Megan's Granola

This is the best granola you will ever make or ever want to eat. It's from the Internet, and while I've played with the ingredients, the original recipe is still the best. Give some away and you'll have friends for life.

Servings: 30

Difficulty: Easy to moderate (lots of nut chopping and a little judgment about when the granola is done but not too done)

Ingredients

8 cups rolled oats
1 1/2 cups wheat germ
1 1/2 cups oat bran
1 cup sunflower seeds
1 cup finely chopped almonds
1 cup finely chopped pecans
1 cup finely chopped walnuts
1 1/2 teaspoon salt
1/2 cup brown sugar
1/4 cup maple syrup
3/4 cups honey
1 cup vegetable oil
1 tablespoon ground cinnamon
1 tablespoon vanilla extract
2 cups raisins or sweetened dried cranberries

Instructions

1. Preheat oven to 325 degrees.
2. Line two large baking sheets with parchment or aluminum foil.
3. Combine the oats, wheat germ, oat bran, sunflower seeds, almonds, pecans, and walnuts in a large bowl.
4. Stir together the salt, brown sugar, maple syrup, honey, oil, cinnamon, and vanilla in a saucepan. Bring to a boil over medium heat.
5. Pour over the dry ingredients and stir to coat. Spread the mixture evenly on the baking sheets.
6. Bake in the preheated oven until crispy and toasted, about 20 minutes. Stir once halfway through. (This is important to keep edges from getting overcooked.) Cool. Then stir in the raisins or cranberries before storing in an airtight container.

Strawberry Cake

I didn't think I would be a fan of strawberry cake but this is light and delicious—perfect on a summer day. It takes a little more time than your average cake, but it is worth every extra minute.

Servings: 10–12
Difficulty: Moderate. This one takes time.

Cake Ingredients

24 ounces organic frozen or very ripe fresh strawberries, hulled (and thawed if frozen). Frozen tastes fine in this recipe.

1-2 teaspoons sugar (optional)

1/4 cup milk, at room temperature

6 large egg whites, room temperature (4 whole eggs can be substituted, but the cake will be lighter with the egg whites)

1 tablespoon vanilla extract

2 1/4 cup cake flour, sifted

1 3/4 cup sugar

4 teaspoons baking powder

1 teaspoon salt

12 tablespoons unsalted butter (1 1/2 sticks), softened (not melted)

Instructions

1. Thaw frozen strawberries. Pour into a fine strainer placed over a bowl and let sit. Lightly toss strawberries occasionally to remove any pockets of excess liquid. Reserve the liquid for another use or discard.

2. Place strawberries in a food processor or blender and puree.

3. Reserve 3/4 cup puree for the cake. Use leftover puree to fill the cake or fold into frosting if desired. It's also great spooned over ice cream.

4. Preheat oven to 350 degrees.

5. Prepare 2 8-inch pans with baking spray with flour (or simply butter and flour pans).

6. In small bowl, combine puree, milk, egg, vanilla and mix with fork until well-blended.

7. Using a mixer, combine sifted flour, sugar, baking powder, and salt. Beat at slow speed and add butter. Mix until combined and resembling moist breadcrumbs.

8. Add the puree mixture and beat at medium speed for 1 minute or until full and evenly combined.

9. Scrape down the sides of the bowl and hand beat for 30 more seconds. Divide the batter evenly among the pans and smooth tops.

10. Bake for about 25 minutes or until a toothpick inserted in the center comes out clean.

11. Let cakes rest in pan for about ten minutes and turn out onto wire racks.

12. Let cakes cool completely (about 2 hours).

Frosting Ingredients

2 sticks of butter, at room temperature
6 cups powdered sugar
5 tablespoons milk
2 teaspoons vanilla extract
1/4 teaspoon almond extract
Pinch of salt
A little puree for color or food coloring if you like

Note: This makes a lot of frosting. I cut the recipe down by 25% and had plenty.

Instructions

1. Place all ingredients in your mixer bowl.

2. Beat on low just until you have no more dry streaks of powdered sugar. Add food coloring if you want at this point.

3. Beat on high and whip for 3–4 minutes until light, fluffy, and smooth, stopping once to scrape down sides.

4. Frost using a pastry bag fitted with a large star tip (or do what I do, which is just slather it on). You can use puree for filling between cake layers, but you will have to make sure the top layer doesn't slide around on you. You might use skewers to anchor layers until the frosting sets up, then remove.

Please turn the page for an exciting sneak peek of

Sarah Osborne's next

Ditie Brown Mystery

coming soon!

Chapter One

It was a typical muggy July in Atlanta—a time when tempers flared and murder seemed just around the corner.

Every summer I dreamed of a cottage by the sea, but the kids appeared to be happy enough with the Glenlake public pool ten minutes from our house. My best friend Lurleen and I made sure they got in the water every day it wasn't raining.

We'd just returned in the late afternoon, and the shade from my giant magnolia tree gave us a moment's relief from the oppressive heat. Jason, aged five, was becoming a swimmer and Lucie, almost nine, already was one. After a sad four months since the death of their mother, Lucie was finally acting like a child again and not a second mom to Jason.

"Stop hitting me with your water wings, Jason. It's not funny. Make him stop, Aunt Di."

"Jason, come here. Let me have those wings. You hardly need them anymore."

Jason looked at me as if he were debating the possibility of running into the house, but I was too fast for him. As a pediatrician, I knew how to capture children, if not with my charm than with the speed of a firm hand.

I took the water wings and scooted him inside to take a bath.

"You can use my shower upstairs, Lucie."

I entered the house two steps behind her. The swim had been refreshing but already I was perspiring from the humidity that passed for summer in Georgia.

The air conditioning in the house took my breath away. I jumped when I saw Mason settled on my sofa. I didn't work Fridays, but Mason did.

"You look comfortable. Why aren't you tracking down murderers?" I asked.

"I got time off for good behavior."

He must have seen me shivering. "I hope it's not too cold in here. Can you sit for a minute?"

He held out his hand and pulled me, wet suit, towel and all, onto his lap. He wrapped a throw around me.

"That will get soaked," I said.

"You have a dryer don't you? I'll take care of it."

"Really—why aren't you at work?"

"I pulled two all-nighters. I'll check in later. Right now, I just wanted to see you." He pushed my short dark curls away from my face. "You look good enough to eat."

I probably did look like a nice plump muffin, but no matter how I looked, Mason made me feel gorgeous. I slipped off his lap, so I could see him more clearly.

"What are you up to?" I asked.

"A man has to be up to something because he wants to see his girlfriend in the middle of the day?"

"Yes, if that man is a detective with the Atlanta Police Department."

For a moment, Mason looked hurt. "You really don't know what day this is?"

I searched my memory and shook my head. "It's not my birthday or yours. Jason had his, and Lucie's is in September. I give up." I looked into his tender gray eyes, rubbed his bald head and gave him a kiss. "I really don't care why you're here, I'm glad you are."

"It's exactly four months since we met," he said. "You forgot."

"I'll never forget that," I said.

It was the worst night of my life and my children's lives. It was the night their mother Ellie died. Mason Garrett, the detective on the case, gave me the news. He was kind and gentle, and my view of him had never changed.

I cuddled up to him wet bathing suit and all.

"I can't believe it's only been four months," he said. "I feel as if I've known you forever."

"I feel the same way."

"You mean that?"

"Of course." As soon as I said that out loud, I realized where Mason was headed. When would it be the right time to ask me to marry him or at least to move in together? The children, I'd say, as I said every time he brought up the issue. The children needed stability right now, no new upheaval.

We were spared this conversation by Jason who ran into the room with his mitt in one hand and a bat in the other.

"Wanna play ball, Uncle Mason?"

"You got a ball?" Mason said glancing around.

Jason searched the room. "Hermione," he shouted.

My wonderful, patient shepherd-collie mix trotted into the room, head held high with a softball in her mouth.

"Jason," I said. "I told you to put that up where Hermione couldn't get it. She thinks it's her toy now and she'll chew it up."

Jason pulled it from her mouth. "It's fine, see?"

It was fine except for a few teeth marks.

"If it gets chewed up," I said, "the next one comes out of your allowance."

Mason stood up. "I think we men better leave, before your aunt Di starts yelling at us." He ushered Jason out in front of him.

Hermione trotted after them into the front yard. From the porch I watched Mason lob the ball to Jason who threw it back with the fierce attention of a five-year-old boy. After Lucie appeared, ready to play short stop, I went inside and took my own shower. I was barely dressed when I heard Hermione barking.

Mason shushed her and turned to someone in our yard. "Can I help you?" he said.

I was running down the stairs when I recognized a familiar voice. "I wondered if Ditie was available."

I came out on the porch, a towel in one hand, trying to do something with my curly hair that would go its own way no matter what I did.

Before me stood Phil Brockton, the IV, in a Civil War uniform no less. Despite my best efforts not to notice, he looked incredibly handsome. Six feet tall, one hundred eighty pounds, straight dark hair that fell casually over one eye—elegant in his gray uniform.

"Phil? I thought you were going to call me when you were coming to town for a reenactment."

"I did call you and emailed you as well, but you never responded, so here I am."

It was all true. Phil had emailed me a few weeks earlier and given me the date he was coming. I hadn't responded because I didn't know what to say. He called and I deleted the message almost as soon as I received it. Somehow I'd managed to 'forget' those communications.

"I'm on my way to a planning party and thought I'd stop by. I hope you can come tomorrow. It's the first of the Atlanta reenactments."

Before I answered him, I introduced him to the three people who were staring with their mouths open.

"Philip Brockton, this is Mason Garrett and these are my children Lucie and Jason."

Mason and Phil reluctantly shook hands.

"You're the boyfriend police detective, right?" Phil asked.

Mason raised one eyebrow and nodded. "You're the doctor obsessed with the Civil War who took off for New York abruptly after residency."

This wasn't going well.

Phil looked at me. "What have you told this guy about me?"

"Never mind," I said to both of them. "Remember the children. Phil, why are you here?"

"The Battle of Resaca is tomorrow. I'm hoping you can come. For old times sake."

"Like Civil War old times sake?" Mason asked. "Or something else?"

I gave Mason a look that was meant to say I could fight my own battles. Phil was the only man I ever thought I might marry before Mason. He'd stood me up seven years earlier—not at the altar but by leaving town and moving in with an oncology nurse.

"Why didn't you just call me, Phil?" I asked.

"Things got hectic, Ditie. Besides I wanted to see you. What do you think? Can you come?" He looked around at the family group. "Everyone's invited." He said that more as an afterthought.

"I don't know, Phil."

"A lot of the old gang will be there from med school—Harper and Ryan Hudson, Sally Cutter, Andy Morrison. I don't know if you remember Frank Peterson—he was a year older, but he and I got to be friends."

"To be honest, Phil, the only person I'd really like to see is Andy. I haven't kept up with your other friends, and didn't Sally drop out of school second year? I'm surprised you're still in touch with her."

"Yeah, we're friends. She loves this reenactment stuff. Please come."

I looked at Mason. He didn't look pleased.

"I'll see if Lurleen can watch the kids, and I'll have to see if I can come in later to the refugee clinic. I work there on Saturday mornings, so I don't know if I can come, Phil."

"I'd love a chance for you to see me in action. Maybe we could visit before things got started."

"I'll see."

Phil left, and Mason turned to me. "Why are you doing this? I thought you were over this guy."

I looked at the children who were standing still, staring at us.

"Not now," I said. "I just took a shower and already I'm perspiring. Let's go inside. I think we all need to cool off."

I headed for the kitchen. "How 'bout some lemonade? We'll make it fresh. Jason, get me six lemons from the bowl by the sink. I'll cut and you can squeeze, Lucie."

I turned to Mason. "Maybe you can find a family movie for us to watch later."

Mason didn't say a word, just headed for the family room.

Lucie leaned toward me and whispered. "Something's wrong, isn't it Aunt Di? You have that look."

"That look?"

"You know, the look you have when you're worried and don't want us to know, when you get those wrinkles in your forehead and your mouth goes all serious."

"Oh, Lucie." I hugged her. "It's nothing to worry about. It's just that a man I knew years ago turned up on my doorstep, and it shocked me a little."

Jason was walking toward the island trying hard to balance lemons in his small hands, intent on not dropping any. I placed them on the chopping board, and he counted them out.

"Look Aunt Di, six."

I smiled at him. "Perfect."

"That man who came to see you," Jason said, "was he wearing a costume for Halloween?"

"That's months away," Lucie said, "in October."

I could see Jason's lip start to quiver. He never liked being criticized by his sister.

"He was dressed in a Confederate Civil War uniform," I said. "He came to Atlanta to play a part in a pretend battle."

Jason looked completely bewildered.

"He looked funny because he had on the costume of a Civil War Colonel." That got nowhere.

"Jason, you remember how much Danny likes to talk about the Civil War, the war that took place over a hundred and fifty years ago."

"Danny calls it the War of Northern Aggression," Lucie said proudly, "where the Northern states got mad at the Southern states and everybody fought everybody. We read about it in school, and they called it the Civil War."

"I love Danny like a brother, but we don't see eye to eye about everything. The Southern states wanted to leave the United States and form a separate country. You've heard about Abraham Lincoln?"

Lucie nodded.

"Lincoln was president and he didn't want the United States to fall apart," I said. "He fought a war to save it and eventually to free the slaves."

I'd lost Jason half way through the conversation. He'd wandered off to the living room and was trying to teach Hermione a new trick.

"That's enough history for one day. You can talk to Danny about it this evening. He and Lurleen are coming to dinner."

I sliced the lemons, and Lucie squeezed them into the pitcher. We added sugar and ice water and stirred like crazy. Lucie tasted it and agreed it was sweet enough. I carried glasses outside and the three of us settled on the porch swing. Hermione flopped at our feet. Majestic, my imperialistic cat, found his way onto my lap.

I listened to the children talking to one another, bickering over who could throw the ball farther, and I let my mind wander.

Phil Brockton, the man I hadn't seen in seven years turns up on my doorstep expecting me to drop everything and run to watch him play soldier. Just like old times. When I could be of use to him he wanted me around. He even let me think he loved me. Then he moved to New York leaving me high and dry.

I sighed. Lucie looked at me.

"It's nothing," I said. "I guess I'm bothered that Dr. Brockton showed up."

"Did you love him, Aunt Di?"

"Whatever made you ask that, honey?"

"You have that look you give Uncle Mason sometimes."

"Good grief, Lucie. Do you spend every minute studying my face?"

Lucie blushed. "It's not hard, Aunt Di. Even Uncle Mason says he can tell what you're thinking before you say a word." Lucie sat quietly for a moment. She started picking at the wooden planks in the swing.

"What is it, Lucie?"

"It's just . . . if you loved him once, maybe you still love him. Uncle Mason wouldn't like that, and I wouldn't either."

"Not to worry, Lucie. I'm not in love with Phil Brockton."

"And you are in love with Uncle Mason?" she asked smiling.

"Say, I think you have a wobbly tooth in that mouth of yours. Let me check."

I poked around in her mouth and tickled her until she was giggling so hard she nearly fell off the swing onto Hermione. Majestic had jumped ship at the first sign of a disturbance and Hermione had the good sense to move away.

"My turn," Jason said. "I have a wobble tooth, too."

He darted away before I could catch him and we all ended up in a pile on the lawn when Mason joined us outside.

"I can't leave you guys alone for a minute," he said as he shut the screen door. "I expected more of you, Hermione."

She disentangled herself from us and trotted up to Mason in hopes of a good rub, which she got.

Lurleen and Danny arrived and we made plans for an ad hoc dinner. Danny and Mason would grill some steaks. I would handle the salads, and Lurleen would watch the kids. She was always my back-up. When her aunt died and left her a fortune, she'd quit her job working for Sandler's Sodas and spent almost as much time with the kids as I did.

Over dinner I told Lurleen and Danny the story of Phil's abrupt arrival and his request that I watch a Civil War reenactment in the morning.

"Oh boy," Danny said, "would I love to see that!"

Danny looked just like a kid at that moment, all six feet four inches of him.

"You could come with me if you don't have work to do," I said.

Danny was a former cop and now private investigator who set his own hours. "I'm free tomorrow."

"It'll be a longer day for you, Lurleen. I'll have to stay late at the clinic once I get there."

"I don't mind," Lurleen said. "No offense, Danny, but the idea of watching grown men play war doesn't really interest me."

"It's not playing war, Lurleen, it's creating living history," Danny said.

"*Ah, mon dieu,*" Lurleen said. She returned to her own unique version of French when she got frustrated.

"I'll have to get to work by ten or eleven," I said, "but you can probably stay as long as you want, Danny."

Mason had been silent throughout the meal. I looked over at him.

"Would you like to come?"

"Can't. I have to work tomorrow."

His response was curt, and I didn't have the inclination to draw him out.

I told Danny I'd be going early to talk with Phil and that he should plan to get there before nine when the battle would begin.

Mason barely said two words to me before he left for the night. Worse than that he barely kissed me good night. What was wrong with him? He couldn't really be jealous about a relationship that ended seven years ago.

* * * *

I left a little after six the next morning to get to the Resaca battlefield by seven. It was due north, and there wasn't a lot of traffic in the way. Danny would join me around eight. I'd never seen a reenactment, and to be honest, the idea intrigued me now. In med school it was the last thing I had time for. Perhaps having a boy of my own made me realize something new about the excitement of guns and battles. I suppose to be equally honest the idea of seeing Phil once more in uniform also interested me. Not for the lost relationship. We were never a match although I didn't realize that at the time. Still, Phil was a handsome man, and I didn't mind seeing a handsome man in action.

When I arrived I saw hundreds of men dressed in blue and gray on the field. I found the tents with women inside and asked where I might find the Confederate organizers of the event.

"We're Confederates, dear. We know the men. Who is it you might be looking for?"

"Phil Brockton," I said.

"Colonel Brockton? He's a fine man. My William is under his command. They are over yonder under the cluster of trees."

She never broke out of her role and pointed to a cluster of pine trees a hundred yards away.

I spotted Phil about the same time he noticed me. He motioned me to stay back and I watched as he sketched something in the dirt to a cluster of his men. Then he strode out to meet me.

"I'm glad you came, Ditie. Pretty impressive, huh? Wait until the action starts."

He was in charge of maintaining and positioning the cannons on the confederate side. He let me walk with him and gave me a history of the battle as we walked.

"General Sherman and our man General Johnston fought on this field— happened in May 1864—so it wouldn't have been so hot. Sherman wanted to hold the railroad and telegraph lines south of Dalton, and he did. We didn't win this one," he said, "but we fought bravely. They lost more men than we did."

I looked over the green fields and rolling hills. It was hard to imagine dead and wounded men strewn over that land.

We came to the first set of cannons. Phil inspected each one, shining a flashlight into the bore. "We mostly use 12-pounder smooth bore Napoleons if we can get hands on them. This one's a beaut."

I tried to look excited when Danny ran up and took over. "Gosh, I've never seen one of these up close." He ran his hand along the green five foot cannon. "They used solid shot in this?"

"Or canister in close quarters," Phil said.

Danny turned to me. "The cannister casings are filled with steel balls, sawdust, anything they wanted to put in there, Ditie. They could do a lot of damage over a wide area."

I nodded. It did at least help me understand what was going on, but I was ready for the battle to start. "I think I'll join the women. You two carry on without me."

As I was walking back to the tents Ryan and Harper Hudson caught up with me.

"I'm surprised to see you here, Mabel," Harper said. "I heard you were back in town, but I never knew if you'd taken off again. I never expected to see you at a reenactment—I thought you hated them in med school?"

"They took up more time than I had then. I guess I came to see what Phil has always been so passionate about."

"Can we take that to mean you and Phil might be getting back together now that he's divorcing his wife?" she asked.

"Our relationship is ancient history. I didn't know he was in the middle of a divorce, but I've moved on. I'm here because Phil invited me."

"We're here," Harper said, "because we just love this kind of thing. Don't we, hon?"

Ryan shrugged and gave me a kiss on the cheek. "Nice to see you, Ditie."

"I have to be a Federalist, today," Harper said. "Too many Confederates reenacters showed up. I don't mind. At least I'll be on the winning side of this one."

Phil saw us clustered together and ran over to us. "Hi Harper. I don't think we need you today in uniform. Sorry. It looks like a new cluster of Federalists showed up."

"That's fine. I'll watch my man in action." She motioned to Ryan but winked at Phil.

Danny yelled over to me, and I left them on the field. Ryan and Harper made a handsome couple, both tall and fit. Harper was blond, Ryan's hair was a light brown. They looked like Ken and Barbie in uniform. I thought they had a dermatology practice in Buckhead, but I'd never bothered to look them up when I came back to Atlanta. They were more Phil's friends than mine.

I waited for Danny to catch up with me.

"This is really fantastic," Danny said. "Phil said I could participate the next time he's in town. Man, I'd love that."

I nodded. Together we found a spot on the hill under a tree that provided a bit of shade and waited for the action to begin. We could see Phil gathering his men. Someone stepped out of line and offered a prayer. Then Phil got everyone situated. Several men wandered off with guns at the ready. A massive row of Confederate soldiers faced the Union forces twenty yards away. Six people including Phil stood near one cannon.

"Did you bring your binoculars, Danny? I forgot mine."

Danny handed them to me. I made a survey of the people near the cannon. I thought I saw Sally Cutter, but I couldn't be sure. Andy was recognizable with his hat off and his red hair flying in the breeze, laughing with someone standing next to the cannon, Frank Peterson perhaps.

Wait a second! I saw someone else I recognized talking to Phil.

"That is Carl Thompson! I swear it is!"

"Should that mean something to me?" Danny asked. "Is he famous?"

"Phil and Carl hated each other in med school. Carl hated everything about the South, and that made Phil hate him. They traded barbs throughout first year and stopped talking after second year. I wonder what could have brought about this great reunion."

Some signal seemed to start the battle. Bugles blared and shots were fired. Smoke filled the field. I watched as Phil's crew stepped up in a ritualized dance. One man stuck a long stick into the bore of the cannon.

"A sponge," Danny explained, "to make sure there are no left-over sparks from a previous shot."

Next someone put something in the tip of the bore. Another tamped it down.

"Black powder," said Danny. "And now, see that rope Phil is holding—that's the lanyard. It's attached to a wire that's fed into the powder through what's called a vent. When it's pulled out friction makes the powder ignite and the cannon fires."

"Thanks for the artillery lesson, Danny."

He looked at me as if I were mocking him.

"No, I mean it. I can understand what's happening now. Everyone has their role."

Danny nodded.

The action stopped for a moment. It looked as if Carl and Phil were having a discussion while everyone else stood around waiting for something to happen. After a minute Phil handed the lanyard to Carl, left him on the right of the cannon and stood to the left of the gun.

I watched as Carl pulled the lanyard and the gun banged.

"What the hell?" Danny yelled. He grabbed the binoculars out of my hands. "That wasn't supposed to happen."

When the smoke cleared, even I could see something was terribly wrong.

Several of the people around the cannon had been knocked off their feet and the cannon itself was split.

Oh my God. Phil stood up, looking dazed. Carl had been on the other side and I couldn't see what happened to him. I *could* see that everyone was looking in that direction.

I asked Danny to let me look and he handed me the binoculars.

I watched as Harper came running across the field. She helped Ryan to his feet. I saw Sally and Andy look to the other side of the cannon. Even from where we stood I could hear Sally's scream. Frank stood silently several feet from the shattered cannon. Phil had gone to where Carl lay and returned shaking his head.

I ran after Danny as he raced onto the field. He motioned me back and pulled out his cell phone. I assumed he was calling 911. I didn't see Carl. I didn't need to. I could see from everyone's expression he was dead.

"We need a medical examiner out here, now!" I heard Danny shout into the phone.

About the Author

Sarah Osborne is the pen name of a native Californian who lived in Atlanta for many years and now practices psychiatry on Cape Cod. She writes cozy mysteries for the same reason she reads them—to find comfort in a sometimes difficult world. TOO MANY CROOKS SPOIL THE PLOT is the first novel in her Ditie Brown Mystery series. She loves to hear from readers and can be reached atdoctorosborne.com.

CPSIA information can be obtained
at www.ICGtesting.com
Printed in the USA
LVHW111534020519
616416LV00001B/177/P